UNCONDITIONAL

Q.B. TYLER

Copyright © 2019 by Q.B. Tyler

All rights reserved.

No part of this publication may be reproduced, distributed, or transmitted in any form or by any means, including photocopying, recording, or other electronic or mechanical methods, without the prior written permission of the publisher, except in the case of brief quotations embodied in critical reviews and certain other noncommercial uses permitted by copyright law.

This is a work of fiction. Names, characters, businesses, places, events, and incidents are either the products of the author's imagination and used in a fictitious manner. Any resemblance to actual persons, living or dead, or actual events is purely coincidental.

Cover Design: NET Hook & Line Designs
Editing: Kristen Portillo—Your Editing Lounge
Interior Formatting: Stacey Blake—Champagne Book Design
Proofreading: Leslie Middleton

Playlist

Halo—*Beyonce*

A Drop in the Ocean—*Ron Pope*

Love on the Brain—*Rihanna*

Run To You—*Whitney Houston*

Xo—*Beyonce*

Body and Soul—*Anita Baker*

Floating—*Alina Baraz*

I Wanna Love You Forever—*Jessica Simpson*

Because You Loved Me—*Celine Dion*

If You Could Only See—*Tonic*

Make You Feel My Love—*Adele*

Dangerously in Love—*Beyonce*

(Everything I Do) I Do It For You—*Bryan Adams*

Helium—*Sia*

By Your Side—*Sade*

Can't Help Falling in Love—*Haley Reinhart*

Turning Page—*Sleeping at Last*

All of Me—*John Legend*

Blue Jeans—*Lana Del Rey*

Stand By Me—*Ben E. King*

For the people on *my* "home team"
There will never be enough words to explain the love I have for you.

CAL

Ten Years Prior

PIERCING BLUE EYES FULL OF SHOCK AND TERROR FLY OPEN THE second I open the closet in her tiny room. I drop to my knees as the wind expels from my lungs and I find myself struggling to breathe. She's shaking so hard, a pink polka-dotted bunny stuffed in her mouth as she tries to mask her cries. I can practically hear the pounding of her heartbeat slamming against her tiny ribcage. She's wearing a pair of pink pajamas that I know aren't keeping her warm on this cold October night and I know if I touch her hand, they'll be as cold as ice.

She scoots back further into the closet, bumping into a few pink toys that look older than me in her effort to put space between us. She pushes them toward me in an attempt to deter me from coming closer, so I proceed with caution.

Holy shit, she was here this whole time?

My mind goes through a million scenarios, wondering if this young girl was a witness to the devastation just below.

"No, hey, I'm here to help; I'm a police officer." I coo at her as I reach a hand out for her. Her skin is pale, but you can't tell due to how red and blotchy her face is. The only part of her face that isn't red are her lips which look slightly blue from the arctic temperatures of her bedroom. Her chocolate hair is pulled into two French braids that go down her back and her blue eyes are swimming with tears. She blinks several times as she lets the bunny fall from her mouth.

"Mama?" Her voice is soft and high pitched and I can hear the tears building in her throat. She must have been hiding because she knew something bad was happening.

But how much does she know?

Did she see the tragedy unfold?

Did she witness her father murder her mother?

I clear my throat. "Mama isn't…" I blink my eyes trying to figure out how to explain the gruesome scene downstairs to a terrified child.

I hear commotion downstairs and I know it's the fire department, EMTs and officers from all over the state scouring the premises for clues. When homicide-suicide got called in over the radio, *everyone* reported for duty.

I've been in the police force for just under a year, after getting my Associate's degree right after high school and spending a year fucking around, wondering what the hell I wanted to do with my life. At twenty-three, I am one of the youngest on the force in Ferrell County inside a small town in Oregon. The town had a few more than three thousand people and it definitely isn't my scene, having been born and raised in Portland, but this is where they need me.

"There's a lot of people downstairs right now…but we're gonna go," I whisper softly. "I'm going to take you somewhere safe, alright? Where no one can hurt you."

She cranes her neck to try and look behind me and shakes her tiny head one more time. "No."

No? She can't possibly think she can stay here. "Sweetheart."

"Madeline." She corrects me and her angelic voice floats around me again.

"Is that your name?"

She nods and pushes something towards me. *A book.* A small smile finds my face when I recognize the cover. The Eiffel Tower and young girls in two straight lines or however it goes all wearing yellow hats and matching clothes.

"Like her." She points. "Mama loves it. She reads to me every night. But you can call me Maddie."

I nod again. "Maddie is a pretty name. . I'm Cal."

"Cal." Her voice wavers slightly, but after a moment she sticks her hand out. "How do you do?" I chuckle at her politeness before I take her tiny hand that's as cold as ice and shake it. Her hand squeezes mine and I wonder if it's because she doesn't want me to let go or if she's just trying to warm her hands.

I hear someone coming up the stairs and it puts me on high alert when I hear them announce themselves. "Stand down," I growl over my shoulder, knowing that another large man was *not* what this girl needed to see. I was larger than a number of the guys on the force. At six-four, and in the shape of my life, I was someone most people didn't want to fuck with. The list of people who showed up to spar with me in the ring at the station has dwindled to practically nothing over the past few months. I'm intimidating enough to a small child, I'm sure.

"Is there a child?" I hear whispered. "Should we send in Daniels?" I roll my eyes as I think about Officer Aria Daniels. She was the officer who was always called in whenever there were any hostile domestic situations involving children. She hated it.

"You guys are so sexist!" she would claim with her hands firmly planted on her hips. But kids loved her. They felt safe with her. And that's all we cared about. That *they* felt safe.

"Fine." I grit out before turning back to Madeline. "A lady is coming. Okay?"

"Mama?" Her eyes light up as she moves closer to me and

peeks her tiny head out of the closet and tries to peer around my body. Her eyes dart to mine as if to say *are you lying? Because I'm not amused.*

Even as she's blinked the majority of the tears from her eyes, her gaze pierces mine. They're so young and innocent. It feels like there's a vice grip around my heart as I think about her going into the system. Her growing up without her parents—well a mother...*because fuck her dad*. But her mama. The mama she so desperately loves. "Mama!" She screams, her eyes shut and I wince at the ear-splitting volume of her wail.

"Maddie... sweetheart... please don't cry." I reach out for her slowly and she flinches but she lets me slowly rub her back just as Aria appears in the doorway.

Objectively, Aria was a knockout with green eyes, dirty blonde hair, and curves that stop men on the street in hopes that she is just celebrating Halloween early, parading around in a uniform that is just a *touch* too tight. Aria is that hot girl cop fantasy that probably every man and a few women have had when they come into contact with her.

Except me.

Not only is Aria a royal pain in my ass who consistently acts like she's my mother, but she's been dating my brother for the past few months, and it seems that they are pretty into each other.

"Oh, you are so sweet." I hear her soft voice float into the room and then she's kneeling next to me in front of Madeline. "What's your name?"

Her eyebrows furrow slightly and flit to me. She shakes her head before planting her lips firmly together, a sign that *I am not talking to you*. "We are going to go downstairs now, okay? It's time to leave. Do you want to ride in a police car? I'll turn the siren on." I smile at her, knowing that the bribe usually always worked for children.

"That's bad," she whispers. "The siren on is bad. And it's loud," she says as her eyes are trained on me. She puts her hands up and covers her ears.

"It's not as bad when you're in the car." I tell her, and I don't know why I feel the need to argue with a traumatized seven year old.

"Is Mama coming too?" she asks, and she scurries back to the closet to grab her book and her bunny.

"No, sweetheart," Aria answers and my neck snaps towards her. I shoot a glare at her as if to say *why the fuck did you tell her that?*

She shoots me one back as if to say *I know what I'm doing.*

As we have this engagement with our eyes, an ear shattering cry fills the room and my head darts over to Maddie, as she falls to her knees in a fit of sobs, her hands covering her face.

"See what you did," I growl at Aria.

"She's too old for me to lie to her face. I need her to trust me."

"Well she hates you," I growl at her.

"Oh stop," she snaps at me before she goes to pick up the small hysterical child whose life, unbeknownst to her, was slowly changing with each passing second.

Maddie, however, is *Not. Fucking. Having. It.*

"GET AWAY!" She swings at Aria and scoots closer to me. "You are not my Mama!" she screams and before I even have a chance to shoot Aria a *look what you did* glance, Maddie has attached herself to me and wrapped herself around me as best as she could. Her arms and legs are wrapped around my right leg like ivy, with her cheek pressed against my shin. I pull her from me slightly and stand up so I can collect her in my arms properly.

"I need you to keep those eyes shut until I say, okay?"

She regards me warily, her eyes studying my face for any answers as to why I would be asking that.

"Why?" She asks.

"Please? And then if you're a big girl, you can have...ice cream?" I'm not sure what I can really entice her with, but I was under the impression that most children could be persuaded to do just about anything for the promise of ice cream.

"I can't have ice cream before dinner," she says as she plays with my badge, her blue eyes staring transfixed by the shininess.

"We can break the rule just this once."

"Okay, deal. Chocolate." She gives me a smile before squeezing her eyes shut but opens one eye as best as she can. "Don't forget my bunny and my book...please," she adds before shutting her eyes again and placing her head on my shoulder.

"Of course," I point at the items on the floor and nod at Aria before I head out of the door, a smug grin finding my face that for once Aria didn't know what was best.

"Are your eyes closed?" I ask her now. My hand finds the back of her head as I carry her down the stairs and through the living room. Madeline Shaw can't be a day older than seven; she is so tiny, I'm almost afraid I'll crush her in my arms as I carry her out of the house. I press her face against my chest, so she doesn't see the devastation. Her parents lying in pools of their own blood, her mother's eyes wide with fear, her mouth agape with shock. It's something right out of a horror film.

Homicide-Suicide.

The living room is small, the bare minimum furniture is scattered throughout. An old couch that I'm sure has some type of bed bugs lines one wall. A television that looks older than me and a lounger that is covered in blood, line the others. Blood spatters the left wall and there is a rug in the center of the room that looks like more than a few feet have walked all over it. I rub her back slightly, my heart shattered that this sweet girl had to endure these conditions.

Is she so frail because she wasn't being fed?

Once I get her outside, I tell her she can open her eyes and she does on command, her eyes darting around her front yard. "You don't have siblings, do you?" I ask, wondering if there was possibly another child hiding. "A brother or sister?"

"No, just me." She points at herself proudly. "Are you my big brother!?" Her eyes are wide and filled with excitement and I wish I didn't have to be the reason the look leaves her face.

"No…" I laugh at her huge jump to a conclusion. "No, I just…" I look back at the house. Officers from all over Oregon are surrounding it and taking pictures. I step over the bright yellow crime scene police tape just as I hear someone scream, "There's a child!"

"Fuck," I grumble.

Her mouth drops open and points at me. "You said a bad word," she whispers. "You have to sit on the naughty step."

"I'm a little old for the naughty step," I argue.

She furrows her brows together and a smile finds her face. I prepare myself for a sassy as hell response about not *ever* being too old for the naughty step when a group of people swarm us. Her eyes are scared, and she grips me harder, before pushing her face into my neck again. "Who are they!?" Maddie cries, her fingernails dig into my shoulder and I hold her tighter in my arms.

"She's unharmed," I tell the EMT. She was hiding, but she's shaken up. Give her some time," I tell them as I press a hand to her back.

"We still need to—" one of the EMTs starts.

"I said she's fine. Now give me a minute," I bark at her.

"You need to let me do my job," she argues back and I look down at the small child who is still gripping onto me for dear life.

I pull her back to look at me. "Maddie, sweetheart just go with the nice lady, she's just going to check you over okay?"

"No! Don't leave me!" she wails against my chest and wraps her tiny arms around my neck. She perks her head up, the tears swimming in her eyes and threatening to move down her little face. "Please, I'll be a good girl!"

I've dealt with children before, and never had I felt the pain of one of them. Never once did I feel a thump in my chest that I couldn't ignore as the tears fly down her face. I felt bad, of course, but Maddie's pleas make me want to do something, *anything* to make them go away. "Just for a minute, okay? I'll be right here." One of the EMTs manages to get her out of my grasp and she begins to kick against them in an attempt to get down.

She reaches both arms towards me. "No...CAL!"

CAL

Present Day

MY EYES SHOOT OPEN JUST AS I HEAR HER SCREAM FOR ME AND IT takes a second for my heart to slow as I realize that it's not real. I rub a hand over my face. These nightmares are back in full force. The nightmare that I didn't get to Maddie in time.

That her father took her from me first.

I sit up in bed as I think about the seven year old that is sleeping down the hall. The seven year old that is now... *seventeen.*

When we got to the police station later that day, Maddie stuck to me like glue. She wouldn't let go of my hand for anything. It remained encased in mine for most of the day, and when they tried to separate her from me to place her with a family for the night, she *lost* it. She didn't have any family; she was alone in the world, which meant she would be staying with strangers. She had friends her age, but the parents of her close friends didn't seem too keen on taking in the orphaned girl with the dead parent complex for any extended period of time.

Before I could stop myself from speaking the words, I mentioned that she could come home with me. I still remember those huge, blue eyes, the color of the ocean, looking up at me. The fear had been so evident in them it gripped my heart. *"You'll take care of me?"* she'd asked, and I didn't have the heart to tell her I meant just for the night.

Just until Social Services lined someone up.

Just until she came to terms with the new normalcy of her life.

She was the kid with the dead parents. The kid that survived the most gruesome and terrible tragedy that this town had ever seen.

She'd be gone within a week.

∽

Ten years ago

We pull up to my townhouse that I'd bought with the savings I had from working my ass off plus a little help from my mom. It wasn't large, but it was enough space for me. A two bedroom, two and a half bathroom, with a finished basement is plenty of room for me and if I happened to settle down with a wife anytime soon. I look down at the little person who I swear has been gripping my hand for dear life since I met her. She pushes some stray strands out of her face and grips her bunny tighter. "Your house is pretty. I like the flowers."

I roll my eyes as I think about my mother planting them to give the house some "warmth."

"Pink is my favorite color," she adds as we move towards the door. I have a small suitcase of her things in my other hand, and as soon as we get inside, my suitable sized house suddenly feels so small with her in it.

She swallows and looks up at me as if to say now what?

I have no fucking idea. "Are you hungry?"

She shakes her head, but I know she needs to eat something. It's been a long night and although the social worker brought her some child-friendly snacks, she hasn't had a proper meal.

"You should eat something, Maddie."

She purses her lips together and looks towards my kitchen. "Okay, what do you have?"

I do a mental check of what's in my refrigerator, which I'm pretty sure is beer and condiments and maybe a frozen dinner. My mother usually comes over every once in a while to make sure I wasn't eating out for every meal but I don't think she's been over this week.

"We can order something?"

She looks up at me, pools of blue widen and she smiles. "Pizza!" A dimple appears for the first time, and I'm pleased that I put it there.

After she's eaten, I can tell she's tired as the exhaustion of the day is probably catching up with her. "You ready for bed?"

She wipes her mouth with the back of her hand, smearing the sauce further into her skin. "I should take a bath."

Shit. I hadn't thought of that. "You sure you don't want to just go to bed?"

"I need to take a bath before bed. My jammies are clean."

I want to ask if she's sure about that given that I was familiar with the conditions of her house and the fact that clean wasn't a word I would use. "Fine, bath. Just let me call Aria."

"The lady cop?"

"Yes."

"Why?" Her eyes, despite what she's been through today are filled with innocence and curiosity and it makes me want to keep her this way forever. Untarnished by the bullshit in the world. Untouched by evil and darkness and hatred and malice. I find myself hoping that she'll find her way back into the light before the darkness of losing both of her parents on the same night consume her.

I wasn't sure how to tell her that I didn't feel comfortable bathing her. That she shouldn't feel comfortable having me bathe her. That she shouldn't be naked around any boys until she's thirty. But I figured she'd endured enough trauma for the day so I take the easy way out.

"Aria has the good smelling bubble bath."

I pick up the phone and walk out of the room, preparing myself for the shitshow of talking to Aria about my impulsive decision to take in a domestic violence victim. I can already hear her nagging. "She's going to get attached, Cal! Hell, you're going to get attached!" But that's where she's wrong. I'm not going to get attached. This is only temporary. By next week, I will be a distant memory to Madeline Shaw as she settles into her new life.

I'm sure of it.

∾

Present Day

I walk into the kitchen to find Maddie typing furiously at her laptop.

"What are you doing up so early?" I've pulled sweatpants on over my shorts and a sweatshirt over my torso as I've caught her ogling me one too many times. I don't think she means to let her eyes rove over me appreciatively, but that doesn't stop my cock from twitching in my pants.

My body is traitorous under her lustful gaze, and it's getting worse. It's like my dick doesn't know the difference. Never mind that she is seventeen or that this is Maddie. My cock only sees how she's blossomed into quite possibly the most beautiful woman I've ever laid eyes on.

"You look like shit," she tells me. "Not sleeping well again?" She gets up from the table and grabs a mug from the shelf. She holds it out for me and I can't help but take in her attire. She's wearing one of my Academy t-shirts and sleep shorts that are way too short making her toned legs go on for miles. Toned legs that she formed from ballet. *And now I'm thinking about her in those tiny fucking leotards she parades around in from time to time.* She is short, far shorter than me, but her legs are ones of tall models that seem to go on for miles. She usually wears her chocolate brown hair long and wavy down her back, but right now she has it pulled up into a high ponytail revealing a pencil behind her ear.

I snatch the mug from her. "Why are you awake? I usually have to pry you out of bed with the jaws of life in the morning." I turn my back to her as I recall threatening her with every punishment I could think of as I yelled for her to get out of bed to get ready for school.

"I hated my English paper. I woke up at three and decided to rewrite it." *Forever the perfectionist.* Maddie loves school and has a thirst for knowledge that you don't see in many high schoolers. Certainly, not of the popular variety.

"You've been up since three? Maddie, it's six, that's not enough sleep."

She snorts and when I turn around, I see her powder blue eyes are trained on her computer. "It's fiiiine."

"It's not fine," I growl at her, hoping she gets the message that I'm pissed. "You have practice tonight, don't you? You hate having class when you're running on no sleep. Your bitchy ballet teacher won't get off your back for sloppy *ronde de jambes*...your words." I wave my hand dismissively as I recall her ranting.

"Competition class is canceled, so I'll come home after and take a nap before later, happy?" She looks at me from over her computer, testing me. Provoking me.

Okay, Madeline, I'll bite.

"And what's later?" I ask her. Maddie and I have dinner together on the nights I don't have to work and the social butterfly doesn't have plans. She became rather popular after her therapist and I pushed her to get out there and start actually *enjoying* high school instead of just going through the motions until graduation. Up until she was about fifteen, she rarely left the house and spent all of her free time with me. *Something I did miss if I was being honest with myself.* She'd grown up from the little girl I rescued that night; I was pleased that I'd had the front seat and maybe a hand in her transformation. Now she was an intelligent, charming, young woman who I'd grown to love more than anyone.

"I told you. I have a date."

I cross my arms in front of my chest and stare down at her. Maddie has dated a few guys here and there but it was never serious. I'd made sure Aria had the *talk* with her when she'd come to me with tears in her eyes that she didn't know how to use a tampon. I'm fairly certain my look of shock and horror matched hers before I managed to get Aria on the phone.

I'd been forced to grow up a lot quicker than I expected, bringing in a child and raising her, but I had zero intentions of doing it again anytime soon. *At least not until I got Maddie off to college.* So, Maddie knew the deal about dating and boys. *Everyone had to be cleared through me and preferably while I was holding my gun.*

"Did you? It's a school night." I raise an eyebrow at her. I wonder if she'll call me out on the fact that it's not necessarily a rule. Maddie gets good grades and does more than what I ask of her—*not that I ask much*, so I basically let her do what she wants within reason. I'm not sure where the line of disciplinarian is, but I thank every God there is that Maddie has given me little to no troubles. I keep waiting for her rebellious phase. For her to miss a curfew or skip school or shoplift, but *nothing*. The most she'd done is drive too fast and swear like a sailor, both of which I'm certain she learned from me.

"You seemed fine with it earlier this week when I mentioned

it. And it's hardly a school night when Thanksgiving break starts the day after tomorrow. Give me a break. Tomorrow is going to be a joke."

"No."

She looks around the room before finding my gaze and a smirk finds my lips, as I think about how rare it is for me to tell her no. "No, what? It's a Thursday. You've never told me I couldn't go out with my friends during the week before."

"You heard what I said, Madeline. No."

She slaps the table. "Are you kidding me right now?! That is so not fair!"

"Life's not fair, sweetheart," I tell her as I take another sip of coffee. "And besides I may have agreed at some point, but that was before Turner told me you were flying through town like you didn't have any sense yesterday." I was pissed when one of my subordinates told me he'd pulled a cherry red Volkswagen over yesterday because it was going 50 in a 25. I almost called her and made her ass come straight home.

"Ugh, snitch," she growls. "Snitches get stitches."

I roll my eyes at her comment. "You're lucky he just let you off with a warning."

"Right, like he would have given me a ticket. Isn't he one of your little pets? That would have just been a waste given that you would have made it disappear." She flutters her eyelashes at me and I narrow mine. In the past ten years, I've flown up the ranks at work and now I'm the Chief of Police across three counties.

"Next time you're pulled over, I'm taking your keys."

She snorts. "Good one." She grabs a carton of eggs from the fridge and a bowl to begin her morning breakfast regimen that's usually only reserved for weekends. "Pancakes okay with you?"

"I'm serious, Madeline." I use her full name so that she

knows I'm not fucking around. And I hear her mumble under her breath in response like she always does. "The car is in my name, therefore it's mine. I just let you borrow it. If you can't adhere to the law, I'm taking it."

"You can't take my car, you bought it for me." She pouts, letting her bottom lip jut out.

My cock twitches slightly and for a second, I let my guard slip and allow myself the thoughts I try to avoid at all costs. The thoughts that slip through the cracks. The flashes that appear out of nowhere and throw me off kilter. The ones that I suppress and hide in the deep dark crevices of my mind.

Fuck. Fuck. Fuck. Abort mission.

I feel my cock rising in my shorts, as my mind begins to proceed with the fantasy of her on her knees in front of me.

Time. To. Fucking. Go.

"I can take the keys if you're out there being a menace to society," I call over my shoulder as I trudge out of the room. Even with my shorts and sweatpants, my dick is far from small and with the way it's rising, you'd be able to pitch a tent underneath it in no time.

I didn't need her seeing that.

By the time I'm back in the privacy of my room, my dick has deflated. I turn on the shower and step into the scalding hot temperatures, wishing I had the balls to turn it to freezing to allow the pelting ice water to turn my dick flaccid.

My mind goes through its list of rationalizations it does every time a wicked thought floats through it. First, Maddie is not my daughter. She's not. Not biologically; and while I was her legal guardian, I hadn't legally adopted her. She calls me Cal. Not Dad, or Father or…*Daddy.*

Oh Goddammit. I look down when I feel a rush of blood head south.

Stay the fuck down.

Second, Maddie doesn't see me as her father. Maybe her big brother. Or *Superhero* like she has me listed in her phone. But I'm not Dad.

Then what the hell are you? You feed her, clothe her, you have her listed as a dependent on your God damn health insurance. Don't try and justify your perversion, Grayson.

I let my head fall back against the tile as the water runs down my chest, my abs and trickles down my dick that still isn't completely soft again.

I'm going to motherfucking hell.

Two

Madeline

I'M PULLING ON MY SUEDE KNEE-HIGH BOOTS WHEN I CATCH A glimpse of the dark, ominous sky. It looks like the heavens are ready to open up at any minute with the storm that they've been predicting for a week. The normal gray sky looks almost black and a shiver snakes down my spine as I think about my aversion for bad storms.

"It's going to be fine, Mads." My thoughts are interrupted by Cal leaning against the door jamb, and I let out a sigh of relief that he's not in uniform today because that had the power to turn me into a quivering mess on sight. Not that the casual suit he's wearing is making it easier. His light brown hair is wet, like he's just gotten out of the shower, slightly disheveled but sporting its usual wave. A lock of his hair falls slightly over his eye and he pushes it back in that sexy way that all men are taught to in school or something. "But that's another reason I don't want you going out tonight. I can't protect you when you're God knows where." He nods towards the window. Cal is classic overprotective and he worries whenever I go out; more than a few times I've caught one of his minions following me around.

I turn my head back towards the window and then back to him again. "You know I hate storms. Always have." I swallow.

"I know. And *you* know I won't let anything happen to you, right?" He moves through my bedroom and stands right in front of me, entirely too much in my space. I smell the woody cologne he wears and the spearmint mouthwash he uses, and I suddenly find myself struggling to breathe. His hand reaches under my chin and raises it slightly higher to meet his gaze—brown eyes that I know better than I know my own. That I trust more than anyone. The warmth of his hand floods me, making me feel like I need to shed every layer of clothing so he can touch every inch of my bare skin. *Particularly the wet flesh between my legs.* "You trust me, don't you?"

"Yes?" I whisper, but it comes out more like a squeak. All the conviction has left my voice in response to the thumping in my sex.

I find myself staring at his mouth as one side raises in a sexy smirk. His lips part and his tongue slides across his bottom lip and I don't even try to hide the groan. "Cal…" I breathe out.

He narrows his gaze slightly, his warm brown eyes, darker than usual and filled with something I can't quite detect. "You want me, don't you, Madeline?" He pushes a hand through my hair and cups my jaw. His hand firm but gentle as his thumb strokes my bottom lip.

I let out a sigh, and my legs almost give out but he grabs me to keep me upright. "I love when you use my full name."

He leans forward, while I'm still in his arms. His breath tickles my lips. "Madeline." I let out a whimper. "Maddie." His lips bypass mine and trace kisses down the side of my face. "You're exquisite. I can't wait to get inside of you, baby."

"Oh my God, me too." I groan as I wrap a leg around him and begin to rub against him. Just as our lips are about to touch a crash stops us.

"MADDIE!"

I return to the here and now just as things were about to get good in my most recent fantasy. One that I'd conjured up in my mind while on the way to school this morning. I look up at the person who had the audacity to interrupt my thoughts, to see my best friend, Sasha Parker, who had just slammed her hand on the table, and is glaring at me with her signature irritated expression. "Are you even listening?"

I blink my eyes a few times and look around at the table of our friends, all of whom are staring at me after Sasha's outburst. I shake my head. "No, sorry. What?" I sink my teeth into the apple I'd gotten and give her a bored look.

"Am I not entertaining enough?" She waves our friends off as if to say, *mind your business*, and they go back to their conversations.

"Not particularly, no. What do you want?" *I want to know where things were going to go with me and Cal, and YOU had to interrupt.* I bite my bottom lip so I don't actually say those words aloud, as no one, and I do mean *no one* knows about my secret feelings for Cal. The last thing I need is more time with a shrink. Or worse, being forced to leave Cal altogether. I fight the tears in my eyes as I think about the terrifying feeling that I always had in the back of my mind that at any given moment someone would come and take me away from him.

It used to be so bad that I had nightmares about it for years. Nightmares that could only be quieted by Cal holding me in his arms, rocking me back and forth.

I dreamed of the night my mother died.

I dreamed that my father found me before he killed himself.

I dreamed that social services came for me while Cal was at work and I didn't get to say goodbye.

Of course, this was all when I was younger, I'd long since grown out of that irrational fear after Cal had assured me hundreds of times that *no one* could take me from him. I know that isn't how he meant it, but I held onto those thoughts. Particularly while my hand was between my legs.

I'm his.

In some form, at least.

You okay? she mouths and I nod, blinking the rest of the tears back. She purses her lips slightly like she doesn't believe me but doesn't push the subject.

"Are you coming to Jeff's tonight?" Her jet black, curly hair falls around her as she leans forward and raises her perfectly shaped eyebrows up and down.

"Ummm, no." I take a sip of my water and watch as everyone turns to me.

"Why not?" Melanie Andrews asks. Melanie is so desperate to be Sasha's best friend it's actually kind of sad. I let her have it because as much as I love Sasha, she's too high maintenance for me sometimes, and Melanie handles it much better than I care to. She tucks a red hair behind her ear and leans forward with her hand under her chin like I have some juicy story for not wanting to come to the party.

"Daddy Cop said no?" Sasha cocks her head to the side and her curls brush over her shoulder.

I roll my eyes. "You know I hate when you call him that." *Mostly because I follow about a hundred Daddy related Tumblr blogs that drive me out of my goddamn mind.*

They are hot as hell.

"I don't see the big deal; school's out for a week starting tomorrow and Jeff's parents come back Saturday!" *Translation: We're going to get fucked up.*

"As riveting as getting drunk off cheap beer in his basement sounds, it's supposed to storm and you know I get a little skittish during them."

"But Mike was bringing his friend from his rec lacrosse team to meet you. Come on, Mads, you have to meet him. He's gorgeous and smart and like All-American or whatever." She waves her hand and her boyfriend takes notice.

"Ummm, hello?" Mike, her boyfriend of the last three years, says from next to her and she turns her head to look at him, her eyes sparkling and shooting him that look that makes him putty in her hands.

"Yes, hi, what's up?" She blinks her eyes several times.

He narrows his eyes at her and taps her olive button nose. "I've got my eye on you."

"You've got your eyes on my ass, calm down." She waves him off and turns to me and I chuckle at their back and forth. "You have to come, please!" She puts her hands together and her bottom lip juts out in a pout. "It'll be so fun. Just tell Cal you're coming to my house."

"That's not exactly helping. Cal doesn't trust you, Sash." I giggle as I think about the few times I did get into mischief. Sasha Parker was always a step behind me.

Her hand finds her chest and she scoffs. "Well, I never! I am offended."

I raise an eyebrow at her. "Are you?"

The bell rings, forcing all of us to get up and head back to our classes. Sasha falls into step with me as we head to our fifth period calculus class. "Maddie, you're really not coming?"

"I mean Cal said I couldn't go out."

"Ugh, fine." She scoffs and pulls out her phone. "This is so lame. I'll see if we can move the party to tomorrow. Can you come then?"

"I'll see. Why is it *so* imperative that I'm there, Sash?"

"Because! You're my best friend and it won't be as fun without you." She hops from one foot to the other and does a little shimmy. "Listen, if you don't come, the party will die." She puts a hand over her forehead and pretends to faint.

"Anyone ever tell you, you're dramatic?"

"Anyone ever tell you, bite me?"

I chuckle and wrap an arm around her neck. "Come on, crazy, let's get to class."

"Or we can ditch?" She shoots me a mischievous look and I just shake my head at her as we make our way down the hall.

I spend most of my calculus class the same way I do when I get bored: trying to keep my mind from drifting to Cal. It doesn't help that I could probably teach this calculus class, and according to my teacher, I'm not quite being "challenged" enough. You know what's challenging? Trying to focus on derivatives when all you can think about is the man you live with working out in the basement without a shirt. I'm fairly certain I saw God the first time I watched him do chin ups.

I clear my throat as the moan threatens to escape my lips and the girl next to me gives me a questioning look. I give her a thumbs up letting her know that I'm fine but mostly to mind her business.

Is this what all women in love, *or in lust* or whatever *this* is, deal with?

I am in motherfucking hell.

∽

I pull to a stop in front of my house and let out a sigh. It had started to rain while I was on the way home, and by the time I pulled into my neighborhood the sky had turned the darkest shade of gray and now I was in the middle of a torrential downpour. I check my front and back seats, searching for my bright yellow umbrella. I don't see it anywhere. *Fuck*, I cringe as I remember leaving it by the door yesterday. I slap a palm over my forehead and groan as I accept having to walk the forty feet to the house, all the while getting drenched. I'm just about to reach for the handle to make a run for it when my door opens. I yelp and send my foot flying towards the person on instinct when he grabs my leg.

"Hey, easy there! Geeze, who did you think it was?" I look up into warm brown eyes and my heart jumps. *God, he's gorgeous. How is it possible for a man to be that good looking?*

Tall and built like he'd spent the majority of his twenties in the gym, Cal Grayson is every woman's fantasy. I know this because I see it in their eyes at every grocery store, school function, or hell, even the gas station. It's gotten to the point that I hate bringing him around all the catty and very horny, single *and not so single* dance moms when he comes to my ballet recitals. It felt almost pornographic looking at him in a swimsuit, and watching him workout sends a shiver down my spine and a dull roar between my legs that I can't ignore, but pretend I do.

He has a smile that has the power to control my mood and is so lethal it makes my knees weak. It's one of those genuine smiles that reaches his eyes, and if you aren't careful, your heart. It's often masked by a dusting of stubble that sometimes grows into a beard that makes him look like this sexual mountain man or lumberjack or whatever the fuck would make a woman's ovaries beg for his child. *I can't be the only woman in love with him.*

"Shit. What are you doing home?" *Great, this puts a delay on my plans to finish the rest of this fantasy and at least two orgasms.*

"Preventing you from getting soaked, evidently. You left your umbrella at the door." I blink up at the man standing next to my car door, holding his huge umbrella and I can't even try to ignore the throb in my sex from the chivalry. "Come on." I grab my backpack and he immediately takes it from me while I grab my purse.

"Thank you," I tell him as we walk towards the house. With

every step, my panties dampen and I feel my cheeks heating up at the growing need to relieve myself. As soon as we're through the door, I ask him again. "Why are you home, though? You're not usually here at three." I look at my watch and then back at him.

"I wanted to be here when you got home." He shrugs and sends a hand through his light brown hair.

"Why? Did you really think I was going to go out without telling you?" I scoff; the lust I was feeling is suddenly gone, replaced with irritation that he doesn't trust me.

"No, but..." he scratches the back of his neck, "they're calling for a really bad storm."

"So?" I knew what he was alluding to, but I wanted him to say it. I wanted him to say that he is here for *me*.

"I know how you get during storms. I just didn't want you to freak out, and Aria is working the night shift tonight."

Aria is one of the few people that Cal allows in the house with me alone. He trusts her wholeheartedly, and while he trusts some of his guys in the same regard, he didn't want to leave me alone with men at a young age, so Aria became a second parent.

She'd taught me all of the woman things that Cal couldn't teach me and she was the only person I felt comfortable talking to about boys. *The very few boys I forced myself to try and date to keep my mind off of someone I had no business wanting.* Cal may have been both my mother and father at times, but Aria was *Mom*. The warm side, the compassionate side, the side that gave me the best hugs and taught me how to shave my legs and how to bake the best chocolate chip cookies.

Once I'd gotten older, and it wasn't a requirement for me to have a babysitter physically in the house with me, Cal would get someone from the station to park outside the house to monitor it. But that didn't help when I got freaked out during the storm.

A clap of thunder takes me back to my first storm in this house.

I shoot up in bed as the crack of thunder is so loud it shakes my bed. My eyes immediately go towards my nightlight, a source of comfort that illuminates the room and makes it not so dark. But I don't see anything. The whole room is pitch black. I look down at my hands and I don't see them. I don't see anything.

Am I dead? Am I like Mommy?

Mommy!

I reach around the bed, searching for my bunny. The tears start to fall from my eyes...I think they're tears. If you can't see them, how can you be sure? I touch my face, and I feel the wetness. I blink my eyes trying so hard to see, but it's so dark. Another crack of thunder followed by a flash of lightning illuminates my room for a second and I could have sworn that I saw every monster come to life.

"Not real. Not real. Cal says they're not real. Your mind just plays tricks on you." I open my mouth to scream for Aria. She's babysitting while Cal is at work, but a voice whispers in my ear.

"If you scream the monsters will get you."

No. No. They're not real!

"You sure?" it whispers again.

I put my bunny in my mouth and scream just as another crack of thunder moves through the house and I jump off the bed, not realizing that I was tangled in the sheets. I hit the ground with a thud. "Owwwwww!" I cry, and I tuck myself into a ball.

The thunder claps again and I squeeze my eyes tighter. I grip my bunny and slide away from my bed, hoping that nothing comes out from under it to grab me. I manage to crawl despite my hurting leg before I curl into a ball in the middle of the floor.

"Mommy, can you hear me?" I sniffle just as the door opens. I scream and cover my ears because I've decided that hearing the monsters is worse than seeing them.

I feel arms around me and I begin to kick and suddenly my hands are away from my ears. "Hey, it's me. I'm sorry, I'm sorry." *I think he's sitting down now because I'm sitting too as he rocks me back and forth. I let out a breath.*

Cal's here. No monsters can get me.

"I'm sorry." *He kisses the side of my head.* "I sleep through storms usually...I should have figured you'd be scared. And then the power went out...did you fall? I heard something."

"*I fell off the bed.*"

"Shit, are you okay?"

"*You said shit,*" *I whisper.*

"Yes, but you know you're not supposed to say that." *He taps my nose. How does he know where my nose is? It's so dark in here.*

"*You shouldn't either.*"

"Fine, but are you okay?"

"*My leg hurts.*"

"Which one?"

I shake the one that hurts and I feel his hand on it as he shines his flashlight. "It's okay I don't think it's broken. We won't have to cut it off."

"Cut it off!" *I shriek with a giggle. We're silent for a minute when I turn to look at him as best I can.* "It's too dark here. Can I sleep in your room with you? Please, I'm scared. Or will you stay here with me?"

"Your princess bed is probably a little too small for me." *He stands up with me still in his arms and grabs his flashlight.* "You can stay in my room." *He starts walking out of the room when I stop him.*

"Wait, my bunny!"

Not that I needed it. When I had Cal, I felt safer than that bunny has ever made me feel.

"You good, Mads?" *Cal looks at me, his hand on my shoulder and I nod.* "Yeah, I just... thinking about that first storm. Do you think the power will go out?" I wince as I think about how dark this house gets with it almost completely surrounded by woods.

"It might, but you know I'm better prepared than I was ten years ago." He'd changed out of his suit and was now in basketball shorts and one of the few Academy t-shirts I hadn't stolen that showed his sharp biceps.

I need an orgasm, *stat*.

"I know, still freaks me out." I grab my backpack from his hand and make my way up the stairs.

I don't know when exactly my feelings for Cal changed from superhero to star of all my sexual fantasies. When I was younger, I would tell him that I loved him, that I was going to marry him, and attack his face with kisses on a daily basis. It was innocent, in that schoolgirl crush way.

And then one day, he touched my shoulder in the same innocent way he always had and I blushed. *Hard*. I couldn't have been any more than thirteen. For a year, I tried to make sense of my feelings, wondering how it was that I was starting to feel these things for a man that had practically raised me.

I'm sick, I thought.

I tried to ignore the thoughts.

And then I discovered what I could make my body do after a little too thorough exploration one day in the shower. Sasha and I had stolen her mom's *Cosmopolitan* one day and decided we were going to figure out what all the fuss was about. *Not together*, but separately and report our findings.

Long story short, I was home alone, thank God, because Cal's name slipped from between my lips the moment I fell over the edge of my first orgasm.

That was three years ago.

I've been fucked ever since.

Three

Madeline

"**I**'M NOT DOING IT." I CROSS MY HANDS IN FRONT OF MY CHEST AS A scowl finds my face. I stare at the beautiful pink bike that Cal had bought me for my birthday and turn my face back to his as he kneels next to me. "I refuse."

He pulls his sunglasses off his face and his chocolate brown eyes meet my icy blue ones. "Maddie, come on. You have to learn to ride a bike without training wheels."

"I tried. I failed." I huff.

"You fell one time." He puts his index finger up in front of my face. "Because you let go."

"You were doing so good, sweetheart. You didn't need me!"

"No." I turn away from the bike and begin walking back towards the house when I feel his hand wrapping around my arm.

"Mads."

"NO!" I scream. "You can't make me."

"I promise it'll be—"

"No." I glare at him. "I fell. Look at my elbow AND my knee!" I show him the scratch on my arm that is so big it has to be covered with two SpongeBob band-aids and the one on my knee that hurts every time I bend my leg. "It hurts, Cal." My lip trembles and my eyes well up with tears. "You swore you wouldn't let me fall."

His eyes are warm and I wonder if he's going to cry too when he wraps me in a hug. I smile and rest my head on his shoulder because even though I'm mad at him, he gives the best hugs. He rubs my back and kisses my nose, the hair of his beard tickling my skin and making me giggle.

"You can't stay mad at me forever."

"Yes, I can." I go back to glaring so that he thinks I'm still mad. He smiles and touches my cheeks with his index fingers like he always does when he wants my dimples to pop out.

"Let's try one more time, and then…I'll let you stay up late tonight."

My ears perk up and I look around as I think about his offer. "How late?"

"Past nine o'clock news late."

I put my hands on my hips and cock my head in that way that Cal says "he can't say no to." "I stay up past then anyway."

"You're supposed to be asleep, Madeline Elizabeth." He narrows his eyes at me and I giggle with a shrug.

"Stop buying me books."

His eyes roll in a full circle, and I find myself trying to imitate him. How does he do that? "Fine, ten o'clock news, final offer."

"You got a deal!" I shake his hand and take off for my pretty pink bike with the tassels and wicker basket attached to the front.

A clap of thunder rouses me from my sleep and immediately I'm on high alert. The room is almost pitch black and before I can think I'm reaching for my cell phone and turning on my flashlight. *Fuck, the power went out.*

It was rare that we lost power, with Cal getting a generator installed after the first few times scared me shitless. For the power to have gone out, it's probably a big storm and right on schedule, the thunder claps and confirms my suspicion. The tree outside is scratching against my window, and the rain is hitting the roof so aggressively I'm surprised I've been asleep this long.

A flash of lightning brightens the room and I shut my eyes just like every time for fear of seeing something that would shake me to my core.

I'm out of bed before I can stop myself and padding down the hallway towards Cal's room. Even without my light, I'd know how to get there. I'd memorized that it was sixteen big steps and twenty-two smaller steps between mine and Cal's room. A fact that was necessary when I was bolting for it in the middle of the night. It's been years since I snuck into Cal's room, and I don't know if it's because my feelings have been getting more intense and I'm being led by my hormones, or if the memories of that first storm are still haunting me, but I find myself in front of his bedroom.

From a young age, Cal taught me to always knock on closed doors, and while at the time I didn't realize why, I always listened to his rule. Of course now, at seventeen, I realize why he'd ask me to knock before barging into his bedroom. And because I'm seventeen, with lustful thoughts swirling through my brain about seventy percent of my waking hours. I decide to proceed *without* caution. I push through his door and pad through his room, the carpet plush under my feet, careful to keep my phone pointed downwards as I move towards his bed. I sit on the edge and I feel him shift.

I shine my phone upwards, careful not to blind either of us. "Wha—Mads?"

"Power's out."

He lets out a sigh and sits up, resting his back against the headboard and grabs his phone to check the time. "What did I tell you about knocking?"

I roll my eyes. "What, are you naked under there or something?" I hope he can't see the flash of hope cross my face or my eyes that dart straight to where his dick is hidden beneath the wool blanket.

"No, Madeline, but you know the rule."

"Sorry, but you didn't come to my room when the lights went out. You always come..." I trail off.

"It's been a while since they went out." My eyes are finally adjusting to the darkness of the room and I can make out his eyes now. "Must be pretty bad out there."

"Yeah..." I tell him softly. I bite my bottom lip gently and my eyes flit around the room. "Can I stay?"

He's silent and I briefly wonder if he's going to tell me no. That I need to go back to my room and stop whatever it is I'm doing.

Stop trying to seduce me, Maddie. I swear I hear his body telling me.

"Yeah, of course, I mean... yes. Let me just run downstairs for a second, okay?"

I don't say anything because a part of me is a little scared about being up here by myself. I know my fear is irrational and a little childish, but call it what everyone refers to it as my "brush with death" when I was a kid. There were things that went bump in the night and it scared me. Except these bumps were heard from *within*. The brutalities of my childhood whispered in my ear in the dead of night, making me wonder if I'd eventually meet that same end. The nightmares of physical monsters had stopped haunting my dreams years ago. The nightmares manifest in different ways now. I'm no longer afraid of the monsters under the bed, but the ones that lurk in my brain. The ones that whispered, *you're next*. Ones that are only completely silenced when I'm around Cal.

His hands find my face and he strokes my cheek, as if he can hear my thoughts, as if he is lurking there as well, whispering, *you're not next, Mads.* "Two minutes, okay? Just stay here.

It's your turn in *Words with Friends*. I took my turn after you fell asleep."

My eyes shoot to my phone, opening the game that Cal and I have been nonstop playing since I got an iPhone three years ago. "Okay."

I'm still trying to figure out how I can put this five-letter word on a triple word score when Cal walks back through the door with something in his hand. I can't quite make it out when he puts it on the floor. "What are you doing?"

"I got a sleeping bag."

"What for?"

"Mads…" He trails off.

"You've never made me sleep on the floor before." I frown.

"It's not for you, Maddie. You think I'd make you sleep on the floor?"

"Oh…why are you sleeping on the floor?"

"I just…I don't think…I mean…you're older now and I just…" I hear the implication, and I interrupt.

"Oh my God, Cal. Stop." I try to sound as dismissive as possible so I don't alert that I'm gunning for the exact thing he's trying to avoid.

"No, Madeline. When I'm asleep, my body might still react to…" The room is so quiet I can hear him gulp as he lays out the sleeping bag and grabs a pillow from his bed.

"So, you don't trust yourself with me, then?" I try to catch the words before they leave my mouth, but I'm too late and I snap my lips shut knowing that he's going to react to my comment.

"That's not what I said," he grits out and I let out a sigh before falling back in his pillows. His entire bed smells like him and it speaks to me on the most primal level. I turn my head into his pillow and quietly inhale his scent. A scent that is so ingrained in my body and soul despite the fact that it isn't in my DNA.

"You're being ridiculous," I tell him as I let my eyes flutter closed.

"I know," is the last thing I hear before sleep takes me for the second time.

⌁

I wake up the next morning to the most delicious warm feeling flooding my entire body and heating my bones. My feet, which are notoriously cold even with the fluffy socks Cal consistently buys me are toasty warm and I feel heat wrap around me like a vine. A tingle licks up and down my spine and it feels like a heater is blowing out air directly on my neck. My eyes flutter open and the first thing I feel is a pain in my shoulder. *What the fuck?*

The feeling in my shoulder that I realize is due to falling asleep on the floor is immediately erased when I look down and see arms wrapped around me. I'm basically pinned to Cal's body with the vice grip he has on me, and I briefly wonder how in the hell I got, not only on the floor, but *inside* his sleeping bag with him.

Holy shit. He's going to freak. Especially when he realizes that his morning wood is digging into my back like a spear dying to push its way through me.

I have vague memories of climbing off the bed and snuggling against him, but I could have sworn that was just a dream.

Evidently not.

I manage to peek towards the window and I see it's still storming out. *It's about to be a storm in here as well.*

I'm trying to pry myself out of Cal's arms when the universe decides that *now* is the time to fuck with me. Cal's alarm blares through the air with a shrill pierce, serving as an alert that *something isn't right, Cal Grayson. Wake the fuck up and deal with it.*

His eyes fly open before I've had a chance to untangle myself from him. I've sat up slightly, but our legs are still entangled, his arms are still wrapped around me, and his dick—I shift slightly and inadvertently bump into him—*yep still hard.*

"Maddie?" His eyes are wide and nervous but mostly confused as he lets me go like I've burned him. Like he's been holding onto fire all night and his body is finally reacting to the searing flame.

"I...I don't remember moving down here."

He looks around, still slightly confused and disoriented before focusing back on me. "What the fuck, Madeline?"

"Sorry, I..."

"This is exactly why I got the sleeping bag." His ears are red, a telltale sign that he's embarrassed. His cheeks don't pinken like most people. Instead, his ears are his giveaway. He moves backwards away from me and shakes his head before turning his alarm off, which I didn't even realize is still blaring with the way my subconscious is screaming at me for my stupidity.

"I'm...sorry." Tears well in my eyes as I hear his disappointment, his regret, his...*disgust.* "Please don't hate me. You know I get a little...vulnerable during storms."

"Yeah, I'm more than aware. And when you were younger it was fine that you snuggled up to me. Now...you can't do that shit anymore and you fucking know why. So, don't act like you don't," he snaps.

His posture is combative, despite the fact that he's still sitting and I shrink slightly into myself. I don't say anything, and I try to look anywhere but the heated eyes staring at me.

"Go get ready for school, Madeline." I hop off the floor and basically sprint out the door. I make it to my room and fall back against the door, letting a breath out that I feel like I've been holding since I slipped into his bed last night.

It isn't until my heart has started to slow from the accelerated speed that I realize I left my phone in his room. I groan, thinking about going back in and facing Cal, and I honestly think I'd rather go the day without it. I spend the next thirty minutes showering and getting ready for school, suddenly excited that this is the last day before Thanksgiving break.

I'm pulling my boots on when I hear the door close and my head snaps towards the window. I'm immediately off my bed and bolting towards the window just in time to see Cal already in his car, backing out of the driveway. *What the fuck?*

When he makes it into the street, his black Jeep Patriot stops, and for a moment I swear I meet his gaze through the window. I just only hope he doesn't see the tears forming in my eyes before I turn away. I jog down the stairs, and I see that he's left enough coffee for me and my phone on the table. I pick it up, prepared to text Sasha when I see I have one waiting for me.

Superhero: Have a good day. Be safe.

CAL

It took twenty minutes and a lukewarm shower for my dick to go down after I willed myself not to touch it. I had a paralyzing fear that Maddie's face would flash through my mind the second I wrapped my hand around my dick and I didn't want to risk it. So, I let the cooled water rain down on my cock until it softens enough for me to wash my balls. I let my head hit the tile and shame slides over me; I wish it would slither down the drain like the water.

I was hard. Holding Maddie in my arms. Her soft warm body rubbing against my dick like she had the right to.

I run a hand through my hair as I wonder how in the hell I'm going to face her as I step out of the shower. I open the door of the bathroom, peeking my head out as I didn't put it past Maddie to be sitting on my bed so that we could *talk,* and I let out a sigh of relief when I don't see her anywhere in my room. I move towards my door and lock it, suddenly feeling like a seventeen year old is preying on me like she's the hunter and I'm the *hunted.*

You're being dramatic, Cal. She was scared and you make her feel safe. Protected. It's always been this way. Nothing's changed.

My cock stiffening under my towel refutes that thought, confirming my suspicions that in fact, everything has changed.

"Hey hey!" Aria drops into my chair on the other side of my desk and props her foot up on the wood surface as she takes a bite of the protein bar that she treats like a major food group. Her hair that is usually pulled into a slick bun is wild and free around her shoulders with sunglasses perched on top of her head.

I tap her foot with my pen and she rolls her eyes and crosses her legs. "Listen, what are you doing tonight?"

"Why isn't your hair up?"

"Chill out, boss man. I just got here."

"You were due at eight. Why are you just getting here at nine-thirty?" I look at my watch.

"Because your brother wouldn't let me out of bed." I go to tell her that I so didn't want to know when she holds up a hand. "And told me to tell you to take the stick out of your ass before I knock it out of you, *little* bro." I blink my eyes at her several times and she giggles. "Listen, I didn't say it, he did."

"Don't make me put you on parking duty."

"You wouldn't." She frowns and I shoot her a look willing her to test me. "Not when I have such good news for you."

"It better be a lead on that mysterious fire in the warehouse across town." I wince, wondering if foul play was involved and thus no real suspects as everyone had covered up the evidence.

"No. Well... maybe, but that's not what I was referring to."

"Maybe?" I ask wondering, what the lead is.

"Focus, Cal."

"I *am* focused!"

"No, listen. I want to set you up with someone."

I groan. "Aria, no. We've been over this."

"Cal! Henry approved this one!"

I give her a stern glare as I remember the last three women Aria has set me up with. They were all disasters. One was a neurotic schoolteacher that treated me like I was one of her students. The other was thirty year old party girl who got so wasted on our date that she spent the night puking up the tequila shots she'd assured me she could handle. And the final, a preacher's daughter that was currently going through her rebellious phase about seven years too late, and practically pulled her tit out at dinner and told me she'd suck my dick in the bathroom before we'd even ordered appetizers.

No, no, and fuck no.

Once upon a time, I would have fucked all three and not thought twice, *and yeah maybe I did fuck that last one*. But I never dated all that much, and I brought even fewer women around Maddie. I never wanted her to get the wrong idea about me, or that these kinds of women that felt *disposable* to me were the kind of women *she* should strive to be.

I wanted better for Maddie.

I wanted everything for her.

"Come on, Cal. She's really sweet. We do yoga together."

Since when did flexible become synonymous for sweet? "What does that have to do with anything?"

"Come on, Henry says you haven't gotten laid in forever," she points out.

"I hate you both, and I'd love if you could keep my sex life out of your pillow talk." I slam the pen I'm holding down on the stack of papers and shoot her a look.

"You don't have a sex life, Cal. I hate to break it to you, hon. And Margie wants grandchildren sometime this millennium."

"Then *you* and Henry give them to her." I feel a pang of guilt over my comment and Aria and Henry's past, but luckily Aria doesn't react, so I continue. "Besides, I already gave her one." Even as I say the words, they bother me. *Maddie isn't your child.*

"You and I both know, she doesn't see Maddie like a grandchild. She's like the daughter Margie never had."

"She certainly treats her like a grandchild." I recall every single time that my mother has let Maddie get her way. Every time Maddie would throw *Margie lets me do it* in my face when I told her no. The way they would talk on the phone for hours, the way her face would light up when she came over to babysit. I'm still slightly pissed at my mother for teaching her to play poker and then proceeding to give her a "Poker for Dummies" book that hustled me out of forty-five dollars and a week's worth of ice cream for dinner.

She was nine.

"The point iiiiiis," Aria drawls, "you need to meet someone. You're a young, good-looking guy, with a good job and good credit and you own your house and you have your shit together! I see the way women fall at your feet. Why are you keeping everyone at arm's length?"

"Why do you think, Aria?"

"I know and that's the point I'm trying to make. You can't keep letting Maddie control your life." She tucks a hair behind her ear and looks at me with that signature look that pisses me off. *Stop fucking momming me, Aria. I already have one.*

"She doesn't control my life, A, but I made her a promise. I made a vow to put her first."

"And that's admirable, but at some point, you have to put *you* first again. She's almost eighteen and eventually she'll be out on her own." My cock stiffens and deflates in that one sentence. Hardens as it thinks about her being eighteen and then softens just as quick thinking about her out on her own. *Away from me.*

My mind floats back to a time when she'd told me that time would *never* come.

"Hey, Cal?"

I look over to where Maddie is doing her homework to find that she's set her pencil down and is staring at me with a worried expression.

"What's up, Mads?"

"Can I live here forever?"

"Forever?"

"Yeah, I mean…even when I go to college and get married and stuff?"

I chuckle at the ten year old at my table. "You don't want to move out? Get your own place? Have independence and all that shit?" I wince. I've been trying to get better about not swearing so much, especially around Maddie, but it isn't exactly working and now she's swearing like a sailor too.

"I can still have independence from my bedroom."

"We'll see how you feel in a few years, okay?"

"I'm serious. I want to live here forever. I don't have to go, do I?"

I look in the eyes of my favorite human and even though I know one day she'll be humming a very different tune. I shake my head as I know that day isn't today, and hurting Maddie's feelings was never my intention. "You can stay forever, kiddo."

"Perfect."

I swallow down the hot coffee. It burns my tongue and all the way down my throat to try and combat the burn from Aria's words that one day Maddie *would* leave.

"Alright, yeah. What's her name?"

Maddie is sitting on the couch when I get home, flipping through the channels as her computer balances on her knee. It's 6 PM, and I'm meeting Henry, Aria, and my *date*, Penelope, across town at seven. I frown as I pick up the mail that is sitting on the table. "I wasn't expecting you home?"

"You weren't? You know I usually tell you if I'm not coming home." She doesn't look up from the computer.

"Right. Well, I guess I mean, I was expecting you to have plans." I can't remember many Friday nights that I didn't get home to Maddie running around like a chicken with her head cut off because she couldn't figure out what to wear, or her hair wouldn't curl or Sasha was *so motherfreaking late.*

"Oh. Well, Sasha wants me to go to this party with her, but I'm not all that interested."

"Why not?" Not that I'm not thrilled. Sasha Parker is trouble and she and Maddie together are double fucking trouble. Even though Maddie rarely gets into mischief, I know she's in a phase where she's experimenting with too much fucking alcohol and it pisses me off.

"You're okay with me going to a party? Usually, you make me take a chaperone."

"That you ditch in two point five seconds."

"Like they can't find me." She rolls her eyes. "But no…I just thought we should talk about…this morning."

"Nothing to talk about, Mads."

"Oh? Is that why you left without so much as a goodbye?"

"I said goodbye."

"You know that's not what I meant."

"Maddie, there's nothing to talk about. Besides, I'm going out with Aria and Henry." I head up the stairs and within an instant, she's behind me, following me up. Her perfume engulfs me instantly. A scent that has the power to arouse me if I didn't focus. I walk faster to try and put some space between us.

"Can I come?"

"No."

"What? Why not? I can always come when you guys go

out." I pause and turn around to face her after turning on the light in the hall. She bites her bottom lip and for a second, I see a flash of hurt, but maybe it's just my imagination because it disappears instantly. "It's not just you three?"

"No, it's not."

"A date?"

I nod, wondering why I feel guilty for having a date. Why I'm letting *Maddie* make me feel guilty for having a date. *Why should she care? Why should I care that she cares?* "So, you're not going out?" I ask her. "I'll have Peters stationed out front."

She shakes her head and follows me into my bedroom and suddenly it feels three times smaller with us in here together. Flashes of this morning, my body wrapped around her petite frame come crawling back into my mind and wake up the sleeping demon inside. Fire ignites through me, and I feel my ears heating. *Get rid of Madeline before I make my appearance, Officer Grayson*, I can practically hear my dick screaming at me.

"Is she pretty?" She crosses her arms in front of her chest and I'm grateful that she's wearing a t-shirt and not accentuating her breasts with those thin tank tops she wears from time to time.

"I don't know." This isn't the first time she's asked me about a potential date, but it is the first time that it feels weird talking to her about it. Like I'm betraying her. *I have got to get a fucking grip.*

"Blind date?" She snorts. "Well, that's stupid. Aria and Henry don't even know your type."

I snap my head towards her, confused. "What?"

"They don't! Margie even agrees." She sits on my bed.

"You and my mother gang up on me for everything, I swear to fuck."

"It's because she likes me better."

"I'm aware." I glare at her before crossing my arms and cocking my head to the side. "But back to the first thing, what makes you such an expert on my type?"

She shrugs and plays with her hands in her lap. "I've got eyes."

"Okay, and what do they see?"

She purses her lips and shakes her head, a sad smile finding her lips. "You need to figure that out yourself, I think."

"So ominous." I let my hands drop. "I gotta take a shower. Do you mind?" I point at my door and she sighs and stands up.

"Have fun on your date or whatever." I don't have time to question her attitude because my phone starts ringing in my pocket. I put the phone to my ear just as I hear Aria's blaring warning to *not be late, motherfucker.*

I move down the steps, pulling my suit jacket over my button up and look at the young girl seated on my couch having changed into her pajamas. "You're really not going out?" I ask her.

"I'm really not." She affirms.

"Alright, I'm calling Peters." She doesn't even argue with me, knowing that it's not an argument she can win.

"Or you could just…not go." She shrugs and I narrow my gaze at her, wondering where that's coming from.

"Why?"

She bites her bottom lip and takes a moment to stare at the television before turning to me. "Because I don't want you to?"

Under normal circumstances, I would take time to unpack that statement. Try to dig to the root of her issue with me going out, but this morning coupled with Aria's advice that I need to start putting myself out there makes me ignore that feeling in my gut that tells me to talk to Maddie.

"Maddie..."

She scrunches her nose, and if I didn't know any better, I would say that she's trying to prevent herself from crying. "You look nice," she says softly before she moves off the couch and up the stairs without another word.

∞

I pull up to the restaurant across town, having just checked in with Peters for the second time since I left about whether everything is okay. He'd promptly told me to relax, have fun, and *fuck off* before hanging up the phone.

The waiting area is large and dimly lit by lanterns that line the ceiling. The waitstaff is walking around taking orders for cocktails when I immediately spot Aria and Henry, the main focal point of the room, as everyone's attention is drawn to them, *like always*. Aria and Henry look like a superstar couple when they go anywhere. Heads turn when they walk by like they belong in a Ralph Lauren catalogue under "perfectly dressed couple."

Of course, their relationship looks much different from the inside.

Aria jumps up, her champagne almost spilling over the side, and waves me over. "Yay! You're here! And on time!" She twirls her finger in a circle. "Turn for me."

Henry nods at me and rolls his eyes, as if to say, *she does this shit to me too*. "Baby bro," he says with a jerk of his chin. I nod back, even though a part of me is slightly irritated that he'd signed off on this charade. My older brother is a few inches taller than me but with significantly less muscle. His hair is darker and his eyes are more reminiscent of our father's, a dark blue, unlike the brown of mine and my mother's.

I spin around and look back at Aria. "Do you approve?"

Her bright red lips quirk up in a bright smile. "You look great. Proud of ya, champ."

"You act like I can't dress myself."

"You can't. Did Maddie okay this?"

A lump forms in my throat hearing her name and I immediately turn my head for a waiter with any kind of alcohol to loosen the knot. "Nah, she wasn't really around when I left."

"She wasn't home? Where is she?" I immediately hear the mother in her voice.

"No, she was, but I only saw her briefly."

Aria's eyebrows furrow, but she doesn't press further when a waft of very strong perfume floods my nostrils. I take a step back, hoping to put some space between myself and the oppressive scent when it just moves *closer*. I turn my head to see a woman with reddish-blonde hair, sparkling blue eyes, and bright pink lips coming at me. A smile finds her mouth and her eyes as she sticks her hand out. "Hi, I'm Penelope."

"Cal." I know how to perform even when I'm not particularly in the mood, so I turn on the charm. "It's a pleasure to meet you, Penelope." I smile and cock my head to the side, my obvious move that allows me to unashamedly check out a woman who would then think I was interested.

It inflated their ego and made them feel more comfortable. Even though I was far from interested in this moment. I can't stop the nagging thought that keeps flaring up that Maddie is upset that I've gone out but I try to put it out of my head. We make our way to the table, my hand resting on the small of Penelope's back as she yammers on about being so excited to try this restaurant. If I'm being honest, her voice is grating on my goddamn nerves. We are sitting at a table near a window, allowing us to stare into the forest behind the restaurant which is illuminated by hanging lights.

"I'm so glad we did this." Aria smiles as she takes another sip of her champagne. Henry nurses his whiskey ginger and I fight the urge to text Madeline to make sure she's okay. As if she can hear me, my phone vibrates in my pocket. Aria and Henry are no strangers to my having to respond to messages, so I don't think anything of it when I pull my phone out. "Excuse me a second."

I frown when I realize it's not Madeline and really *is* work-related. *Whatever, this actually could wait.*

"Everything good, boss?" Aria asks with a raised eyebrow, and I nod.

"So, Aria says you're the Chief of Police. Do you like it?" Penelope's voice chirps from next to me.

"Yeah, it's great. Love it. I've always wanted to be a cop, always wanted to help people, and the power to make a difference is a responsibility I don't take lightly."

"Wow," she tucks a hand under her chin and smiles up at me, "that's really admirable."

I nod. Maddie admires me. She's told me time and time again that I'm her hero. That she believes I was put on this Earth solely to change her life and the lives of so many other people. She is immensely proud of me, and I wear that pride with honor that shines brighter than any badge I have. "Thank you."

"She also said you have a…umm…kind of daughter?"

I chuckle and my heart races as it always does as I prepare to explain to a potential romantic interest about Maddie. I don't explain it to everyone, but a few people know the story of what went down in that shack across town all those years ago and are curious. I could practically hear the ovaries bursting every time I told the story, but I typically ignore it, as Madeline's story isn't one that did much besides gut me.

Her shaking body in my arms. Her fear of abandonment. The way she screamed for me when they tried to separate us. It took me to a dark place that sometimes takes me a second to break from. I scratch my beard as my eyes scan the restaurant, looking for someone that could bring me a drink. "Yeah, Madeline. She's not my daughter."

"But she lives with you?" I don't think I hear the malice or judgment but it is borderline, so I already feel the defense coming as I prepare my statement.

Aria and Henry exchange a look, like they know that it's too early to go down this road and that I'm seconds from reading her for giving her unsolicited opinion. "Yes." I give her a look, warning her to watch her next step, which she must understand because her eyes widen and she shakes her head.

"I didn't mean…I was just curious that's all."

"Curious about what? Do you go around asking people that adopt children that go through traumatic experiences why they felt the pull to take care of them?" Even as I hear the words, I know why I'm defensive, but I ignore the blaring light that tells me I no longer have those feelings for Maddie. That she is slowly shifting categories in my life and there is nothing I can do about it. I never technically adopted Maddie, so I don't even know why I feel the need to make that analogy, and Aria and Henry must wonder too because they look at me curiously.

"I…sorry." She lets out a breath and looks at Aria. "Ummm, I'm going to go to the ladies room."

She and Aria depart the table and Henry shoots me a glare. "Calm the fuck down, Cal. What is wrong with you?"

"You know how I feel about people giving their opinion about Maddie."

He pinches the bridge of his nose and squeezes his eyes shut. "She was just asking, and you bit her head off, preaching from some soapbox about adoption, when you never even adopted Maddie." He eyes me from over his glass as he takes a sip.

"Sorry," I grumble, realizing that maybe I was too quick to snap at her. It wasn't her fault that I'd been wound up tight as fuck after this morning. *Hell, more like the last fucking year.*

He leans forward and his eyes narrow worriedly. "What is with you, man?"

"Nothing."

"Is something up with Maddie? That's the only time you're really in a bad mood. Unless it's something work-related, but Aria said things have been mild lately."

I roll my eyes thinking about how my brother and his wife think that my mood could be controlled by a seventeen year old girl.

Almost eighteen, my mind decides to remind me and right on time, my cock jumps in my pants.

"I need a drink," I say, looking around the restaurant. My face falls slightly when I see Aria and Penelope approaching the table. I was hoping to get a drink in before they returned. I figure now is the time to smooth things over if I don't want Aria to chop my dick off tomorrow, so I turn to her and smile. "Sorry about that…I guess I've had a lot of opinions thrown at me for my decisions the last ten years."

"Oh," her eyes widen and she smiles like she wasn't expecting my apology but thrilled she was getting it, "no worries, I understand. I didn't mean to be intrusive."

"All good. Should we get some drinks?"

⁓

We're heading out later that night, after dinner, and Aria and Henry are moving towards their Uber after they both indulged in a few too many drinks. I, on the other hand, stuck to one and then switched to water, despite Penelope goading me into taking a few shots with them. "I hope you're not driving."

"No umm...I can call an Uber?" she says.

I'm instantly annoyed by my gentleman instinct kicking in when I just want to go home and check on Maddie after her radio silence all evening. When she was younger and I'd been on dates, she'd rapid-fire message me, asking me how it was going and to take a picture of the dessert menu so she could pick out something for me to bring her.

Things were so simple back then.

Didn't stop me from ordering her a piece of carrot cake.

"I'll take you home."

"Oh, are you sure?" She looks up at me through her eyelashes and gives me a shy smile that I see through instantly.

"Yep, come on."

Twenty minutes later, I'm pulling up to her apartment building and she hesitates with the door handle as I unbuckle my seatbelt to get out to walk her to her door. "Do you want to come up?"

"Maybe some other time, Penelope." I smile at her, trying my best to let her down gently. "I have to be up early and—"

"I get it." She cuts me off, and a part of me feels like a dick, but another part—an even bigger part—overwhelms me, and that part only cares about being a dick to Maddie.

I make my way around my car to help her out and walk her towards her front door. "I had fun."

"Me too, Cal." She hugs me, and as she pulls away, I press my lips to hers, trying to soothe the rejection she might be feeling as best as I can. Even as I do it, it feels wrong. I feel nothing and it irritates the shit out of me. She's a good kisser and I can't even appreciate it. Her arms immediately wrap around my neck as she pushes herself closer to me, sliding her tongue through my lips and coaxing mine into hers. I let this go on for a considerate amount of time, before I pull back, leaving a huge smile on her face. She gives me a small wave and I notice her perfume lingers even after she disappears inside.

I drive at the speed of a racecar driver to get home, and when I pull into my driveway, I nod at Peters on the way in. I'm not surprised to see a light on, knowing that Maddie always leaves it on for me so it's not pitch black when I get home. I don't expect her to be awake at 1 AM, so I'm shocked when I see her sitting on the stairs as soon as I walk in the house.

"Mads? Why are you awake? And sitting here?"

She blinks at me like she isn't sure she heard me or isn't sure how to answer. Shame and guilt encroach on my senses, and I try to push them away with the belief that I have no reason to feel guilty. "I brought cake." I hold up the bag and again she doesn't respond.

"Maddie, what's wrong?" I move closer to sit next to her on the step, but that must have been the wrong thing to do because she backs up and shakes her head.

"I smell her all over you." She scrunches her nose like it's offensive.

"Sorry, she was wearing a lot."

"I...I can take it to the dry cleaning...your jacket. Because it's...strong." I can't read her mood, so I just nod graciously. "Did you like her?"

"She was nice."

"That's not what I asked."

"Maddie, what's going on with you, huh? I feel like you're so angry with me and…"

"Because you're angry with me!" She stands up in front of me and furrows her brows at me.

I furrow my brows, confused. *When am I ever mad at you?* "What? No, I'm not. Why would I be mad?"

"This morning?" she asks weakly.

Oh. Right. The whole reason I even agreed to this fucking date. To further emphasize the line that Maddie and I didn't need to be crossing. *Ever.*

"I'm not mad. It was an accident. We're good, Maddie. Always." I smile at her, hoping that makes *her* a little less mad at *me*. Except her eyes show that she's *pissed*.

"Did you kiss her?"

"What?"

"There's lipstick…" She points at my face and I can see the hurt as clear as day on her face.

Fuck. Fuck. FUCK. I didn't even think to check the mirror between dropping her off and getting home.

"Maddie, you're out of fucking line." I stand up, officially over this conversation. But not quite for the reason I was expecting. I'm over it because she's jealous and I hate that she is. I hate that she doesn't know me well enough to know that she is the only woman that matters to me.

My mind tries to ignore that I just thought of her as a woman. But my dick hears it loud and clear.

My mind continues to race as I put her cake in the fridge.

"Excuse me?" she snaps at me.

"You heard me, Madeline. So, what, I kissed her? Why does that fucking matter?" I hope she can hear the translation in my words. *It doesn't matter. It doesn't matter. You. fucking. Matter. Don't make us do this tonight.*

She blinks her eyes a few times and shakes her head. "You're right. Shit. It's…your business."

Fuck that. "Maddie…" I reach an arm out for her, suddenly pissed at myself for the tone I took with her as I witness her shutting down before my very eyes.

"Thanks for the cake. I'm going to bed." She backs out of the room slowly, like I might attack her if she makes any sudden movements before I hear her bolting up the stairs and closing her door.

Five

Madeline

I CAN FEEL THE PHYSICAL ACHE BEHIND MY EYELIDS THE NEXT MORNING when the sunlight peers through my blinds. I spent the entire night in tears after what happened between me and Cal and not just because I was upset and feeling what I believe to be some sort of heartbreak, but because I was humiliated. I acted like a jealous girlfriend and he fucking called me on it.

How the hell am I supposed to face him ever again?

I'll admit it, I was jealous. Seeing the pink on his lips mixed with her scent all over him made me feel territorial as fuck. It pissed me off that some woman had tried to stake her claim on him. A claim that I had somehow twisted myself into believing I'm entitled to.

You can't fucking have him, Maddie! I had been so blind with jealousy that the words were leaving my mouth before I could stop them.

Cal doesn't want you, Maddie. Why the hell would he want some dumb kid?! A kid who's sheets he had to change when she wet the bed.

Even though it was only once, it happened, and what makes you think he'd ever see you in a way other than that girl? Maybe one day as an adult, but certainly never as a partner.

I pry my eyes open and groan when the harshness of daylight hits my face. I submerge my face in my pillow and groan again. My eyes feel swollen and tired and I can already bet that they're red along with my splotchy skin that comes with my crying. The house is quiet, and I'm assuming Cal has already left for work, so I pad out of my bedroom and down the stairs to look for coffee without even a glance in a mirror. When I get downstairs, I'm stunned to see him sitting in the kitchen, reading the newspaper, and for a brief moment, I think about darting back upstairs to hide.

Great.

I walk by him, mumbling a *Morning* and grab a mug to pour myself a cup of coffee.

"Hey." His voice is smooth. Like warm honey pouring over me and sinking into my bones.

I turn around and put the steaming cup to my lips. "Hey."

He frowns and stands up, making his way over to me. "Your eyes are so red." He touches the skin under them and it might as well have been a direct line to my sex because it throbs under his innocent touch.

"I uh—I was up late reading on my phone."

He nods like he doesn't believe me and takes a step back. "I told you to stop that. You're going to ruin your eyes."

His scolding doesn't do anything but exacerbate the pulse. *God, what is wrong with me?*

"Right. Sorry."

"Hey, listen about last night…" he starts and I shake my head, not wanting to go down this road again and already feeling the familiar prickle that causes my tears to form.

"Cal…" I interrupt, "can we not?"

He stops and I take a minute to admire his looks. Dark jeans that hug him in all the right places and a Police Academy hoodie makes him look like a young college student and not a thirty-three year old man. His eyes seem to be doing the same to me because when mine find his, they're glued to my chest. I feel myself getting hot under his gaze and just when I thought I couldn't get any more turned on, he takes a step forward. "What's going on with us, huh?"

You mean besides the fact that I'm so desperately in love with you that I can't fucking see straight? Nothing.

I think about blowing him off. Making him feel like he's crazy and that nothing had changed between us. I think about sidestepping the question with a joke. But inevitably, I go with the truth.

"I don't know." I bite my bottom lip and stare up into his stormy eyes. Eyes that for the first time seem like they may not have all the answers. His hand reaches out and pulls my bottom lip from between my teeth and I gasp. I stare at his hand as he lowers it slowly and I feel his eyes on my face, but I don't meet his gaze. He takes another step towards me and my heart begins to race. A loud thumping in my chest that matches the one between my legs. He's right in front of me at this point and he lifts my chin slowly to meet his gaze. His thumb finds my bottom lip again, and he traces the skin so lightly I barely feel it. *But I see it.*

"Cal." My voice comes out like a whimper. He must have been in some sort of trance until now, not realizing how dangerously close he was to taking us over a line we couldn't come back from because a growl leaves his lips and he takes a step back.

He shakes his head. "I need to go in for a little while. Will you be here?"

"I...I was going to go to the grocery store with Margie... since Thanksgiving is next week?" I say weakly, my body fully preparing to give out the second that Cal isn't in the room. I feel like I'm wound so tight that I'm seconds from shattering into a thousand confused pieces that I have no hope of putting back together.

"Right." His eyes dart to my necklace, just like they always do when he knows I'll be away from him. The heart pendant around my neck is actually a tracker that Cal gave to me when I was about nine. There had been a flare up of gangs a few towns over that were crossing into our small peaceful county. Cal didn't have jurisdiction there, but he was moving up the ranks fast, and there was talk that a man he'd put in prison was the brother of one of the gang members. Within hours of the first threat, I had around the clock protection, and I was told I could never take this necklace off.

"Cal, I'm scared. What if the bad guys get me?"

He kneels in front of me and pulls his sunglasses off, allowing me to see his concerned eyes. Like always, my eyes move to his shiny badge and I touch the metal. "You know I would never let anyone get to you. I would die before I let anything happen to you."

My eyes widen and I throw my arms around his neck and let the tears flow at the thought of him dying. "You can't die. If you die, who will take care of me?"

"Hey hey. We've talked about this." He pulls me away and gives me a kiss on my forehead. "Aria and Henry will always take care of you. Or Margie. Okay? You have a family now, Maddie. One that would never turn their back on you or hurt you." Until Cal, the only experiences I really had with family ended in death, so I wasn't too big on the term 'family.' But I was big on the sweet man that had taken me in and let me turn his life upside down the past two years, so if he said we were family, I was in.

"You're my family."

He smiles and taps the necklace he just put around my neck. "This stays on, Maddie. No excuses."

"Okay."

"I'm serious. Sleep. Bathing. Doesn't come off, ever. Got it?"

"Okay, but why?"

"It has a tracker in it, so if anything ever happens…" He trails off and shakes his head. "If we're ever separated, this will tell me where you are, okay?"

I hold the magic necklace in my hand and squeeze it. "Ooooh. Do you have one too?"

He chuckles. "No."

"But how am I supposed to know where you are?"

"For now, I think only you need the tracker, alright?" He raises an eyebrow and I furrow mine.

"That's bullshit."

"Language, Madeline!" His eyes widen but I can see the humor in them, and I put my hand over my mouth and giggle.

"Well, it is!"

I finger the necklace and he nods in response, like a language that only we can understand. "Say hey to Mom for me."

I nod. He turns around and moves out of the room, and just as I'm about to let out a sigh of relief, he stops. His back is to me and, even under the sweatshirt, I can see the tension creeping up his back. "For what it's worth, I don't plan to see her again." My mouth drops open at his statement. "It is your business, Maddie, and for you to be upset…it didn't sit right with me."

He doesn't wait for my response before he's out the kitchen and heading up the stairs. A part of me, a very large part, urges me to follow him. To confess to him what the last three years have meant for me. What I could potentially want in the future. I've taken two steps before I freeze, realizing that an impulsive move like this could have catastrophic results. Cal will flip one way or the other.

In a good way or a bad way.

Am I ready for everything I've ever known the last ten years to go up in flames?

The front door slams open so hard I think the door has come off its hinges. I jump what feels like three feet when I hear footsteps moving up the stairs. *What the hell?* I wonder if he's looking for me but doesn't realize I'm lying on the couch, reading.

"MADDIE!" The scream shakes me to my core, a scream so tortured that it speaks to the young girl that hid in a closet while her father murdered her mother. I'm off the couch in a second and flying up the stairs, only to see Cal sitting against the wall in front of my door. His elbows are resting on his knees and his head is in his hands.

"Cal…what…?" I start when his eyes dart up to meet mine. It all happens so fast, but within seconds, I'm up against the wall, his tall frame towering over my small one.

"Maddie…" He lets out a breath. "Fuck. You're…here."

"Of course, I'm here. I texted you when I got home from the store…"

"No, I mean…" He presses off the wall, grabbing his hair and turning his back to me. "DAMMIT!" he screams again.

"What's wrong, what happened?"

"I would literally die if something happened to you." He turns his head slightly so I can see his profile. "Do you get that?"

"Hey, I'm fine, okay? I'm here." I wrap my arms around him and press my cheek into his back. His hands find my arms and begin to rub them gently.

"This girl was so young. Your age when we met." My blood runs cold, thinking about what could have him reacting this way. *No way. He always finds them in time. He's a Superhero.* "He got her too." I feel myself being dragged to the ground and before I realize what's happening, I'm in his lap. "I couldn't save her, Mads."

His voice is broken and laced with anger, sadness, confusion. "Why...why couldn't I get there?"

"It's not your fault, Cal." I press my hand to his cheek and stroke the spiky stubble. "You can't save all of us."

"What if I couldn't get to you? What if..."

"You can't think like that, Cal. You did get to me. You saved me...in so many ways. Who knows what would have happened to me if I went into the system? If I didn't have someone looking out for me..." The tears spring to my eyes just as they always do when I think about *what could have been*.

"I can't stop thinking about what would have happened if I was too late. If he got to you before he killed himself..."

"He didn't." I grab his hand and lace our fingers. "I'm here, see?" I'm acutely aware of the fact that I'm straddling his lap and I think he's starting to realize it as well because he shifts slightly and clears his throat.

"I got you," he whispers and I nod in agreement.

You've always had me.

"Right. Well..." he starts as he tries to move me, but I stop him, pressing my hands to his shoulders to halt his movements.

"Cal," I whisper. My lips are so close to his, I can taste the coffee and the mint from the spearmint gum he always chews. I'm staring at his lips, wanting a taste so badly that I bite my lip to stop from acting on the primal urge. "I got you too."

"Maddie..." His heart pounds underneath my hand and when he tries to move, I hold my ground and push him so that he's lying flat on his back, with me hovering over him. "Madeline," he croaks. His voice is hoarse and I wonder if it's because he's literally straining to keep his dick from rising underneath me. I'm not sure how I ended up in this position, me straddling the man that had raised me since I was seven years old, but I knew I had no intentions of getting up until I rubbed against him *just once.*

This had been my fantasy for the past three years and I was too overcome with lust to care that doing this would change everything with one gentle brush over his hardness between us. I wonder if he could feel the heat radiating from between my legs. I knew my panties were soaked and I was sure that the tiny shorts I was wearing over it weren't doing much to control the deluge.

He coughs, but I've watched enough porn to know that he's trying to stifle a groan. I'm not sure what's going on in his mind, but I'm fairly certain by the glint in his eye it is as depraved as what I'm thinking. *He's not your father, Madeline.*

He's been more of a father to you than your actual one.

I swallow as the words wash over me and spread like wildfire throughout my whole body and congregate between my legs. I bite down on my lower lip, making an effort not to move a muscle. "Yes, Cal?" My eyes bore into his as he lies on his back underneath me.

"You should get up," he tells me, and despite the foot and a half and eighty pounds of muscle he has on me, he doesn't move me from his lap.

Push him, Maddie.

I press my hands to his chest gently and shake my head back and forth. "But...that's not what you want."

"Madeline, up," he growls and I curl my fingers into his shirt and dig into his chest as I move back slightly so that my sex is right against his dick.

I try to ignore the racing in my heart as my pulsing clit has totally taken control, and before I can stop myself, I've rubbed against his cock.

"Maddie, please..." His voice is pained and I was fully planning to stop—*maybe*, but when I open my eyes, Cal's are closed and I can tell he's gritting his teeth.

"Just...do this for me. *Please.*" I beg as the fire between my legs becomes greater with each stroke. His cock is fully hard at this point and I feel my clit peeking out between the lips of my sex. Slick and swollen and desperate to be touched without two layers of clothes.

"Maddie, we can't..." His face is red beneath his beard, bringing out a trace of auburn in his facial hair. "Please...get up."

"You can make me." It's a gamble, yes, but one I'm willing to take. His hands tighten on my thighs and I know it's time to up the ante. I rub again, stroking his dick with my pussy up and back slowly, teasingly. "But I think I can make you come."

"Madeline..."

"Maybe you should stop saying my name. It's fucking with your head."

"You dry humping me is fucking with my head. Saying your name is keeping me from leading us somewhere we can't come back from."

I freeze. "Like what?"

"You know what." His voice is low and it vibrates through my body.

"Like fucking me?"

The magic F word must make him come to his senses because he's sitting up in an instant and gripping my forearms. A familiar smell wafts around us and I wonder if he can sense it too. Sex. *My sex.* Arousal. My orgasm forming on my pussy and dripping into my panties. He licks his lips and his eyes darken from their usual brown to almost black.

"Cal." My eyes drop to his mouth and I feel his gaze searching my face.

"Maddie." His tone almost sounds like a question, but I'm

not sure the answer. *Is he asking me to stop? Or asking me to keep going?*

"I've wanted this...for so long."

"I don't know what *this* is, but this is wrong."

"I won't tell anyone. Not even Sasha, I swear."

"That's not the point, Mads...I'm..."

"Not my father." *Maybe that forbidden aspect of our relationship turns me the fuck on, but it might kill Cal.*

"I'm supposed to protect you."

"Who says you're not?"

"I can't...like *this*."

"Would you rather I let another boy do it?" I'm pushing him and I know it. I know Cal is overprotective when it comes to me. He wants to keep me in a cage until I'm married.

"You let another boy touch you and I'll ruin the fuck out of his future," he snaps.

"Why?"

"You know why, Madeline. No one is good enough for you."

"What about you?"

"I'm not an option."

"I think I get a say..." I move in his lap. "Your cock surely wants one."

He groans and falls to his back, shutting his eyes and putting a hand over his face and I note he still hasn't moved me. "You can't say things like that."

"Cal, I know you like to have control over every situation, but for once, I need you to just... relax." His chest is rising and falling so rapidly, and I swear I can hear his heart pounding beneath my hands.

"Keep your fucking clothes on." He growls and I nod. *Fair.* I close my eyes and begin to rock back and forth against him again. "Open them." I assume he means my eyes and when I do, his gaze locks with mine instantly. His hands move to my hips, gripping them as I move back and forth.

"Fuck. That feels good."

"Does…it?" He chokes out, and I nod.

"I'm going to come."

He clears his throat, and when I meet his eyes, they're filled with lust. "Tell me when."

I nod and his hands move up my hips and rest under the t-shirt I'm wearing. He strokes the skin just above my belly button as my hips begin moving more erratically as I chase the orgasm that was just out of reach. "I'm going to come, oh fuck!" He wraps his hands around my waist again, moving my body faster against his cock. "I want to wait for you." I whimper as my toes begin to curl.

"No. Come, Madeline. Come for me, right now."

Come for *me*. Those three words are so much louder than the rest and have a direct line with my clit which feels like is about to splinter into a million pieces. "Oh, God, Cal!" I scream as I squirm and writhe on top of his cock. My body feels like I've stuck my finger in a light socket and I've short-circuited every single nerve in my body. I drop to his chest, my head resting over his heartbeat. My limbs feel like they weigh a hundred pounds, boneless and useless, and I'm fairly certain I've lost my sense of sight because when I open my eyes everything's blurry and unfocused. It isn't until a tear trickles down my cheek that I realize that I'm crying as my body searches for the equilibrium after the most intense orgasm of my life. "Oh my God, that was incredible," I moan.

"Holy fuck," I hear before I'm flipped on my back and he's rubbing against me between my open legs. I wrap my legs around him hoping that he'll get the message and move closer to me, and he must be driven by his cock, in this moment, because he leans down and hovers over me. His lips an inch from mine. "I kiss you and it's over."

"What is?"

"Everything we've ever known."

"I'm willing to risk it."

"You can't breathe a word of this to anyone. No one can know I touched you like...this."

"I know."

"I'd lose everything. I'd lose...*you*."

"I know that too." My heart hammers faster at the thought of being away from Cal. He's been my hero, my knight in shining armor, and the love of my life for so long and the lines have been blurry for a while now. *But from the looks of it, he's catching up.* "I won't tell anyone. Our secret."

I see the very smallest hint of a nod, and then his hands are moving up my body and cupping my face. "You're so fucking beautiful."

"When did you notice?" I ask, dying to know when things changed for him. When I was no longer the girl that he saved from the most horrific tragedy of her life.

"You don't want to know."

"Yes, I do."

"A year ago..."

I gasp. "What...?"

"On your seventeenth birthday. You ran over to me and jumped in my arms to thank me for the car...I...I almost dropped you." My heart skips in my chest and a thousand butterflies shed their cocoons in my stomach. He rubs against me again and I feel my body start to hum with pleasure as it builds again.

"Do you think about me when you touch yourself?"

"Yes, but I never let myself come...not thinking about you.

Never about you." He lowers his head almost shamefully and I press a hand to his cheek.

"Why is that a bad thing?"

"I'm a monster, Maddie. I can't believe I'm doing this to you. I promise, I'll pay for a really good therapist one day."

I chuckle. "Don't make jokes while your dick is pressed against me."

"I make jokes when I'm nervous. You know this."

"Why are you nervous?"

"Because this is...*you*, and I've been fighting the urge to come since you first straddled me ten minutes ago."

"Stop fighting it, Cal. Let go." I grab him by the back of the neck and pull him closer to me and lean up slightly, letting him know what I plan to do and then our lips touch.

Not in an awkward way like most first kisses are. Not in a slow passionate way like when you kiss your lover after not kissing them in so long. But in a rushed, frenzied way that is aggressive and hard and rough. He bites and I bite back. His tongue sweeps between my lips, and I meet him with rabid urgency. I'm so desperate for his taste on my tongue, I explore every inch of his mouth. It's sloppy and wet and loud and, quite frankly, the hottest fucking kiss of my life.

He presses my arms above my head, holding them there, and laces our fingers together as his tongue penetrates my mouth in a way I wish his cock was doing to my pussy. He bucks against me with wild reckless abandon, fighting for the orgasm he's spent God knows how long fighting and then he does. Long and hard. I know the second he does because he groans in my mouth and his kisses get even more frantic—if that's possible. Our kiss doesn't stop when his orgasm wanes. If anything it gets even more wild and uncontrolled. We're a tangle of arms and legs, threaded together in the most delicious puzzle, our pelvises pressed together as they yearn to be connected. I push my hands through his lush, wavy brown hair and I find myself fantasizing about grabbing on to it as his head disappears between my thighs. *Perhaps my favorite fantasy of all time and I wonder if I could push that into becoming a reality.*

"Cal," I moan when he pulls away to suck on a place on my neck, "please."

"Please what?"

"Please, can we lose the clothes."

"No," he growls and just like that, it's like a bucket of ice water has dumped all over us, breaking us from the sex haze. He's off of me, putting space between us for the first time since we started and he backs away from me. "Holy fuck, I can't believe I let that happen…"

"Cal…" I move towards him and he puts a hand out to stop me from coming closer.

"No, Madeline. Stay."

Tears rush to my eyes and my bottom lip trembles. "But…?"

"I'm not your boyfriend. I'm…fuck I don't know what I am anymore. But this can't happen again."

"Why?"

"You know damn well why." He stands up, and I can see the evidence from both of our orgasms all over his gray sweats. His erection has gone down, after his thunderous orgasm, but the dark gray spot tells the story of our tryst.

"I'm…I'm sorry," I tell him, because I am. I love him and I hate myself for ruining everything. For letting my forbidden fantasy control everything. Ruin everything. I expect him to tell me I had nothing to be sorry for. That it was his fault. That he could have moved me. *Anything.*

What I did not expect was for him to walk away without another word.

Six

Madeline

I don't see Cal for the rest of the day.

Not for lack of trying.

I'd walked by his bedroom at least twenty times, hoping that he'd open the door and talk to me. I know he was holed up in there mad at himself, and me, and probably the world.

My hand hovers over the door waiting to knock when I let it fall.

He doesn't want to see you, Maddie.

I back away from the door and trudge back to my room passing an array of photos of Cal and me and his family...*my family*. I stop at one picture in particular. Cal and me on my first trip to Disneyland. I was so excited and couldn't believe when Cal surprised me.

The gravity of what Cal and I did hits me full force and the fear that things will never be the same between us comes creeping into my brain. *Or worse, that he'll hate me forever.*

I don't know if it's the stress and the intensity of the day or the fact that I am really exhausted, but I fall into a troubled sleep.

The sound of the front door closing wakes me up out of my sleep and I notice that my room is pitch black. I turn over on my side and blindly search for my phone, rubbing my hand all over the sheets. I find it and bring it to my face. I tap the home button illuminating the space around me.

Eight-thirty on a Saturday? Cal didn't usually go in this late, but maybe something happened? I frown when I don't see a text from him as it's rare for him to leave without saying goodbye to me. Ever since I was young, he'd made a point to tell me he'd be back. I still remember the first time he left me with Aria while he went to work.

Cal kneels in front of me and pulls my bunny from between my teeth. "I have to go to work for a little while, okay?"

My teeth chatter slightly, not because I'm cold, but because I'm so terrified of him leaving me all alone. "Will you be back?"

"Yes, of course, I'll be back. I don't like that I have to leave you at night, but it's really important."

"Superhero stuff?"

He smiles and nods, that twinkling in his eye that makes me think that he is really made of magic. He's the handsomest boy I've ever seen. "Superhero stuff."

"Can I come too?" The shiny silver of his badge catches my eye and I reach out and run my finger over the metal.

"No, too dangerous for you. But you'll stay with Aria, okay?"

"Will you wake me up when you get back?"

"It'll be very late."

My lip trembles and the tears form in my eyes. "Please? I want to know that you came back."

"I'll always come back, Maddie. I promise."

"If you don't, I'll be all alone. Who will take care of me?" I lower my chin sadly as the tears slip down my face.

"You'll never be alone." He shakes his head at me and lifts my chin, wiping the tears from my eyes. "I'll wake you up when I get in, alright?"

"You promise?"

"Promise." He taps my nose and pushes his index fingers into my

cheeks trying to get me to smile, and I do after a few moments, breaking out into a full-on grin and then a laugh as he stands up. He waves at me before he's gone out the front door. I run to the window and watch as he pulls off, waving at him the entire time as he disappears into the night.

I peek my head out the window and I see the usual cruiser sitting just off the driveway. I grab my phone and dial the number I know by heart and I'm instantly irritated when he doesn't pick up the phone. He knows I worry when he doesn't answer, and I know sometimes he physically can't, but I'm pretty sure this is not one of those times given that he just left the house. So not only am I the worried girl I've always been when I can't reach Cal, but now, I'm the worried girl who thinks it's because he's ignoring her after what happened earlier. My phone comes to life in my hands and I eagerly answer it. "You left without saying bye? Are you joking?" I snap as soon as I answer.

He sighs and I can hear the hum of the engine, making me think that we're on speakerphone. *Shit, I have no idea if anyone is in the car with him.*

"I'm sorry, Maddie. It was an emergency and I knew you were sleeping." He pauses and then continues. "I'm alone in the car."

I nod like he can see me. "Are you coming back?" I whisper, my memories weighing on me like a ton of bricks.

"Always." The one word seeps into my bones and warms me after all of his coldness today.

"Will you wake me when you get in?"

"It'll be late."

"You know I don't care."

"Maddie…"

"What, Cal? So, you go to your very high-risk job without so much as a goodbye and now you won't wake me up when you get home safe? I didn't agree to those terms," I sass.

"Fairly certain the terms changed today," he grumbles and it feels like a punch in the gut.

"Is that what this is about?"

"What the hell else could it be about, Madeline? I can't believe I let that happen. It can't happen. Never again."

My hand tightens around my phone and my pulse quickens in response to the anger coursing through me. "And you had to do this over the phone? What, you couldn't face me?"

"Not at the moment, no." I don't say anything and the silence between us stretches to what feels like a full minute. *Would things be awkward between us after what happened?* "I don't want you going out."

"Why?"

"Because it's already late."

"It's eight thirty." *And I feel like I'm essentially being I don't know, dumped? Rejected? Whatever this feeling is, it sucks and I need Sasha or hell, Aria.*

"And if you had plans, I'd know about them. Stay in the house, Madeline."

"Can I go to Aria and Henry's?"

"Aria got called in."

I let out a sigh. "Can Sasha come over?"

"No."

"Why?"

"Because the last time she came over when I wasn't there, you two got drunk as hell."

We were bored! "Lock your liquor cabinet."

"You picked the lock!" he argues.

I huff. "This is ridiculous. Fine."

"Thank you. I'll see you when I get home."

"Bye." Regret unfurls in my chest the second I end the call as I think about the fact that I didn't tell him to be safe. I type out a text to him, my finger hovering over the send key, before I close my eyes and send.

Me: Be safe. I love you.
Superhero: Back at you, Mads.

It wasn't the first time I'd told Cal I loved him, and he was no stranger to saying it back, but it's the first time I've said it since his tongue was down my throat.

⁓

The sounds of rattling in the kitchen rouse me from sleep. I made a point to watch a movie in the living room versus my bedroom, knowing I would fall asleep on the couch and make it so Cal had to wake me up when he got home. *He'd never leave me to sleep there all night.*

"Shit," I hear from the kitchen followed by the slam of a microwave. I'd whipped up some stir fry while he was gone, knowing he'd be hungry when he got back, and I assume that's what he's trying to do. I sit up, throwing the blanket off of me and pad into the kitchen where I see him sitting at the table with his head in his hands and a tumbler of a brown liquid—probably whiskey in front of him.

"Rough night?" I ask.

His head snaps up and you'd think I was naked by the way he looks over my body. I'm wearing a sweatshirt and leggings, so it's not like he has flesh to feast his eyes upon. I look down to see, feeling slightly subconscious, but when I meet his eyes, they're filled with something I don't recognize.

Want maybe?

"Not as rough as this afternoon," he grumbles.

"I'm so sorry that it was so hard for you. I won't give you the arduous task of having to kiss me again, swear." I was tired of his moody teenage girl attitude.

That's my role.

Instead, I'm handling this with way more maturity, making me wonder who exactly the adult is here. I move towards the microwave and open the door, knowing that he always leaves it in there too long and sure enough his food is practically steaming. The plate is hot and I snatch my hand back from it, the heat searing into my skin and shooting up my arm. "Fuck," I groan as I wave my hand to try and cool my fingers. He's by my side instantly, pulling my hand to the sink and letting it run under the cool water which does nothing for my heated skin that's responding to his touch. "You always leave it in there too long."

"Sorry." He pulls my fingers out from under the water and holds them in his hand before pulling the wet hand to his lips, sucking the excess water from my skin. He presses kisses to each of my burnt fingertips before letting it gently fall. "Better?"

No, this was most certainly not better. What about you sucking my fingers is better? "You're giving me serious whiplash."

His eyes widen and he takes a step back, probably remembering that touching me is what got us into trouble earlier. "I can't think when I'm this close to you. I make bad decisions."

"Was touching me so bad?"

"No...yes...you're smart enough to know it has nothing to do with *you*. Kissing you was...amazing. Touching you, feeling you...I can't get it out of my head," he tells me as he sits back down and grabs his drink.

"But...?"

Bringing his drink to his lips he shoots me a look. "But…it can't happen again, Maddie."

"Why? It's just kissing…"

He cocks an eyebrow at me and looks me up and down like he's trying to show his attraction for me and how difficult it is to *just* kiss me. "You and I both know that what happened here this afternoon is a slippery slope."

"What if I promise not to push for more?"

He snorts as he grabs his plate that's cooled down and sits at the table. "Yeah, okay, eventually you'll want more." He pushes his food around his plate and looks up at me. "Eventually, *I'll* want more."

"So, that's it?"

"That's it. I'm your legal guardian. I can't…we can't…No." He shakes his head.

"You didn't adopt me. I'm not your daughter."

"That aside, you're *seventeen*. I'm an officer of the law. I know better. I shouldn't have even touched you the way I did." He drops his head into his hands and pulls on his hair.

"Then don't have sex with me until I'm *eighteen*. Besides half the states in the US say I can give consent at seventeen *or* younger! I can get married even earlier with like parental consent." *So, you basically.* He shoots me a look and I roll my eyes. "Lighten up! God, you're still so easy to rile up. You act like I won't be eighteen, in less than a month."

"This isn't funny, Madeline," he snaps.

I sit down next to him and slide my legs over his knee and prop an elbow up on the table. "I'm sorry, I get the whole making jokes when I'm nervous thing from you, I think." I smile before I grab his drink and take a tiny sip.

He chuckles and his hand finds my lips, drawing his thumb over the skin. He doesn't say anything for a while before he murmurs, "You're so beautiful." He strokes my cheek, cupping it gently and I rest my hand over his.

"So are you."

His eyes rest on my lips, tracing over the fullness and my tongue darts out to wet them.

"Fuck." His eyes shut and when he opens them, I can see the war in his eyes over what to do.

He lets out a breath and adjusts himself, and I swallow past the lump in my throat seeing him grow under his slacks. I look up and his hooded gaze is penetrating me, seeing me, *knowing* me. I can't look anywhere except his eyes and how close he's getting to me. I'm not sure who started moving first, but before long we've met in the middle, our tongues in a battle neither one of us care about winning. He tastes like whiskey and the spice from the stir fry and a hint of the raw virility I tasted earlier. His tongue is experienced, demanding and rough against my timid one who hasn't done this but so many times. We're still far enough apart from our positions at the table and I'm too nervous to move closer for fear of breaking the haze and scaring him off again. But he makes the move, standing up and separating us for a second before pulling me into his arms. I wrap my legs around his waist on instinct before we're on the move up the stairs our lips never separating. "I need you in my room. It'll freak me out too much being in yours."

"Yes, please. Take me to your bedroom," I moan as we cross the threshold and tumble onto his bed. I'm in my pajamas, but he's still in a dress shirt and slacks. I want to tell him to change before we ruin these just like we did his sweats from earlier, but I worry that he'll panic at the thought of getting naked in front of me. "Cal," I moan as his lips find my neck, sucking at the skin and I relish at the idea of having a hickey. My usually flawless skin purple and blue with indents of his teeth in the flesh.

"I won't mark you here." His voice is low in his throat and it makes my whole body tingle. "Maybe somewhere less visible."

"Like…between my legs?" I can feel my cheeks heating with embarrassment *or maybe arousal?*

"Shit, like exactly there."

I take deep breaths, trying to slow my breathing as I think about him leaving a hickey. On my fucking pussy. *I've died and gone to heaven…*

Or maybe hell.

"I bet your clit is so pink and pretty. I bet you taste so fucking sweet." He bites down on my neck again and I yelp.

"Do you want to try it? I don't think it's that sweet." *So much for not pushing him, Mads.*

He pulls back to look at me. "You've tried it?"

"Sure." I shrug. "I was curious."

"Fuck." He groans before he sits back on his heels and rubs his palm over his forehead. "I can't eat you out." The crassness of his words slithers down my spine in the most deliciously sinful way. *I can't believe he said that!* "It'll destroy the rest of my resolve."

I sit up on my elbows and blink several times. "Okay," I whisper softly. "Can we go back to kissing?"

"No."

Dammit, Maddie, you had to get greedy!

"Touch your pussy," he demands, his eyes are dark and feral, like he's preparing to rip me apart with his teeth.

"What?"

"Slip your fingers under your leggings. Don't take them off and don't show me your pussy. But just finger yourself for me… and I'll taste you from your fingers."

My eyes widen and my heart skips a beat in my chest before it returns to the steady thrumming between my legs. "You're serious?"

He nods and moves to sit against the headboard. "Come here."

I do as I'm told and he pulls me so that my back is flush against his chest, my ass pressed right up against his cock. His legs are spread and I'm settled between them feeling his cock jump every few minutes. His lips find my ear before he bites down gently. "Pretend it's me."

"I always pretend it's you." I turn my head slightly and he presses a kiss to the corner of my mouth. I already rubbed myself to two roaring orgasms twice today in response to what happened earlier, but I know I could get off in probably two minutes flat after the last several minutes. I slip my fingers under the waistband of my leggings and press my fingers inside my pussy.

"How does it feel?"

"Wet. Slippery."

"Fuck. You're probably soaked, aren't you? Your panties are drenched."

"I'm not wearing panties."

"Oh God." He grits his teeth. "Do not show me your pussy, Madeline Shaw, I fucking mean it."

I whimper at his use of my full name. I pinch my clit and I shudder in his arms as my body begins to climb. "Holy shit, Cal. Oh God, touch me. *Please.*"

"Please don't ask me to do that." His voice is hoarse and just as pleading as mine.

My mouth falls open as I throw my head back, a guttural moan escaping my lips as I climb higher and higher towards the climax. I add another finger fucking myself with two while my thumb continues to stroke my clit. "Caaaaal." My eye twitches behind my lids just as it always does when the orgasm brewing is particularly powerful and for a second, I feel like I'm paralyzed. Nothing works except for the three fingers inside of my pussy. I can't think, I can't speak, I'm not one hundred percent sure I'm even breathing. I'm vaguely aware my left hand is digging into his thigh and my hips are moving on their own against my hand. "I'm going to come."

"Yes, you fucking are," he groans in my ear, and for a brief moment, I wonder if he's been talking this whole time and I've just missed it. "Is it my fingers inside of you? My tongue? Or my cock? Tell me, Maddie. What are you thinking about?"

"Your...t—tongue. Oh God! Yes!!" I scream as visions of Cal's tongue flicking my clit pushes me over the edge. His lips are on my temple, trailing down my cheek and I vaguely hear him tell me that I'm a good girl. That I'm perfect. And nothing in the world is more beautiful than me. I feel exhausted with it being my third orgasm that day when I feel him pulling my hand out from between my legs. I barely catch a glimpse of it, glistening with my juices when his lips wrap around them.

"I knew I shouldn't have tasted you. But I couldn't help it. I had to know." I hear him still sucking on my fingers and that bundle of nerves between my legs that is still pulsing suddenly intensifies. *Holy shit, am I not done?*

"Cal...*please* touch me."

"No, Maddie. If I touch you, I'll want to taste you and if I taste you, I'm going to want to fuck you. I *can't* touch you. I *can't* fuck you."

"But..."

"No, Madeline." He tenses beneath me and I briefly wonder if he's coming to his senses and is about to make me move from his lap. I turn to face him and sit between his legs.

"Can I touch you?"

He swallows and shakes his head. "Please don't."

"What if...just like earlier?" I ask as I place my hands on his thighs. I slowly move them up higher until they are bracketed around his dick. I squeeze and I see his cock jump. "What if I just sat on it right now…and rubbed on it for a while. Would that be okay?" He swallows and I don't take it as a no so I make my move, climbing into his lap and straddling him. "This isn't wrong."

He rolls his eyes shut and puts his hands over them before scratching his beard. "This is all kinds of wrong, Maddie."

"We aren't having sex." *Yet*, my mind adds and I pray on all that's holy that my subconscious is correct. That eventually we'll get there.

"You rubbing against my dick until we come is pretty high up on the list of things we shouldn't be fucking doing." I can hear the hesitation in his voice but I also hear the lust.

The want.

I can see the war behind his eyes over what to do, so I push him just a little harder.

"Shhh." I begin to rub against him and I can feel the juices from my orgasm getting all over the inside of my leggings. The seam of the fabric grazes my clit with every swipe and I wonder if I'm going to come again. "You're so hard. God, Cal. Is it all for me?" I wrap my arms around his neck as I begin to move faster against him. His hands find my hips and begin to control the speed, pushing and pulling me harder on him.

"Yes." He hisses. "It's for you." His face tucks into my neck and I feel my nipples hardening as I brush against him. "Please don't hate me one day for this," he whispers so low that I almost miss it.

But I don't.

I pull him away from my neck and shake my head. "What?" I stop moving and look him square in the eye. "I could never hate you. Jesus, Cal, I love you. This isn't a crush or infatuation or some bizarre hero complex. I am full blown in love with you.

Don't you get that?" His eyes trail my face, my guess is, looking for a sign that I'm serious or that I'm unsure. I grab his face in my hands. "I know you may not be feeling what I'm feeling but…"

His lips cut mine off with a kiss so scorching I want to rip my clothes off. I begin to move again, to match the movements of our mouths. "I'm right there with you," he whispers against my lips.

CAL

I HAVE OFFICIALLY LOST MY MIND.

That is the only thing that would give plausible reason for my behavior the last three days.

Touching Maddie

Kissing Maddie

Tasting Maddie.

Fuck. Fuck. Fuck.

It wasn't enough for me to touch her or kiss her or let her rub against me until I came in my pants like a fucking horny teenager, but I had to suck her orgasm off her fingers. I had to run my tongue over each of her tips, my brain memorizing the sweet taste of her arousal.

That was three days ago, and I can't get that taste out of my mind. She tasted salty but sweet and I swear I keep running my tongue over every inch of my mouth in search of any hint of her flavor that may have lingered.

I knew it was a mistake to taste her even if it wasn't from the source because all it did was unleash this beast lurking inside of me. One that wants to devour her. Pin her to the mattress and fuck her till she doesn't know her own name.

Till she doesn't know mine.

Till she calls me *Daddy*.

I wanted that precious gift she has tucked between her legs

and I wanted to claim it as mine. I know from Aria—and because no guy has the balls to be sniffing around the police chief's "little girl"—that she's still a virgin...and I want to be that man that has the first taste.

I want to drive my cock so far into her sweet cunt that she'll never want anyone else but me.

That's the dangerous man that I've been trying to keep at bay. The one that has the power to ruin everything.

Ruin *her*.

Maddie, however, seems to be more than willing to spar with the beast and is doing her best to bring him out of hiding, which is why her warm body is pressed against me and wiggling against my morning wood.

Her soft sighs are doing nothing but making me harder and just when I'm ready to kick her out of bed so I can get some hold on my self-control she spins in my arms and stares up at me with those soft blue eyes.

She blinks several times, like she's trying to convince herself that she's in bed with me at 6 AM. "Morning."

I try to pull out of her grasp but she holds tighter and snuggles closer to me, sliding her leg through mine and bumping my cock with her thigh. Her lips find my neck and she leaves feather-light kisses all the way from the back of my ear to the top of my shoulder and then back again.

I grip her around her waist and pull her closer despite the voices in my head telling me to put space between us. "Why are you up so early?" I turn my nose into her hair and breathe in her scent. Her shampoo smells like coconut and lime and I've grown accustomed to smelling it all over my pillow.

"Your mom will be here soon..." she trails off, "to start cooking."

"Why did we agree to have it here this year?" I groan.

She sits up and half of me is grateful that she doesn't sit in my lap. *The top half.* She pulls her hair over to one side exposing her slender, flawless neck to me and all I can think about is sinking my teeth into the skin and leaving a mark. Then make her wear her hair up so the world can see that someone claimed her. She belongs to someone who is possessive enough to leave his mark on her as a warning to fuck off.

I feel the beast clawing its way up my throat and urging me towards her. I'm vaguely aware that she's speaking something about Thanksgiving and how we all thought it would be fun to have it here when I have her hauled into my lap and my lips on her neck. "Cal," she whimpers, and just like that, I'm hard as a fucking rock.

Maddie has said my name probably a million times over the course of the past ten years and now, all of a sudden, my name falling from those pouty lips has me harder than granite. "Say my name again." My voice is so gruff, I don't even recognize it but the shiver that moves through Maddie alerts me that *she* does.

"Cal," she yelps as I bite down on her flesh. I run my tongue over the skin, doing my best to soothe the sting of my teeth. Her hands find the back of my head and she pulls at the hair as she cocks her head more allowing me further access. I love how she opens herself up to me; whatever I want from her she gives me so blindly. She feeds the beast, and if I was a better man, I'd tell her to stop. Tell her to run. But I won't. Because the beast in me is only responding to the one in her.

The one that's been unleashed already and doesn't seem to want to let me go without a fight.

"Cal, as much as I want to continue this, your mom said… Ah!" I bite down and she gasps.

"Don't talk about my mother while you're sitting on my

dick." I'm still sucking on her neck when she finally removes my lips from her. She puts her hands on my chest and stares at me with a scolding glare, but I can see the lust lurking beneath. Her eyes are dilated, but I can't keep my eyes off the purple mark forming on her neck. I press my fingers to the space, admiring my work and shoot her a wicked glance.

"And how am I supposed to explain a hickey?" She bites her bottom lip because I know a part of her is turned on that I left a mark. *My* mark.

"Make something up. I don't care what."

"I'm going to have to say it's some guy."

"I *wouldn't*." It's a warning that I hope she heeds. "Find a scarf," I growl at her. If she thinks I'm willing to go along with some charade where some other man gets to touch her, she better think again.

"I don't know where this caveman side of you came from." She leans forward and presses her lips to mine. "But I think I love it." She hops off the bed before shooting me a conspiratorial wink. "He'll be *much* easier to break."

By the time I get downstairs, my mother is already in the kitchen, much to *my dick's* and my disappointment. I'd had plans to sneak up behind Maddie and kiss her senseless until someone arrived. But it was probably for the best. Maddie still had three more days left off from school and with the way things were progressing between us, too much time alone together would probably end with my dick inside of her.

Feelings of shame flood my brain. *No.* I'd drawn that line in the sand. Under no circumstances could I fuck her.

This is just a phase. A weird phase where she's figuring out how to transition me to the next phase in her life.

And what are you doing? my voice of reason, who'd been pretty fucking quiet up till now, finally speaks up.

I'm...trying to navigate a relationship with a soon to be eighteen year old girl that no longer reminds me of the girl I rescued when she was seven.

I'm a cop, and I know the rules of fooling around with an underage girl. I cringe at the rationalizations that are already creeping into my brain: that I haven't touched her, I haven't seen her naked, I haven't fucked her. Yes, we've kissed *a lot*, and I've made her come...and she's made me come...

"Mom." I smile, as I enter the kitchen, trying my best to shake off my previous thoughts. Warm brown eyes that I swear have the ability to bring world peace smile at me from behind her glasses. Her hair is beginning to gray, but she'd been dying it for the past few years to combat that, so it is still the honey amber color that I've seen my whole life. She'd already taken her shoes off and is wearing the slippers she keeps here and has poured herself a glass of orange juice, that I wasn't one hundred percent sure didn't have champagne in it...*or vodka*.

My mother has had an ongoing relationship with alcohol ever since my dad split, and while it wasn't enough for Henry and me to admit she had a problem, it lurked in the shadows of all our family dinners and interactions. "Cal! Hi, honey, happy Thanksgiving!" she chirps as she pulls me into a hug and squeezes. "My darling boy, you look good." She puts her hands on my cheeks and squeezes them together to purse my lips. "Last few times I've seen you, you've looked tired. You look so well rested. No bags." She points under my eyes.

I keep my eyes off of Maddie who is in the corner peeling potatoes, trying to ignore the fact that the reason I've been sleeping so well has been because she's been sharing a bed with me.

And what we've been doing before we succumb to sleep.

"Thanks, Mom, you look good too. Where's Grant?" I ask about my *not quite* stepfather. Grant Donovan has been my mother's boyfriend since I was about seven years old, so for all intents and purposes, he is my stepfather.

"Oh, I sent him to the store. I forgot milk, and you didn't have any! Mads, I could have sworn you told me you had milk?"

"We *do* have milk, Margie." She doesn't turn around to look at us, but I can already see the sassy look on her face.

"No, that is water, dear."

Maddie spins around and puts her hands on her hips and furrows her brow. I notice her hair is down, though she's wearing a headband to keep her hair out of her face and a scarf to cover her neck over a t-shirt and sweatpants.

"Told you," I tell her because, quite frankly, that skim milk shit is water.

It's nearing noon. Grant and I are sitting in the living room watching the Lions game when I hear commotion in the hallway.

"That's probably your brother," Grant says and I immediately prepare for the worst. Grant is the manager at the largest bank in the city, has no kids of his own, has never been married, and has showered my mother with the love and attention that she didn't get from her first marriage. They'd been living together since I left home, and I'm glad that my mom has someone to share her life with. Henry isn't as accepting as I am, and the two have butted heads on more than one occasion.

"Can you two keep your shit together today?" I grit out as I take a sip of beer, indulging in alcohol since I have no plans to leave the house today. I work Christmas and New Year's, so

Thanksgiving is the day I took off unless there is an emergency.

Grant rubs a hand over his forehead. "I don't have it in me for your brother's dramatics today."

"Careful," I warn.

"Why can't he be as cool as you, huh?" He pushes a hand through his full head of gray hair and lets out a groan.

Henry walks into the living room and immediately sits in the adjacent recliner without even a look in Grant's direction. "Lions were winning when we left, they still have it?"

"Yeah, but Philly is on the three-yard line."

"Fuckers," Henry grunts.

"Hey, Henry." Grant nods towards him and Henry looks at me before giving him a crooked smile.

"Grant." He nods.

I roll my eyes at his petulance. "Where's Aria?" I haven't heard her high-pitched giggle once, so it's safe to assume she isn't here yet.

"Oh, she'll be here later, she wanted to go to the gym first." He's waves me off as he continues to stare at the screen, his eyes not looking at me once while he talks, allowing mine to divert to the kitchen in hopes of catching a passing glimpse of Maddie.

When Maddie and I are in the same place, I've always been hyper-aware of where she is at all times. In the beginning, it was because I was so paranoid that something would happen to her. Child Protective Services was around quite a bit in the beginning. Not because they thought I was a poor choice, but they wanted to make sure that I was the *best* choice for Maddie. With me being a police officer, as well as Aria's constant presence, not to mention the fact that it was obvious that Maddie had formed a connection with me, eventually they backed off, but I was still scared shitless over raising a kid.

As she got older, that paranoia morphed into a sense of

protectiveness. And now I feel that protectiveness morphing again into something else.

Possessiveness.

I want her near me. I want to feel her skin under my fingertips. I want her sitting in my lap, tucked under my chin as I rub her back. I want to feel her lips tracing my neck and her hands playing with my hair.

I look at Henry and Grant who are staring at the screen, and suddenly my need to have eyes on Maddie overwhelms me and I'm off the couch. "Want anything while I'm up?"

Grant shoots me a look that says *you're leaving me alone with him?* Henry shoots me a similar look but more along the lines of: *I'm going to fuck with him while you're gone.* I sigh and shake my head before heading into the kitchen.

Luckily, my mom has her back to me as she prepares the pie she's making, so my eyes are free to roam over Maddie. I trail my eyes up the back of her legs and her perfect round ass that make my hands flex on their own accord as I remember gripping it last night. I wish I could see her sweet face, her lips, that tiny dimple that pokes out, her button nose, and those blue eyes, but her back is to me as well. She must feel my gaze because she turns around and meets my eyes instantly.

"Nothing is ready yet." She cocks her head to the side and puts her hands on her hips. I can see the smile in her eyes and the one pulling at her lips, but luckily, her voice breaks me of my trance of openly staring at her just as my mom spins around.

"We'll be ready to flip the turkey in a few though, so hang on." She tells me as she holds up a finger.

I've managed to keep it together for the most part until Maddie goes upstairs to change, and it takes every ounce of self-control not to follow her. I don't move from the spot and actually breathe a sigh of relief when she comes bouncing back down the stairs in jeans that look like they're painted on her and a black turtleneck. A smirk finds my face as I realize why she has to cover up her neck, and I swear she shoots me a wicked look when our eyes briefly meet.

The sound of my front door opening reminds me that Aria isn't here, and I smile knowing that Maddie will be thrilled to see her. *And I need another reason to not get reckless.* Aria would sniff that out in a second. Maybe I could pull the wool over everyone else's eyes, but Aria is perceptive and she can read Maddie like a book like only a mother could.

"Happy Thanksgiving!" I hear squealed from the kitchen.

I hear my mother meet her with equal enthusiasm, reminding me to start counting how many drinks she's putting away, but my ears immediately perk up when I hear her ask "Who's this?"

Aria brought someone? My eyes immediately go to Henry, but he must not have heard because his eyes are glued to the television like he didn't just hear his wife's voice.

"This is Penelope…" I'm off the couch in an instant.

No fucking way. I'll kill her.

I immediately enter the kitchen to see Aria and the girl I went on the date with last week. My eyes pass over them both and immediately find Maddie who's staring at Penelope like she just might drive a carving knife through her.

"Oh hey, Cal. Look who I brought!" Aria smiles, though it fades when she sees the look I'm giving her.

Suddenly remembering that I do have some manners, and I can't immediately pull Maddie out of the room to tell her that I had no fucking part in this, I speak up, letting a smile find my face to greet the woman I really wish wasn't here. "Penelope... hey."

"Hey, sorry to totally intrude..."

"That's exactly what you're doing." Maddie's words pierce the air and the room goes silent before Margie smacks her arm.

"Don't be rude, Madeline. She's a friend of Aria's," she scolds.

"Yeah, Mads, chill. She's new to the area and doesn't have family here. I didn't want her to be alone on Thanksgiving. Besides, we all had fun when we went out, right Cal?" Aria shoots me a look that says, *don't let Maddie jump all over her.*

The room suddenly feels way too small, and Maddie's anger is taking up most of the space. *Keep it the fuck together, Maddie.*

No. I can almost hear her.

"So, Penelope, that's a pretty name," my mom interjects as she tries to smooth the obvious tension, though I'm sure she hasn't a clue why the air is frosty in the first place. "Where are you from?"

"Los Angeles," Penelope says with a nod. I'm only half listening as she goes into some story about growing up there when much to my reluctance, I pull Aria out of the room. I'm hoping that being in my mom's presence will keep Maddie somewhat in check, though I'm probably about to blow all that to hell.

"What the fuck?" I snap at Aria and cross my arms over my chest. "Your life is about to be hell next week." I point my finger at her and she smacks it away.

"What!" She presses her fists firmly into her hips. "You made out with her, she told me!"

"A pity make-out because she invited me up and I said no. Why would you bring her here?" I don't hide the exasperation or the irritation in my tone. My nerves are so tense you could snap them, and this is after Maddie had spent the last three days sucking all of the stress out of me through her kisses.

"Why not?"

"Because it's going to give her the wrong fucking idea. Introducing her to my mother? To fucking Maddie? You know I don't take that shit lightly," I growl.

"Look she knows she's here as my friend...not your *girlfriend*. But I thought maybe you guys could get to know each other a little better."

"No."

She stares at me confused. "What do you mean, *no*?"

"It means no, and if you had bothered to ask, I would have told you that I wasn't interested."

"Ugh." She scoffs and rolls her eyes. "I forgot you've still got some fuckboy in you."

"Watch it," I scold her like I do when we're at work and she forgets that I'm her boss.

"We aren't in uniform, so you can kiss my ass."

"Aria, you always do this shit. You always think you know best and you can just control my life like you have *any* fucking say. Back off, *Daniels,* I mean it." I grit out her maiden name like I always do when she pisses me off.

Hurt flashes across her face briefly before I see it harden. "You're being a dick."

"And you're leading that poor girl on," I snap. Not that I particularly care, but I can't very well explain the root of my irritation, so this is the only card I have to play.

"*I* didn't make out with her! You didn't tell me you weren't into her."

"Did Henry know I kissed her? No. Because it didn't fucking mean anything."

She rolls her eyes and shakes her head. "Fine, I'm not going to ask her to leave though. And Margie will kick your ass if you do."

"Maddie will probably handle that."

She crosses her arms over her chest. "And what's that about? I've never known her to be bratty like that."

"She's not being bratty," I snap without thinking. I'm always defensive when it comes to Maddie and rarely let anyone discipline her. Aria is the very small exception and even that needs to be cleared through me. "She doesn't like being blindsided. You know that."

Aria narrows her eyes at me, and I immediately try to clear my brain of the last few days as if she could read the crude thoughts that I've been having about Maddie. I should relax though, never in a million years would Aria ever come to that conclusion. "You let that girl have too much power."

True. "That's not what this is about."

"Oh? You're flying off the handle because of Maddie's reaction. You spoil her."

"And you don't?"

She runs a hand through her hair before putting it up. "That's not the point. The point is you let her have too much say in your life. You always have."

"That's what it means to raise a child, Aria. You put them fucking first." The instant the words leave my mouth, I regret them. Not because I didn't mean them. And God knows I do. I do put Maddie first. But to think of her as a child makes my stomach turn. I've been trying to rationalize my choices since the moment I pressed my lips to hers, and now the voice of reason is loud and abrasive and slithering up my spine and grabbing hold of my senses. I storm away from her and up the stairs to my room, not even bothering to go in the kitchen to excuse myself.

You're sick, Cal. You're hurting Maddie for your own selfish gain. Where's this going? Are you going to marry her? Fuck her? Breed her? That will go over really well with your family and everyone in town that considers you a hero for what you did for the poor broken orphan. All of my hard work and recognition and accolades will be tarnished. They'll think I touched her when she was too young to know better.

They'll think I *raped* her.

And let's just say for argument's sake that no one ever finds out. I manage to keep it from everyone until this relationship or whatever it is plays its course. Then what happens? We go back to the way things were?

No. The relationship I had with Maddie before we started all of this is over. We can't go back to that. Not after kissing her and touching her and...tasting her.

Fuck.

Sounds of sniffling break me out of my thoughts and before I can tell myself that this is the worst idea, I'm closing the door to Maddie's room behind me. "Go away, Cal. I can't do this with everyone downstairs. Not with your girlfriend down there."

"She's not my girlfriend and you know that," I tell her as I sit down on her bed next to her. "I've never known you to be insecure. You know you're my number one girl." I'm trying to keep my hands off of her, but her crying makes me feel like someone has wrapped barbed wire around my heart and every time she sniffles my heart constricts and the wire tightens.

She wipes her eyes and avoids my gaze. "It's different now."

"So, let me get this straight, now that we're...*here*, you think that you mean less to me than you did before?" I raise an eyebrow at her and her watery blue eyes meet mine.

"She's...pretty."

"She's not...you."

She gasps slightly, air moves through her slightly parted lips and her cheeks turn pink. Her tongue darts out to wet her mouth and I shake my head slightly. "Later," I whisper.

"Please," she whimpers, "just for a second."

I swallow, and in that moment, I damn my soul to the pits of hell. I free the beast from the confines of his cage, letting him run wild and free to take what he needed. I don't care about what my family would say, what my job would say, what anyone would say. I'm certain that Maddie is mine. That despite the tragedy in her past that brought us together way earlier than I would have liked, she was meant for me. And she is going to have to go downstairs and watch another woman flirt with me.

I would give her this and whatever else she needs later.

I put her face in my hands, cupping her cheeks gently. "Hey, look at me." She does instantly, as if her body has been trained to obey my every command. I rub my nose gently against hers, inhaling her sweet scent. I let my tongue dart out and trace her bottom lip, then her top lip before I press mine to hers, swallowing a delicious moan that makes my cock twitch. I pull away after no more than a second, not wanting to get carried away. "Wait five minutes before you come downstairs." I stand up and open the door before I peek my head into the hall, grateful that no one is upstairs. I can hear rattling in the kitchen and Henry and Aria talking and I'm certain that Grant is still glued to my sofa.

She nods before she stands up and wraps her arms around me. "I love you." She looks up at me and gives me that smile that makes my heart stop. The smile reaches her eyes and her sweet dimple pops out. I haven't explicitly told her I loved her since we'd crossed these lines, but I hope she knows. I hope she knows with every kiss, every touch, every moment I risk my entire life just to hold her in my arms in a way I knew I shouldn't, I hope she knows that I'd give up everything to love her forever.

Eight

Madeline

THE TENSION IS SO THICK IT SMOTHERS US LIKE A WEIGHTED blanket. Things are always pretty tense whenever Grant and Henry are in the same room, but usually just the right amount of alcohol can loosen that situation. *Unlucky* for all of us, Henry hasn't hit that sweet spot yet, so he is still brooding at the end of the table. I've never really understood why Henry hates Grant so much. From what I can see, he's a good man that has treated Margie like a queen after their father left her heartbroken. I've always liked him, and from the jump, he has always been sweet to me. He'd helped Cal pick out my first car and anytime I saw him he was practically shoving money in my pocket.

On top of the usual "you're not my Daddy and I'll never like you" tension between Henry and Grant, I'm grappling with my own issues of having this outsider at dinner. I'm trying my best not to appear like the jealous girlfriend, but I'm pretty sure I'm failing miserably.

But really, why is she here? I stare across the table at her and cock my head to the side. She is really pretty, but she looks completely over the top for a Thanksgiving dinner, making me believe that she's here for more than just "Aria's friend with nowhere to go."

She wants Cal.

Her strawberry blonde hair is pulled up into a top knot with a few strands hanging. She's wearing a face full of makeup complete with a deep plum lipstick and overly done smoky eye. She's wearing a long sweater over a pair of leggings and heeled boots that make her legs go on for days, and she towers over me.

I've barely said anything since we sat down to dinner, contrary to my normal behavior which is me talking up a storm about anything and everything. The table is practically silent until Aria, whose looks I've been avoiding since the second I snapped at Penelope, stands with her wine glass. "I'm going to get some more wine. Mads, can you come help me?"

"Get more wine? Sorry, I think you forgot the part where I'm not twenty-one yet." I raise an eyebrow at her and take an obvious sip of the water in front of me.

She taps a finger against the side of her glass, irritated, and narrows her gaze. "Like that's stopped you, help please!" I don't miss the growl that escapes Cal's lips over her comment and it immediately sets my body on fire. Visions of him growling as he plows into me from behind crowd my brain and I bite my bottom lip. *Do not look at him, Maddie.*

I roll my eyes before standing. "Would anyone like anything while we're up?"

"Put some more rolls in the oven." Margie points at the empty basket of her infamous buttery bread that had the ability to incite a riot when we were down to the final few.

I'm barely through the foyer when Aria is pulling me away from the kitchen and up the stairs to my bedroom. I can already hear the lecture about reigning in my attitude when she closes the door behind us. "Okay, what is your problem?" she whispers and puts her hands on her hips.

"Nothing!"

"You're pouting like a moody teenager."

"I *am* a moody teenager."

"You never act like it. Something's up." She crosses her arms and I wonder if she could read my mind because immediately her face softens. "Mads, I know you...better than you know yourself."

"You *think* you do." *There's no way you have any idea about what's going on with Cal and me... you'd freak the fuck out.*

"No, I do, and I get that you hate the idea of having to share Cal, but don't you want him to be happy?" I almost choke on her words. *What the hell does that mean?*

"What are you talking about?"

She sighs and sits on my bed. "I know that you're a little... *possessive* about Cal, and that's totally normal. Girls and their dads...especially when there hasn't been a mother figure love interest for their father..." She waves her hand. "It's Psych 101, hon, and you're the textbook definition."

"Okay, first of all, don't psych major me. Secondly, Cal's *not* my dad."

"Maybe not technically, but he's a father figure, and I wish you'd stop denying that. He's done a lot for you, Madeline."

"I'm not denying anything, and Cal knows that I am beyond appreciative of everything he's done for me, so I don't know why you're insinuating that he doesn't know that."

"Okay, don't get so sensitive, and how about we fix the attitude?" She shoots me her signature *Mom* look, and it is times like this that I know Aria wishes she had children of her own.

I try my best to suppress the fantasy forming in my mind, but a flash happens before I can stop it, and I can't stop the smile from tugging at my lips. Me. A positive pregnancy test. Cal kissing me *and my belly* when I tell him the news.

"What's so funny?" Aria asks and I shake my head as I remember that I'm supposed to be irritated with her.

"Nothing, Aria. I just don't think Penelope is the right girl for Cal."

"And you're probably right, but don't you think that's up to him to decide? He holds your opinion in very high regard, Maddie, but give him a chance to figure out how he feels before you force your opinion on him."

"I didn't force anything."

"Oh please," she snorts and stands up to wrap a hand around my shoulder. "You're seventeen, and you already don't see the power you hold over a man. Lord, bless the soul you end up with."

"I resent that." I glare at her, though I can't stop the smile from creeping onto my face.

"Speaking of which, what are we doing for your eighteenth besides getting you on a legitimate poker table? I was thinking about a nice dinner?" I was so excited to go to a casino for the first time; I've been practicing my poker game for weeks.

"Dinner sounds good too." A gasp leaves my lips as I have another idea and I clap my hands together and bounce on the balls of my feet. "Oh! Can we go to a sex shop too?"

Aria stops in her tracks and turns around, closing the door that she'd just opened. "Sex? Wait how, when, what, WHO?!" she shrieks.

"No no no. I just mean because I can…" I shake my head. "Virgin still! Swear!" I grab Aria's pinky and link them just as we always do.

"Oh phew." She puts a hand over her heart and chugs the last of her wine. "You almost…" she lets out a breath. "Okay, yes, you and I can go if you must. I don't even know where there is one, to be honest though. We might have to go to Portland."

"Road trip!" I do a little shimmy and she rolls her eyes.

"Attitude. In check." She points at me. "I mean it, Mads.

You're a sweet girl, I'm just asking that you give her a chance."

"Fine, can I have some wine at least?"

"One glass." She holds up her index finger and points at me.

"One? Well screw that, can I have something harder if I'm limited to one?"

"Yes, that's probably better anyway, at least you can pretend there's no alcohol in it. Mix it with something dark."

"Cal knows I drink, Aria."

"Doesn't mean either of us are too happy about it. Do you just not give a shit that you live with a cop?"

"What's he going to do, arrest me?" I cock my head, ignoring the thoughts of him using his cuffs on me to secure me to his bed like I'm in one of those sexy BDSM novels Sasha and I read.

We make our way downstairs just as Margie pulls the rolls out of the oven. "I was wondering where you two went off to."

"Just some girl talk." Aria grabs my jaw and squeezes before planting a kiss on my cheek.

"And I wasn't invited?" Margie pushes her glasses to her head and narrows her eyes at us.

"I was getting yelled at," I whisper before I grab a bottle of vodka out of Cal's liquor cabinet.

"Oh perfect, make me one, will you?" Margie hands me her glass and Aria puts her hand over mine stopping me. "And why are you yelling at my girl?" She looks at Aria the way grandparents look at parents for scolding their own children.

"Mom…Maddie is not making you a drink."

"Why not! Last I checked, I'm actually old enough to drink." She points at me as I stir the ginger ale into the healthy pour of vodka with a spoon.

Aria rolls her eyes and pats my butt to send me out of the kitchen with the drink I made myself. "I'll make you one, you go back in there," she tells us. I could hear the implication. *This* drink is going to be weak as fuck.

I move back down the hallway and into the dining room to see Penelope laughing with Cal about something. She'd claimed the seat next to him and I sat across from them, forced to watch her stare at him with stars in her eyes.

"Everything okay?" Henry asks as I sit back down in my seat.

"Yup." I take a long sip of my drink, and I can already feel Cal's penetrating gaze on me.

"Madeline." He grunts and my eyes flash to his.

"Mmmhmm?" *Yes, Daddy?* My mind automatically thinks and I can't even stop the flush from moving up my body.

I wonder if he can read my mind because something crosses his face that could possibly be construed as lust from my vantage point." What's in that?"

I shrug. "Nothing."

"Don't lie to me."

"It's ginger ale, calm down."

He reaches his hand across the table towards me. "Let me smell it."

"No, I think I'm good."

"Excuse me?" He gives me that look he's given me on a few occasions when I am testing him, and I shiver with delight at the thought of what he might do to me later. He'd never laid a hand on me, but suddenly the idea of being over his lap while he spanks my bare ass has me clenching my thighs together under the table.

"Oh Cal, relax. She's at home," Aria interjects as she walks back through the room and runs a hand through her hair.

"You okayed this?" He stares at her.

She shoots him a look back like *I know what I'm doing, and did you want to calm her sassy ass down or no?*

I roll my eyes at them both and take another long sip.

His cocoa eyes bore into mine. "That's your *one*, Madeline, and I mean it."

Stop using my full name!

"Oh, calm down, Cal." Margie takes her seat and her drink looks even clearer than mine, making me wonder if Aria's plan to make her a weak drink quickly got derailed when I left the room.

"Calm down? Am I the only one that forgets she's not old enough to drink? Let alone not even eighteen?"

I try to keep the question off my face as I hear his choice of words given what we've been doing the past few days, which in some ways may be more damaging than just a few drinks. I didn't see it that way, but I knew other people would feel very differently.

"She's at home with her family. Would you rather she was out in the street doing it?" Aria asks.

"I'm not condoning this." He points at me. "I'm a cop for crying out loud. So are you." He looks at Aria and she rolls her eyes.

"Not to Maddie, now pass the potatoes." She holds her hand out.

"As much as I've enjoyed being talked about while I'm right here, can we talk about something else?" I hand her the potatoes from in front of Cal, who'd refused to pass them, when Grant speaks up.

"Yes, let's. Let's talk about what we're doing for your birthday, sweet pea." Grant grabs my hand and squeezes. He's sitting diagonally from me at the head of the table, much to Henry's annoyance.

"We?" Henry perks up and Margie, who's within arm's reach, smacks his arm and glares at him.

"Don't start," she warns.

"We already have some plans in place." Aria points at me before pointing around the table.

"Yes, we will be taking down the Meadowfield Casino. I've got my poker face, ready!" I put my hands up.

"I don't believe this." Cal groans. "Is anyone in this family planning to be a good influence on Maddie?"

"You are." I take a sip of my drink and raise an eyebrow at him. "Someone's got to corrupt me a little."

Only he knows the true meaning of my words, and while I thought it might throw him off, he doesn't miss a beat. "I think Grant meant maybe a nice family dinner, you heathens." He looks at all of us and Margie shrugs.

"I'm going with them to Meadowfield. I was invited." She winks at me.

I point back at her and do a dance in my chair. "I need my coach."

"Fine other than going to the casino…" He shakes his head. "Dinner?"

My eyes flit to the only person at this table who better not be invited before turning my gaze back to Cal. "We can talk about it another time. We still have a few weeks."

"You'll be eighteen, that's really exciting." Penelope perks up. She smiles a smile that is probably genuine, and for a second, I feel bad. She's the nice girl in this situation and *I'm* the bitch. If this were a book or a movie or TV show, I'd be rooting for her to get the guy and not me. But life isn't a book or a movie or TV show, and she doesn't have a prayer at landing Cal.

"Thanks." I smile before turning back to Grant without another glance. "We'll be in touch. Just…six, right?" I look around the obvious table of seven and no one says anything, though I feel Aria's glare on me.

"Never a dull moment at Thanksgiving." Margie snorts

from the other end and takes another long sip of her drink. "Okay, who wants pie?"

No Grayson holiday is complete without poker, which is how all of us are locked into a game at the end of the night. Penelope is long gone, having still felt the residual tension from me, and the fact that, besides Aria, no one really seemed to come to her rescue.

"Honestly, Aria, Henry, you don't know anything about my boy, do you?" Margie says as she tosses out a card. "She was all wrong for him."

I giggle to myself because of both Margie's comment and the second vodka drink I'd managed to sneak in while Cal walked Penelope out. I may have stared at them from the window a little too long, but it was enough to know that he didn't kiss her. All he'd offered her was a polite hug, and I was thrilled that she hadn't tried to initiate kissing him.

"Mom! Penelope is nice," Aria says as she throws a card out.

"Penelope is *boring*," Margie added without looking up from her cards.

"You're one to talk about boring significant others." Henry grunts and I pout. *Here we go.* I go to speak up when Cal pins me with a glare, knowing that it is best I stay out of that even if Margie is one of my favorite people and Grant isn't too far down that list.

I listen because I'm a little buzzed...and Cal would always be at the top of that list.

"I raise," Grant replies in response and I throw my cards down.

"Really?" I scoff.

"I know you know how to bluff," Margie speaks up.

"Not with that trash hand." I wave it off.

"Listen, all I'm saying is maybe you ought to let me and Maddie handle the fixing up from now on." Margie points at Aria and Henry. "Because you two are clueless."

"Mom..." Cal's tone is exasperated and I watch him and Grant share a look. His eyes dart to the drink in front of his mother and then the water in front of Grant. Margie is no stranger to sleeping over when she's had a little too much to drink, or just when she wanted to spend time with me. But I take the obvious glance as a sign that he doesn't want that for tonight and all of me hopes that it's because he wants to be alone with me.

There's been a dull throb in my sex ever since he kissed me earlier, and now it's exacerbated by the alcohol that wants his mouth between my legs.

"I fold." Margie tosses her cards. "Maddie, I'm going to put my tree up tomorrow, are you coming over?"

"You know it." I nod, knowing that helping Margie put her tree up had become a bit of a tradition since my first Christmas with Cal.

"Perfect, I got you something!" With my birthday being in December, somehow the entire month had become Maddie's birth *month,* so that my birthday doesn't get swallowed by the holiday season. Spread over the entire month, I get all kinds of gifts, small and large, leading up to the twenty-sixth which is my actual birthday.

As much as Cal hates to admit it, he's spoiled me rotten since that first Christmas. My birth parents didn't have much money, and I was lucky if I got food on Christmas much less presents. Cal seemed to want to erase that from my memory, which meant each year I was surrounded by literal mountains of presents. I never asked for much, and it got to the point that they stopped asking when my response was always, *I don't need anything, I have everything I could ever want!* This year, however, I want something money can't buy, and I fully intended to ask for it.

Aria and Henry, the last of the party are barely backed out of the driveway when Cal has me pinned to the front door with his lips on mine. He tastes like the whiskey drink he'd been nursing the last hour and a hint of pumpkin. *Damn, he tastes so good. Like love and lust and comfort and home all rolled into one.*

"You're going to make me lose my fucking mind." He cups my face in his hands and continues to make love to my mouth with his tongue. He sucks my tongue into his mouth and I meet his kiss with equal aggression. *I never want this kiss to end.* Each kiss feels like another step in our relationship. A new revelation. Each kiss is more passionate and urgent than the last and they all tell me something new about the man I love so much.

"Sorry."

He rubs his nose against mine and presses a chaste kiss to my mouth. "I hate that you think you have a reason to be jealous, but fuck if it doesn't turn me on."

I gasp and pull away from his mouth. "It does?"

"Yes." He grunts and lifts me into his arms and walks us into the living room. "Penelope doesn't mean anything. She's not a threat to you, Maddie. I don't want her."

"Doesn't mean I enjoyed watching her flirt with you."

He sets me on the couch and kneels in front of me, running his hands up my thighs and gripping me hard when he reaches the apex of them. He doesn't touch me there, but he does pop the button of my jeans. "Take them off."

"What?" My eyes widen to the size of saucers. *Is he...now?* My heart slams against my rib cage and my mouth waters at the idea of crossing that line with Cal.

He darts his hands away from me like I've burned him. "Do you not want to?"

My pants are halfway down my legs before he can change his mind. "No, I do. I do! I just didn't..."

He doesn't say anything, just glues his stare to my pussy and helps me pull my jeans off. I am suddenly very grateful for the black lace panties that cover barely anything but my slit and the very thin string that went between my cheeks. "Holy fuck, these are sexy." He plucks the string, letting it snap against my skin and the feeling makes me dizzy. The sexual tension crackles around us and it feels like every single one of my nerves are standing on end.

"Are...are you going to take them off?"

His eyes don't leave my covered sex. "Not yet."

"Not today...? Or not right this second."

"Not today," he whispers, and his eyes float up my body. "Maybe not ever."

"No, Cal." I grab his face. "I want to talk about that."

"About what?"

"I know what I want for my birthday."

He shakes his head and squeezes his eyes shut. "Don't ask me."

"Please?" He backs up slightly and I can see him retreating so I'm off the couch and straddling his lap before he can stop me. "I... I can't promise I'll be good at it but..."

"Hey," he snaps and grips my jaw. "That's not what this is about. Jesus Christ, Maddie, look at you." I frown, unsure of where he's going with this and he shakes his head. "You're a fucking goddess...you're the most beautiful woman I've ever laid eyes on. I'm not supposed to look at you the way I see other men look at you. Men whose eyes I've been threatening to gouge out for letting their lustful gazes fall on you. I'm the one man that's not supposed to look at you like that and...I can't fucking help it."

"You're the only man I want looking at me like that." I press my hands to his chest and rub my nose down his neck.

"I can't hurt you like that, Maddie." His voice is tortured, and I wish I could kiss the pain away.

"Why?"

"Because...I love you too much." His hand runs down my back and I shiver under his touch.

I pull back and stare at him, the tears forming in my eyes and sliding down my cheeks before I can stop them.

"If you love me, then make love to me."

CAL

I AM HANGING ON BY A PROVERBIAL THREAD. I DON'T KNOW HOW I'VE managed to keep myself out of Maddie's pants when she all but begs for it every night she cuddles up next to me, but somehow, I've kept her at arm's length, much to my own disappointment. The need to taste her has gotten so out of control it's almost unmanageable. Letting her rub against me until we both come isn't enough anymore. I need to feel her skin to skin. I need to spread her sweet cunt open like a flower and lick the soft petals between her legs. I want to worship every inch of her skin, marking her with my teeth and tongue and fingers and then my cock. She's a blank canvas I want to paint with my cum. I want to rain my seed all over her perfect tits, her smooth ass, her gorgeous face. I want to worship her…but I also want to defile her.

I want to use her body, fuck every single one of her holes until she's so full of my cum it drips out of her. I want to fuck her like she's a slut. Bend her over every surface in our house and take her so brutally she won't be able to sit down for a week. I want to hate fuck her for making me feel this way. For turning me into this sick bastard that's having these thoughts about the girl I raised. And then, when all of that's done, when I'm done fucking the life out of her, I want to bring her back. Run my lips over every inch of her marked skin, whispering my love and devotion to her in between each kiss as I rock gently into her. Make love to her, teach her the love language that our bodies already know by heart.

She'll take my cock easily because, despite my size, I am made to fit inside of her. Her back will arch, and her nails will claw at my back every time I thrust into her. She'll scream that she wants more, and harder and deeper and faster. That she loves me and that she's wanted this for so long and to promise her that things will never change between us.

But they've changed.

And it'll never be the same again.

It's been a week since Thanksgiving and much to my surprise Maddie hasn't brought up her wish for her birthday. I've been at war with myself on what I should do, and almost seven sleepless nights later, I'm no closer to coming up with a decision. I don't hear anything when I get home from work one evening which is odd because Maddie's car is here.

"Maddie?" I call for her as I toss my keys on the counter. It isn't unusual for her to be cooking dinner or lying on the couch in one of my t-shirts and the tiniest pair of shorts waiting for me to get home so she could climb into my lap and rub the day off of me. I frown, wondering where she could be when I make my way upstairs. I peek my head into her room wondering if maybe she is taking a nap when I see her bed is still made from whenever the last time she slept here.

She's slept in my room with me for the past week, and I briefly wonder if she's just taking a nap. I take a look around her perfectly organized room and step inside. Trophies for various dance competitions sit on three equally spaced shelves on her wall. Directly underneath is a wide bookcase with at least one hundred books, aligned by size, then color, and quite possibly alphabetized. A television is mounted on the adjacent wall and right underneath is a dresser.

I take a step closer, and without thinking, I pull open her top drawer, knowing what's there and grab the first pair I see—a white silky thong with lace trim. I grip the delicate fabric in my hand before stuffing it into my pocket. Feelings of shame wash over me as I think about what I've been doing with her underwear the past week. Ever since I saw her in that tiny thong, I've been stealing her panties and rubbing them over my cock every night after Maddie falls asleep. I wrap the silk around my hand and tug at my cock before releasing my seed into them. Marking them. I want to think about her wearing them after knowing that my cum has been there. A grunt leaves my lips as I adjust my dick and move towards my bedroom.

"Maddie, where are you?" I don't see her in my room but I do see the light on in my bathroom peeking out from under the door. "Mads?" I knock and I frown when I don't hear anything. I push the door open and all of the air leaves my lungs as I take in the sight before me. My dick is hard as granite and I'm trying my best to calm it back down so that I don't attack her. I swallow and take a tentative step forward when her eyes meet mine. Blue, mischievous eyes that have the power to break me. And I believe they are about to exercise that power. *Now.*

"Welcome home, honey." She leans over the edge of the tub and shoots me a wink. "Care to join me?" The words get caught in my throat as I stare at the naked seventeen year old taking a bubble bath in my tub. Her hair is pulled up in a bun at the top of her head, though some strands have fallen and are touching the bubbles that are up to her neck. I can't see anything, but I don't trust Maddie not to stand up and reveal *everything* to me.

I find myself hoping that she will. I've been wondering for a week what Maddie looks like naked. Is her pussy bare? Does she have a landing strip? Does she not do any landscaping? All three thoughts make me hard as fuck. And while hair on a cunt usually does nothing for me, I find myself still hard at the idea of tasting the soft curls between her legs should there be any.

Then, there are her tits. Her asshole. That space between her pussy and her asshole. *Fuck.* I wanted to see all of it. *Now.*

I clear my throat. "Maddie, I don't think…"

"It's a good idea, blah blah blah." She rolls her eyes and settles back into the large jacuzzi style tub that is definitely big enough for both of us. "Fine, do you want to watch?"

I bite my bottom lip, knowing that I need to run from this room and not tempt or torture myself with being in the same room as a naked and wet Maddie. I rub a hand down my face and move closer to the tub and sit on the floor next to it. "How was your day?"

"Good. I missed you." She leans forward and for a moment my heart stops, but I realize she just wants to kiss me. "I won't…" she whispers. "Until you tell me you want to." I nod in understanding and lean in and meet her lips. I hold her head in place as I find her tongue, kissing her like I haven't seen her in weeks and not the seven hours we've been apart. When we pull apart there's a smile on her face. "I love kissing you."

A stab of guilt comes out of nowhere. It flares up from time to time. A voice that tells me that I'm fucked up and, worse, that I'm fucking up Maddie for this. That she'll never be able to have a normal relationship when this is over. Or worse, that these daddy issues that she's working through will never completely go away and she'll end up with some guy twice as old as me. A pout finds her face and I can see the rejection creeping onto her skin so I push my guilty thoughts away and smile at her. "Kissing you has been the highlight of my day."

I don't know how long we've been talking, but the bubbles that had been hiding her body from view begin to disintegrate into the warm water. The bubbles are clearing and I'm beginning to see smooth skin under the clear water. "Maddie..." I turn away as the last of the bubbles surrounding her chest disappears.

"Do you have to go?" Her voice is quiet and shy and sexy as fuck and I feel the beast at the base of my throat dying to come out. I swallow, in an attempt to keep him at bay, but the second I open my mouth, the words fly out before I can stop them.

"No," I growl before I turn to face her. "I want to see you."

Her voice lights up. "You...you do?"

"Yes. Everything. I can't touch you. But I can look. I can memorize every inch of your body and then later, when you rub that tight body against me, I can visualize you naked. I can picture that space between your thighs. Those pretty pink nipples. The curves of your perfect ass cheeks."

She whimpers and shifts slightly, pushing the bubbles away from her and putting herself completely on display. The water has a slight film from the bubbles and her body wash, but I can still make out her curves. She spreads her legs under the water and all I can see is the dark slit between two creamy folds. *She's completely bare.* I groan and let my head fall back, squeezing my eyes shut to sear the visual into my brain. In this moment, I would probably give my life to take one slow lick between her legs.

I grit my teeth shut, so the words don't leave my mouth. The sounds of water sloshing make my eyes pop open just in time to see her stand in my tub, water running down her body in rivulets. I watch enthralled, my eyes unable to look away from the Goddess in front of me. I wanted to catch every drop of water that cascades down her slim body with my tongue. I want to see if she is wet between her legs with something other than water. I wanted to pull her nipples between my teeth to see if they're hard. I wanted to run my finger between her ass cheeks and circle the rosebud there. I want it all, and I can't have any of it. Saliva pools in my mouth and I swallow it down.

I stand up and grab the towel sitting on the sink. She reaches for it and I take a step back. "I just…need a second."

"You can have all the seconds." She purrs as she takes a step out of the tub and onto the floor. She takes a step closer, the water falling from her skin and I back up again. "Don't you want to touch me?" Her bottom lip juts out.

"I shouldn't."

She looks down at her body and then at me, her eyes wanting approval that only my dick can give. "Do I look okay?"

"Okay? Maddie your body is *insane*. You're so beautiful it fucking pains me to look at you and *not* touch you. My dick is so hard it could cut glass."

She bites her lip and reaches for me. I drop the towel and her eyes watch it drop to the floor with a dull thud. "Can I see?"

"Maddie…"

"Just a peek. I won't touch, I promise."

I've been ogling her for the past five minutes, it's only fair, right?

Her hands find my belt buckle and she rubs her hand along the leather and the metal before tugging it gently. "Wait," I growl at her, my hands find her hips and before I can stop myself, I've sat her on my counter and she gasps when the cool marble hits her ass. "I can't touch you when we're both naked…so just give me a second."

"Why not?"

"You know why not, Maddie." I press my lips to her neck, my hands still planted firmly on her hips, and refusing to move an inch. I pepper kisses down her slender neck and chest before I move slightly down. I stop kissing, knowing that I am crossing into dangerous territory.

She squirms and whimpers as I reach her nipple and rub my nose against it. "What are you doing?"

"Memorizing your scent." I move from her right to her left nipple, smelling the sweet vanilla on her skin. I could practically taste her sex that smelled of her body wash but also her wetness forming on her folds. "Part your legs, Maddie."

"Are you going to touch me?"

"Not yet."

"Then no because…I'm wet." I look up at her just as I see the pink flooding her cheeks.

"You say that like it's a bad thing. Like that doesn't turn me the fuck on. Like I don't want to lick up every drop."

"Then why don't you?"

I tell her, "Not now."

"When?"

"Fuck. Maddie…I don't know."

"My birthday?" she squeaks.

I freeze and stare up at her. I part her legs slightly and move the rest of the way down her body until I'm staring straight at her wet folds. *Fuck. Maybe just a taste.*

Her folds are spread, exposing her swollen clit that is staring at me begging me to lick it, suck it, *devour* it. The tip of my nose runs up her thigh and I let it hover over her pussy, breathing in her sweet scent. "Cal." She's white-knuckling the counter and I feel her sex moving closer to me. Her clit grazes my nose slightly and she moans which has a direct line to my dick and it throbs painfully. "Holy fuck. S—sorry. Didn't mean…t…tto." She stammers and I wonder if just that minor brush against me is about to have her coming. "I…I need to put clothes on. Or…

whatever we can do that will make you touch me." Her eyes find mine and I look from her to her glistening pussy.

"Maddie…" I groan as I close my eyes and stand up away from her sex. "I just can't yet."

"Yet?" The hope laced in her voice doesn't just speak to my dick, it speaks to my brain and my heart, and I'm wondering if every part of me is starting to get on the same page as my raging fucking hormones.

God, I'm so fucked.

"You really want this?"

"I really do." She presses her hands to my chest and leans up to kiss me. I pull away and shake my head and she frowns.

"We need to talk about a few things first."

"Like what?"

"Like what? Like what this means for you and me. I can't…" I rub my hand over my forehead and back away from her. I pick up the towel and hand it to her. "What happens to us once we go down that road? Shit, even this?" I point back and forth between us. "Where does this leave us when this ends?"

Her eyes well up with tears instantly and before I can reach out to wipe them, she gets off the counter and wraps the towel around her. "I hadn't counted on this ending." She bites her bottom lip before she leaves the bathroom without another glance.

I think about giving her space, letting her collect her thoughts before I go in and force her to talk to me. But then I remember she hasn't exactly granted me that same courtesy. She bulldozed her way into my heart ten years ago, and then again last week in a completely different way. I've never had a chance to collect my thoughts before I've had to face her, and if she's asking for what I think she's asking, then she needs to know how to talk to me. I follow after her and push my way through her closed door to find her pulling out a pair of underwear. She turns to look at me as she pulls her panties up her legs and lets them snap against her hips. Her chest is still bare and all I want to do is drop to my knees and feast on her tits. "Madeline, if you're going to fucking run away from me every time I upset you, this is never going to work."

"Well, I love you, and I want to be with you and you're talking to me about *when this ends*...so I'm sorry for being a little emotional about that."

"I'm sorry I said that...I guess I'm still playing a bit of catch up. I just think it's going to be a lot harder than you think transitioning this relationship. I raised you, Maddie, and now...This is complicated. And what happens when you go away next year? You're going to want to be free to explore and find yourself." *The last thing she needs is an overprotective...boyfriend? Following her around everywhere. And I know I fucking would. I wouldn't let any of those frat fucks within a mile of her.*

"Who said I was going away?" She sits on her bed and looks up at me. "I thought...I mean I was going to ask if I could stay here with you while I went to school."

"Maddie...you're brilliant and Ivy's are already knocking on our door."

"Ivy League schools are expensive."

"Will you let me worry about that?" I didn't want to tell her that I've been putting money aside for school for her for years, not to mention Margie, Henry, Aria, and Grant are all on board that we'd send her wherever she wanted.

"Since I've known you, you've always put me first. You've given me everything I've ever wanted or needed my entire life. I don't want you giving up anything else for me. I don't want you sacrificing anything else for me. I just want...*you.*" Goosebumps appear all over her body, and my eyes immediately go to her nipples that are turning to hard points.

    I sit next to her and pull her hand into mine and run my lips over it before draping a blanket around her shoulders. "I'll never not put you first, Maddie. No matter where things go between us."

Ten

Madeline

I PEEK MY HEAD OUT BEHIND THE RED CURTAIN, STARING INTO THE SEA OF people in the auditorium. Dozens of eyes stare back at me and it turns my stomach into knots. I don't think they can see me through the tiny crack, but I back away slowly, my lip trembling with each step. "I can't do it."

A hand touches my shoulder and then her familiar perfume surrounds me. "Of course, you can, honey. I promise it's not scary." Aria kneels in front of me and smooths my hair into a bun. Though I don't know how a hair could be out of place, she is hair spraying it down for a full twenty minutes.

"Cal's not here." Tears fill my eyes and one threatens to trickle down my cheek, but then I remember Aria's hard work on my eyes. I look pretty. Like a model in a magazine or a movie star. It's my first recital and my first time ever in front of an audience and all the makeup on my face makes me look like a pretty made up doll. I rub my nose absentmindedly and look up at her. Concern flashes in her green eyes and she tucks a strand of her newly chopped bob behind her ear.

"I know, and you know he wants to be here, but something happened at work." She pulls me into a hug and squeezes before kissing my cheek. "He promised to meet us as soon as he could, remember? And I'm going to take a video. You're going to be so good, Maddie. The best ballerina there ever was."

Somewhere in the distance, they call for me and Aria stands up.

"I have to get to my seat, but I promise everything is going to be okay."

I look up at her and start to rub my eye, but I let my hand fall when I remember my makeup. "What if I fall?"

"Then you get back up and keep going." My eyes widen. I expected her to assure me that I wouldn't. "Everyone falls sometimes...you just get back up and keep going." She touches my cheek and strokes it gently. "Now get out there and show us what you can do."

I'm ushered into a line by a stage mom and a girl next to me, with the same bright pink tutu looks over at me with bright shining eyes. "I heard you talking to your mom...don't be sad, my dad isn't here either."

"Oh, that's not my mom...and Cal's not my dad..." I trail off, still trying to find the words of how to explain who Cal is in my life. I frown when I think about my real dad. "He's better than any dad I've ever met."

I'm brought back into the present by the sound of Catrina's voice. The same young girl with the bright pink tutu is now an older girl with a white tutu indicating she's one of the Russian dancers in the Nutcracker Ballet that our studio puts on every year. "Come on Shaw, you're up." She flicks my shoulder and I stand up with a sigh. "You're being moodier than usual. You're the Sugar Plum Fairy for God's sake, can we put on a smile?" She leans forward into the mirror next to me and purses her freshly painted lips in the mirror. "I can't wait to get out of this; Jacob just got home from college this afternoon and I am feigning for a good dicking."

You and me both. I pout. "I don't think Cal's going to make it."

"Oh, so that's why you're all pouty." She turns towards me before looking around. "Ten years and you still get so antsy when he's not here." She narrows her gaze at me and for a brief second, I wonder if the answers are written all over me. That I want Cal here for reasons different than when I was ten. Before I was scared, and he made me feel brave and like I could take on anything. Now, I just wanted him here because I'm the lead and I want him to be proud of me. I want the man I love and the one that loves me to be here. He'd promised me over and over this morning that he would try his hardest to make it, but he had to go handle something a few counties over and wasn't sure he would be back in time.

"I just feel better when he's in the audience."

"Hmmm." She smooths her tutu down and pulls the straps of her leotard up. "You're sleeping with him, aren't you?"

"What?" I turn my head to hers, my voice loud and piercing and she rolls her eyes and presses a finger to her ear.

"So, that's a yes?"

"No, Catrina. What? What would make you even say that?"

"Well, now, your reaction, and the fact that you're pinker than the Chinese dancer costumes, and two, because no woman could survive living in a house with a man that looked like Officer Sexy without having a taste."

I scoff. "I hate when you call him that."

"Why? Feeling territorial?" *Yes.* She leans forward and runs a finger over my lashes, pushing them upwards. "Tell me you call him that in bed, don't you?"

I roll my eyes and swat her hand away before standing up from my chair. "I don't call him anything in bed because we are not sleeping together! You need to get your mind out of the gutter and stop with the romance books. It's turning you into a horny nightmare." I loved Catrina and her affinity for literally *all* the smutty books, but it's made her believe that everyone is fucking each other. *Or wants to.*

She shrugs. "Fine, whatever." She holds her hands up before skipping off. I look down at my phone just as it buzzes, the sound making my heart sink because I know it's Cal telling me he isn't going to make it.

Superhero: Still in Seattle. I'll make it up to you, I swear. I love you.

The three words make my heart soar. I bite down on my lower lip as I clench, my sex feelings those words almost as much as my heart.

Me: And how do you plan to make it up to me?
Superhero: Talk later, Madeline.

I can read between the lines. *Don't start.* I had tried to sext him once, last week when I was bored in my chemistry class. He was *not* having it and proceeded to give me a very stern lecture when he got home about not putting anything in writing. It made sense because, although texts could be deleted, nothing was ever permanently gone in this day in age.

Me: Fine. I go on soon, talk to you later.
Superhero: Break a leg.

"You were so good!" Aria bounces up and down as I come out of the dressing room and move through the sea of people towards my very loud cheering section. Aria, Margie, Grant, and Sasha were the loudest by *far*. But although they always succeeded in embarrassing me, I wouldn't trade them for anything.

"*Everyone needs a home team*," Aria told me once. "*They're the people that cheer hardest for you even when it's the bottom of the ninth and the bases are loaded and all feels lost."*

Sasha bounces up and down and wraps her arms around me. "I still can't believe your legs can do that. The man that gets you into bed is going to kiss the ground you walk on."

"Sash!" I swat at her as Grant groans.

"What! You're eighteen in like less than a week." Sasha treats my entire family like they're my older siblings and sees them in no way, shape, or form as parental. "Aren't you taking her to a sex shop?" She points at Aria who then shoots me a glare.

"What? She wants to come too!" I smack my best friend in the arm. "You have no freaking chill!"

She wraps an arm around my neck and drags me away from my family and into a corner. "Okay, tell me you can come out tonight."

Visions of how Cal is going to make up for missing my show tonight come barging into my brain like a bright neon light. As much as *no* is on the tip of my tongue, I have to play it somewhat cool and not like I have plans that don't include leaving Cal's bed till morning. *Or ever.* "Out…where?"

"Come on, you've barely been out in weeks and today was the last day of school until after the New Year! Tell me Daddy Cop is going to let you out." Cal and I hadn't spent much time out of the house the last few weeks because out here we couldn't be *us*. Cal couldn't touch me, he couldn't look at me the way he can't help but look at me. He couldn't run his hand down my back and cup my ass. He couldn't trace my neck with his tongue. He couldn't kiss me. All things both of us relished in doing, *often*. So, no, I hadn't really been out of the house.

"I just…" I search my brain for an excuse, but come up pretty empty, "I'm so tired, Sash."

"Bullshit, you can sleep tomorrow. You're coming out. No questions. I'll be at your house in one hour. Please be ready."

I sigh in defeat. "Where are we going?"

"Just to grab some dinner!"

I know my best friend well enough to know, there is more to the story. "With…"

"Mike…" She looks around and gives me a smirk and a shimmy, "and the hot lacrosse guy."

I squeeze my eyes shut, knowing that this is going to be complicated as fuck to get out of. How am I going to explain to Sasha that I can't go on a date?

I see the look she's giving me and let out a sigh.

Okay, how am I going to explain to *Cal* that I'm *going* on a date?

Cal's still not home an hour later and I'm starting to feel antsy about leaving the house without seeing him first. I pick up the phone to call him and he answers on the first ring.

"Hey, Maddie." *Translation: I'm around people. Hi baby.*

I swallow as I run the lotion up my bare legs, wishing it were his hands touching me. "Hey… umm…Sasha wants to hang out."

"Now?" *Translation: I want you home when I get there. Don't go out.*

"Yeah, I just…don't know how to get out of it."

"I don't know that I want you going out this late." I hear someone speaking in the distance and then a voice I recognize coming into the receiver.

"Don't let this old man keep you from going out and living your best life, little G." The voice of Ryan Burns, Cal's right-hand man, comes over the phone. They've been best friends since the first day of Academy and genuinely one of the best guys I know other than Cal. He started calling me little G, as in *Little Grayson*, because to him that's what I am. *Cal's daughter.*

I squeeze my eyes shut, knowing that never in a million years is Ryan going to let this go and now Cal has to be careful about what he says next because Ryan always knows when something is off. It's why he was promoted to Detective at twenty-six.

"Hey Ry, are you guys staying out of trouble?" I reach for my jeans and pull them up over my legs as I cradle my phone against my shoulder.

"You betcha. Now go have fun. But not too much, alright?"

"Ummm...yeah, sure. Can...I talk to Cal really quick?"

"Where are you guys going?" Cal says as his voice comes over the phone.

"I don't want to go, but you're not exactly giving me an out," I tell him. "And I know Ryan just made it ten times harder." I sigh, knowing he can't respond to any of what I just said. "I just want to see you." I sigh, when he doesn't say anything. "Dinner. I'll text you where we go."

"Alright, have fun, Mads." I can hear the smile in his voice that he's probably putting on for Ryan, though I know his heart isn't in it.

"I love you."

"Talk soon." *Translation: I'm fucking pissed.*

⟿

"Can you at least pretend like you're excited?" Sasha says as I slide into her Toyota Camry. It was an early birthday present from her parents, both for turning eighteen and for getting into college. Sasha is brilliant by nature, not by studying, and despite the fact that she skipped more than half of her classes every week, she is still maintaining a good enough GPA to get her early acceptance to a handful of schools.

"I don't want to go out with the lacrosse guy. Speaking of which, does he have a name?"

"Ummm...Bryan? Brock? Brent?" She shrugs as she pulls out of my driveway. "Couldn't tell you. Ask him. And why not?" She points her finger at me. "You've been acting weird the past few weeks. What gives?"

"Nothing, I'm just...exhausted, and I guess a little antsy about turning eighteen. And next year...I don't know, college stuff." I start rambling off the standard things kids our age have to be stressed out about to keep Sasha from getting too close to the truth.

"I know girl, me too. But this is why you have to let loose from time to time."

"I let loose plenty."

"Not recently! I feel like I've hardly seen you since before Thanksgiving. It's almost Christmas. Speaking of which, what are we doing for your birthday?"

Hopefully me and Cal in nothing more than our birthday suits. I roll my eyes at my corny pun and shrug. "I have some plans with everyone, but nothing crazy."

"That's stupid, it's your eighteenth! I'm sure Aria and Cal have something fun planned for you. Like a surprise party!"

"Wouldn't you know if there was a surprise party?" I raise an eyebrow at her.

"Not necessarily, they know I can't keep secrets from you."

Sasha turns on some music and I'm grateful for the sounds of Lana Del Rey to stop the conversation and to quiet the thoughts in my brain. I let her melancholy voice calm me slightly when I feel a text buzzing in my bag.

Superhero: Just you and Sasha?

Me: No
Superhero: Who else?
Me: Her boyfriend and some other guy
Superhero: So, like a date?

This is one of those times that I wish I could be completely transparent. I want to tell him that I feel backed into a corner, and that I don't want to go out in the first place. That I wanted to be home when he got there, tucked in his bed and waiting for him. That I didn't want any other guy. Just him.
But I can't say that.

Me: I wouldn't call it that.
Superhero: Sounds like it…and you know all guys have to be cleared through me.
Me: Cal…

He doesn't say anything and a sinking feeling washes over me that I'm walking into a disaster.

―♾―

Brad Richards has bright blue eyes that almost completely match the shade of mine. His blonde hair is cut short, almost buzzed if not for the fact that it sort of falls in his face in the front. He's tall, much taller than me and Sasha, and even has Mike by an inch, making me wonder if he is well over six feet. He's ripped from what I can see under his letterman jacket that has his name proudly stamped across the back. "This must be the famous Maddie."

I pull my brown leather jacket closer around me. "I didn't know I was famous." A polite smile finds my lips before he pulls me into a hug, much to my surprise. I pull back and put some space between us and give him my hand. "Pleased to meet you."

"So formal." He smiles, revealing a smile with a slight gap between his front two teeth. Objectively, he is still handsome. The slight flaw makes him seem more real and not the perfect All-American boy that he appears to be. He shakes my hand and pulls it to his mouth, brushing his lips over the skin. I slide my hand out of it, wondering why he's so handsy when we literally just met, and he frowns.

I think he's going to say something in response to my aloofness when something over my shoulder catches his attention. His eyebrows furrow and I hear Sasha groan. "Oh, for the love of God."

My scalp tingles in preparation for the storm I know is headed my way. I have no idea how Cal is going to stake his claim over me, but I know without a doubt, that I won't be at this restaurant for much longer.

"Ladies." Hungry brown eyes meet mine. *Well to me they're hungry, to everyone else I'm sure they're the eyes of a cop who doesn't take any shit.* He turns towards Brad and Mike, glowering at my 'date.' "Gentlemen."

"Is there a problem?" Brad looks him up and down, not realizing who he is, and thus getting a different vibe from him. *Please don't start a pissing contest with him.* I'm just about to explain who Cal is when Brad continues, "Because they're with us." He points at me and Sasha.

"Is that so?" Cal looks at me, an evil glint in his eye, and I already don't like where this is going. "Madeline."

I try to stop my body from reacting to his use of my full name but it's no use. My chest deflates, my heart begins to race, and a pulse begins to flicker between my legs. "Brad, this is my… ummm…well…I sort of live with him."

He raises an eyebrow and crosses his arms over his chest, his posture and gaze full of judgment. "Seems a little young to be your dad."

"He's not."

"Brother?"

I shake my head. "No," I say softly.

"Cousin? Uncle? Some sort of family member?"

"We're not...related. I don't...have a ton of family."

"Yes, you do." Cal's voice is smooth and he pins me with a look. *You have family. What do you call Aria and Henry and Margie?*

"I just mean...ummm my parents died when I was younger and Cal took me in."

"Just some random guy?" Brad stares at me and shifts his gaze to Cal in an accusing way.

"God, Brad, shut up!" Sasha glares at him. She looks at Mike, who is privy to my past, much like most people in our town, making me believe that Brad didn't grow up here because everyone in the state of Oregon knows about the Shaw homicide-suicide. "Babe!"

"Yeah, cool it, B." Mike nudges his arm. "He's good," he says pointing at Cal.

"Fine, well we're going to have our date now? I don't really know why you're here." His hand reaches for me, in an attempt to pull me away from Cal, but I keep my feet firmly planted in place and pull out of his grip. A flash of hurt but also anger moves through his eyes and I find myself taking a step back and closer to Cal.

He must sense my apprehension because he takes a step closer to Brad and somewhat in front of me. "I'm here because no one takes Madeline out without meeting me first. She knows the rule and so does Miss Parker, who I'm sure was hoping could get her out of the house while I was MIA." He shoots a look at

Sasha and she rolls her eyes.

"Come on, CG, I need you to relax. Our girl is almost eighteen, you can't baby her forever."

"Watch me." He glares at Sasha, and I have to give her credit, she doesn't back down, holding his gaze for far longer than most. She rolls her eyes and turns to me. "Can you call off your bodyguard please?" She pouts as if to say, *please don't ruin this double date.*

"Can I talk to you for a second?" I try my best to sound irritated with him, trying to play the part of the teenager who's embarrassed, but the truth is I'm irritated with everyone *but* Cal. He'd come for me when I wanted him to and is offering me the out I desperately want to take.

He doesn't touch me as we make our way outside and all I want to do is jump into his arms and wrap my legs around him. "Hi."

"Hey." He smiles and it reaches his eyes making me wonder if he's really not angry with me.

"You're not mad at me?"

He shakes his head. "No." He takes a step towards me and I feel him all around me. "I'm sorry I missed your show."

I shake my head. "I understand."

He touches my chin softly. "I hate when I can't be there."

"You're always there. You're everywhere." I bite my bottom lip. "Thank you for coming."

His thumb rubs my lip and dips slowly into my mouth. "Do you want to be here?"

I shake my head slowly and let my tongue run over it. "I think you know where I want to be."

"I figured I would ask…"

"In case I was lying about my feelings for you?"

"He's your age and not so complicated and…" Fear grips my

heart, hearing his words, and I shake my head.

"Not *you*."

"You want me to take you home?"

I nod emphatically. "Yes."

"Do you want me to come back in with you?" He nods towards the restaurant but I don't think Brad and Cal need any more time in the same vicinity.

"No—" I shake my head just as I hear my name being called. Cal drops his hand from my mouth in an instant and takes a step back from me, trying to cool the heat sizzling between us as Sasha approaches us. Her ash-colored eyes move back and forth between us as if her vision is unfocused before and *now* she's seeing things clearly.

Fuck.

"Hey." Her eyes flicker to Cal, who's raising an eyebrow at her daring her to question what she's walked in on. They sweep back to me because although she talks a big game, I know Cal intimidates her. "Everything good?"

I smile, trying to appear less guilty than I feel. I hate lying to Sasha and keeping things from her. "Yeah, Sash, but I'm really not feeling great, I think I'm going to go." Her brows furrow and shoot to Cal.

"Are you really making her leave?"

"I'm not *making* Maddie do anything, Sasha. She can make her own decisions. It sounds like *you* pressured her into something she didn't want to do in the first place."

"Cal…" I trail off. I shoot him a look telling him to lay off and he rolls his eyes. I try to downplay the conversation we are having with our eyes but Sasha must notice because she clears her throat.

"Can I talk to you for a second?" Sasha asks, before shooting Cal a glare. *"Alone?"*

Cal huffs, irritation flowing off of him in waves as he nods towards his Jeep. "I'll be in the car." I turn back to Sasha, with a plan to lay it on thick of how tired I am from the day when she speaks up first.

"Are you sleeping with Cal?!" she blurts out, her eyes trained on the Jeep parked several cars down.

"No!" I look around, worried that someone might overhear when I realize that even if they did, it's not like they'd necessarily know who we were talking about.

"Madeline." She looks at me, her eyes narrowing and she puts her hands on her hips. "I'm your best friend, if you can't be honest with me who can you be honest with?"

Cal.

"I am being honest."

"Swear on your slippers."

I bite my bottom lip. When I was a kid, whenever I had an ultimate truth, I swore on my ballet slippers. "I swear on my slippers I'm not sleeping with Cal."

She looks at me like she doesn't believe me, which is dangerous because Sasha can be relentless in her quest for the truth. "You know you can tell me anything."

My heart sinks that I can't be honest with her. That I have to lie to her and keep this secret from her. But what if she didn't understand? What if she told someone? "I know, Sash."

She takes a step forward and wraps her arms around me. "You really have to go?"

"Yeah." My eyes are trained on the ground, unwilling to meet her penetrating and curious gaze. She kisses my cheek and squeezes me.

"You do you." My heart thumps in my chest as I swear I hear the double meaning when she pulls away. "Just..." she trails off, "take care of yourself. I know you expect Cal to do that, but make sure you know how to do it too...for when he's not there."

CAL

SOFT, WARM LIPS ATTACK MY FACE AS SOON AS THE DOOR CLOSES behind us. Maddie hasn't even removed her coat when she throws her arms around my neck and pulls me down to kiss her. I welcome her lips hungrily, opening my mouth and meeting her tongue with urgent eager thrusts. She tastes like cinnamon and sex and every time she swipes her tongue along mine my cock tightens in my pants. She wraps one leg around me, pushing her sex against me and opening herself up to me. I grab her hips and lift her into my arms allowing her to wrap her legs around my waist. She yanks her coat off and pushes mine to the floor as I walk us up the stairs, our kisses getting more desperate and frantic. "No fucking dates, Madeline," I growl at her.

The second she told me she was going out with Sasha I knew there was more to the story and then she told me a boy was involved and I saw *red*. Thank God Ryan was off the clock and his woman rang the "I need dick" alarm, so I didn't need to come up with an excuse to go find Maddie and stake my claim. I almost broke that fuckers arm off for thinking he could even breathe Maddie's air let alone touch her.

"I didn't want to go." She pulls back and looks at me. Her lips are swollen and red and glossy and her eyes are shimmering with tears. "You said you weren't mad."

I push her cheeks together and run my lips from her forehead to her chin, kissing her cheeks and nose in between.

"I'm not mad at you. The thought of anyone touching you just drives me fucking insane." I grip her forearms harder as anger whips through me and she yelps. I drop her to the bed and straddle her waist, rubbing my erect cock against her sex. "God, I want to fuck you."

"Because you're jealous?" She sits up on her elbows and pushes me slightly off of her much to my surprise. "You can't be serious. You have nothing to be jealous of."

"You are *mine*, Maddie."

"I've always been yours." She looks up at me through her lashes and bites down on her bottom lip, like she's a master at the art of seduction. "Since I've been old enough to know what it meant to want a man. It's always been you, Cal. I thought I was sick or disgusting for wanting you, but I couldn't help it. I *can't* help it. I want you...I want *this*." She grabs my dick through my slacks and squeezes causing me to hiss.

"Mads," I groan.

"*Daddy.*" A smirk crosses her face.

"Fuck. Don't call me that." I lower my head to hers and press my forehead against hers. God knows I want to hear it. I want to hear her call me *Daddy* while I'm deep inside her...while my mouth is on her cunt. I want to hear the muffled version that escapes her pouty lips when they are wrapped around my cock.

"You sure about that?" she whispers, her breath tickling my face.

No.

I pull away, remembering myself and stand in front of her.

"It hits too close to home." Cum trickles down my shaft and drips into my briefs at the thought of that word slipping through her lips again.

"I know." Her eyes are full of hunger. "It makes me so wet." She gets up on her knees and her blue eyes shine with lust. Her fingers run along my belt and she slides it through the loops. "Please let me see it."

"Fuck." I shut my eyes and take a few steps back. A frown finds her sweet face. "I...I should take a shower."

Disappointment spreads across her features and she sits back down and nods. "I'll wait here."

"Or..." I clear my throat, the words getting stuck there.

"Or?" Her eyes light up and the hope in her voice makes my dick painfully hard.

"You want to join me?" I nod towards my bathroom. She's off the bed and in the bathroom before I can say another word.

My eyes rake over the bathtub that just last week I had watched with bated breath as Maddie bathed and teased me mercilessly. I'm playing with fire, getting into a shower with her, but at least I had a prayer at getting out without fucking her. I knew if I sat in a bubble filled tub, the scent of lavender and Maddie's sex flooding my nostrils, I wouldn't last a minute before I let her sheath herself on my dick. *Without a condom at that.*

"Baby, did Aria ever put you on the pill?" I ask, suddenly feeling a bit apprehensive about fucking her virgin pussy raw and unprotected. My brain has also taken notice that it's the first time I've called her *baby* and by the look on Maddie's face, she's noticed as well.

"Yes." She nods as her teeth find their way into that bottom lip. "Last year. Are you asking because...I need it?"

I clear my throat. "You're about to be naked and wet. I don't know what's going to happen in the next thirty or so minutes..." I swallow. "One look at you and I lose all reason."

"Are you going to make love to me without a condom?" Her voice squeaks slightly and I note the goosebumps popping up everywhere when she pulls her shirt off.

I rub my hand across her chest and unsnap her bra letting it slide down her arms and to the floor with a resounding thud. I slide my fingers through her belt loops and pull her to me by her jeans and then pop the button. I rub circles into her stomach and kneel in front of her as I lower her jeans down her legs. "I don't want anything between us." A growl rumbles in my chest as the urge to plow into her raw takes over.

"Me neither. I want to feel everything. I want to feel your cum shooting into me. I think I can feel it, right?" Her innocent eyes blink down at me as she steps out of her jeans and her scent surrounds me. I stare at her pink sheer panties, her dark slit shining through the fabric. I lick my lips and before I can stop myself, I press my lips to her sex through her panties. "Cal," She whimpers.

"Fuck. I need to get you naked." I stand up and pull my shirt over my head and unbutton my slacks before sliding them down my legs. When I look up, her eyes are glued to my dick and she swallows.

"I knew you'd be big." I follow her gaze to find my dick standing proudly and pointed directly at her as if it knows that's its home. "I've dreamt about you stretching me, claiming my virginity, making my pussy conform to your cock, so it'll never want another."

Fuck me.

I grab her panties and rip them at her hips, letting them float to the ground so she's completely nude. I take a step back; my eyes raking over her perfect body and turn the water on. "Get in."

She walks by me and I tap her ass gently, enthralled by the way it shakes under the smack. She giggles and turns around, her back pressed against the tile and the water hitting her naked body. I swallow as I lower my briefs to the ground, exposing myself to her and I wonder if she can hear my heart pounding in my chest over this intimate moment. Her eyes, staring at my dick, light with excitement and intrigue. I've always been praised for my physique. Hard muscles cover my arms and legs, with abs I work hard to keep in place. Maddie licks her lips and I'm hard at her response to my body.

"Cal," she holds her arms out towards me, "come here, let me touch you." I obey her command and step into the shower, closing the glass door behind me and then we are naked in front of each other for the first time.

I don't immediately wrap my arms around her because my self-control is withering and I'm trying to keep some semblance of it. We've never touched while we've both been naked and I don't know that I'll be able to control myself once I do.

Water trickles down her body in rivulets. I want to kneel in front of her and catch every drop of water that drips off of her with my tongue. Her nipples pucker under my gaze making the points erect and I grit my teeth to stop from pulling them into my mouth. My eyes wander over her perfect body and she shifts nervously.

She must sense my apprehension because she drops her arms. "How far can we go?"

"I wish we'd set some boundaries first, because right now… looking at you naked and wet I just want to pin you to the wall and fuck the life out of you."

"I'm not opposed."

What did you expect, Cal? "Maddie…"

"What? Is this really all about my birthday? I'll be eighteen in less than a week. Besides isn't seventeen the age of consent in like half the states and sixteen in a number of them too?" she argues. *What are you going to do when she's legal?*

"It's about a whole lot of things."

She takes a step forward and I freeze. "Don't be nervous," she whispers as her hands find my chest. She runs them up my chest and to my shoulder and stands on her tippy toes, planting a gentle kiss to my lips. "Do you love me?"

I look down at her and the sincerity in her eyes washes over me like the warm water raining down on us. "You know I do."

"Then touch me. *Please*. I'm so desperate to know what your fingers feel like inside me. What your tongue feels like *there*. Maybe you don't want to fuck me yet. But please, *please* God, touch my pussy."

I feel her words shooting through me like an electric current. "Jesus, Maddie. Where did you learn to say things like that?"

"Porn." She smiles wickedly.

My fingers find her nipple and I rub it between my thumb and index finger. "I feel sick. Thinking of all the depraved things I want to do to you."

Stop touching her.

"You're not sick." She gasps when I flick her nipple. "But these depraved things…tell me."

"These tits," I grumble as I put my hands on both and push them together. "I want to slide my cock between them and thrust over and over until your silky skin jerks me off and I come all over them. I'll come so hard and so much that some gets on your face, coating your pouty lips and I'll watch you lick it off. Lick my cum off your tits because every drop of it belongs in your body somehow. Your mouth, your pussy, your asshole. I want to drain my cock in every one of your holes." I press her against the wall, letting my cock rub against her stomach making me harder than granite. "You think I don't want to touch you? Believe me, baby, the second I touch you with my tongue or my fingers, I'll never stop touching you. I'm fucking dying for a taste of your perfect pussy. This pussy that's belonged to me for longer than anyone would deem appropriate." My hands snake down and spread her puffy lips. "Once I have a taste, I'm never going to want to give you up, Maddie. So, I hope you're not planning to ask me to."

I rub the lips of her pussy, not pushing inside and she shudders at my touch. "Never. I want you. *Forever.*" She gasps as one finger pushes between her folds and rubs her clit gently. "Oh my God," she sobs and I actually see the tears forming in her eyes. "You have no idea how long I've waited for this." She holds my face in her hands. "You make me whole, Cal." Her cheeks turn pink and she looks down at where we're connected. "Please don't ever give me up."

I trail kisses down her face, her neck and over her shoulder as I continue to rub her sex. I feel her words in my heart and my head and my dick and it makes me want to give her everything. Marriage, a baby, everything she could ever want.

Is that where this is going?

One leg wraps around me, opening up her sex even more. "What do you want?" I ask her as I begin to rub her clit harder, I dip a finger into her sex and she's practically soaking which makes my mouth water and cum pool at the tip of my cock.

She looks up at me, emotions swimming in her blue pools that are highlighted by thick eyelashes that hold drops of water from the shower. "Everything," she whispers.

"Be more specific." *Say the words, Maddie.*

"I didn't know that I could ask for it?"

I pull away from her slightly, my fingers still in her most intimate place and eye her curiously. "Why?"

"I mean I don't know if it's possible."

"When have I ever denied you anything? Anything you want it's yours."

"Even...*you?*" Her eyes stare into mine and for a moment I feel like I can't breathe from the rawness of her question. My heart squeezes as the words form and move through my body to sit on the tip of my tongue.

I clear my throat. The hot water, the steam, the naked woman all adding to the intensity of the moment. "Even me." My voice is hoarse and laced with arousal. I've been with a number of women in my past but never have I felt so vulnerable or intimate with a woman in my life. Never has a woman expressed such a need for me that I felt with every fiber of my being. Every part of her calls out to every part of me and I want to protect it and keep it away from anyone and everyone who would say what we have is wrong.

Dirty.

Sick.

"I want it all." Her lip trembles and I lean forward and capture it between my teeth.

I don't respond at first, my mind trying to calm my dick down that's hard and ready to breed the fertile woman in front of me. "You can have it all."

"I...I can?"

"I want it all too," I tell her honestly, my voice barely over the sounds of the running water.

"Fuck me," she whispers. "Put your dick inside of me and give us what we both want. I know your heart belongs to me."

"Always," I grunt.

"I want to know your dick is mine too."

"It's yours, Maddie." I look down and cup her pussy. "Is this mine?"

"You know it is."

"I'll break the neck of any man who thinks it's not."

I rub my cock against the lips of her sex and begin to rock

against her slippery cunt, probing her opening with the blunt tip. "You never have to worry about that."

Say it again. I've never been the type of man that required any kind of validation but with Maddie, I'm fucking desperate for it. "I don't?"

"No, Daddy."

My cock jumps and she whimpers as it tickles her clit. "I had plans to lay you out and make love to your pussy with my fingers and my tongue and make you come over and over until you were loose and languid and drunk on me and then I'd take your virginity slowly, making love to you until your body couldn't take it. But now…" I stare down to where we're connected, where my dick is an inch inside of her. "I want to take you like a fucking animal. Rut into you like a beast and rip your precious body apart and put you back together a new fucking woman." I push slightly harder and I watch as the wind leaves her in a gush. "My. Fucking. Woman."

The word leaves her lips like a prayer and my dick is the holy word. "Yes."

And then in the shower, her legs and arms wrapped around me like ivy, I press my cock fully into Madeline Shaw, the most important person in my world for the past ten years, just as a scream so sexual and passionate leaves her lips that I almost shoot my seed inside of her. She burrows her face in my neck and bites her teeth into the flesh and whimpers as I fuck her mercilessly against the wet tile. "You okay?" I press my lips to her shoulder and I feel her nod.

"Don't stop," she whispers.

"Never. Your pussy is gripping me so hard, it's taking everything not to come yet."

"I want you to." She squeezes and I groan, wishing we were laying down because I have a feeling this orgasm might kill my ability to stay upright. *Fuck, she's tight.* "Come inside me, Cal. I need it so bad, I can't take it." I fuck her almost brutally, drilling her into the tile so hard I wouldn't be surprised if we break through it. My fingers grip her hips as I pull and push her harder on my dick. I look down and see the bright red evidence of her virginity on my dick and I wonder if I've really hurt her. But the beast doesn't care. He wants to rip her open and feast on her insides. Kiss away the fear and terror that lurks within her and swallow any pain she's ever felt.

"I'll make it better. I'll kiss your pussy till it feels better." I grit out, as the orgasm takes hold of my body.

"It doesn't hurt. It feels…so…good…" She stammers between thrusts. Her eyes are squeezed shut, her nails digging into my shoulders and her mouth slightly agape and I know, in this moment, I've never seen anything more beautiful. I could search the world, explore the seven wonders, meet Jesus Christ himself, and I'd never witness anything more magical or powerful than this look on Maddie's face while I'm inside her. "Holy fuck, I think I'm going to come."

"Come on my cock, baby. Touch your pretty clit until your cunt creams all over me."

"Oh, God keep talking." She moans and I feel her hand moving between us.

"You know what's going to happen the second we get out of this shower? I'm going to bend you over and lick you from your pussy to your asshole and then back. Settling on your sweet folds until you come so hard you black out."

"Oh my God!"

"I can feel you quivering. Jesus Maddie, you're so fucking sexy." *How did I have any shot in hell in staying away from her? I want to feel her warmth in my bones and her words in my soul. I want to worship at her feet from now until I took my last breath.*

"I'm gonna... gonna..." Her eyes fly open, blue irises staring straight at me as she goes over the edge. Tears roll down her face just as her eyes flutter shut and roll back in her head. She digs her nails harder into me, her heels digging into my ass and pushing my dick deeper into her if that were possible. "OH MY GOD!" she screams. I swallow them with mine just as I feel myself succumbing to my climax. An orgasm so powerful that it thunders through my chest and comes out my mouth with a roar that sounds more animal than human. I slam my fist against the wall next to Maddie's head, as my orgasm continues pumping rope after rope of thick, hot cum into her womb.

Primal feelings bloom in my chest and I suddenly feel myself hoping that my cum is more powerful than the pills she takes that keep her from getting pregnant. I know it's the high of the orgasm causing these feelings and in twenty seconds when the sense of euphoria wanes, I'll be counting down the minutes till her next period, but for these twenty seconds, I relish in the thoughts of her swollen tits and a round stomach full of my baby.

"I can't wait to get you pregnant." The words leave my lips at the peak of the high. Words that escape me before I can stop them and she gasps in response.

"Me too." She runs her hands through my wet hair and pulls gently.

I swallow hard as my cock falls from between her pussy lips and I press my mouth to hers. "I hope you're not tired," I murmur against her mouth. I make love to her mouth, rubbing my tongue against hers. She nibbles on my bottom lip before biting down harder and I groan.

"Plans to keep me up all night?" She grins as I set her onto shaky legs but I wrap my hands around her hips just in case they give out on her.

"Try for the rest of your life," I tell her with a smile. I turn the water off as it starts to cool slightly and lead her out of the shower.

With the water off, I'm hyper-aware of a noise somewhere else in the house and I put my hand over Maddie's mouth just as she begins to speak. "Did you hear something?"

Her eyes are wide and she shifts them from side to side before she shakes her head.

I open the door to the hallway and I hear the television in the living room blaring. *What the fuck?*

"Stay here." I grab my sweatpants and t-shirt and pull them on as I jog down the stairs wondering who the fuck barged in my house unannounced.

I've made it two steps into the living room when Henry's fist comes flying at my face.

CAL

HENRY IS TALLER THAN ME BY AT LEAST TWO INCHES, BUT I'M MUCH bigger. Years of police training has given me muscle and cat-like reflexes, unlike my older brother who spends his days behind a desk as an accountant. I move just before his fist can make contact with my face and instead of tackling him like I would *anyone* else who thought it was okay to put their hands on the chief of police *before I slapped my cuffs on them*, I take a step back.

"What the fuck, Henry? What—" He comes charging at me again, prepared to take another swing, when I grab his arm and pin it to his side before slamming him against the wall with my forearm pressed against his throat. Fire blazes in his eyes. Eyes with lines under them from staring at a computer screen eighty hours a week.

"What. The. Fuck." I grit out at him.

"What the fuck is right!?" He spits out and I loosen my grip on his throat as his voice is strained alerting me that he's struggling to breathe. I let up so I don't crush his windpipe and take a step back.

"You take another swing at me and I will take you the fuck down," I warn and watch as his fists flex and straighten, knowing that a fight against me isn't one he could win.

"You fucking…" He stares at me with his eyes wide and

harsh. Demanding. Angry. "She *trusted* you. We all did! You're disgusting, Cal. How could you do that to her, you sick fuck?" He looks at the stairs and my heart races thinking about Maddie sitting on the steps hearing every second of this conversation. "You're *raping* her."

"WHAT?" Bile rises in my throat hearing his accusation.

"Legally. And I use that word because you're a goddamn cop. Do I think you forced your dick inside of her? No. I've seen the way she looks at you with stars in her eyes, I'm sure she got on her knees willingly..." I clench my fist and take a step towards him for his disgusting comment. He glares at me, daring me to come forward. "But she's not eighteen and in the eyes of the law it's rape."

"She'll be eighteen in less than a week, Henry." I grit out. A dark thought crosses my mind as I know the law better than anyone. Feelings of shame move through me as I think about what I've done. A lump forms in my throat and a shiver slithers down my spine like a snake.

You should have waited, Cal.

Laws are in place for a fucking reason.

"You expect me to believe...you expect *anyone* to believe you haven't been fucking her for God knows how long?"

"That's exactly what I'm telling you."

"Bullshit. I saw the way you two were acting at Thanksgiving. I knew something was off the way you treated Penelope on our date...And why are we even arguing the semantics of her goddamn age? THIS IS MADDIE!" he screams, his face full of rage and fury as he spits out her name like he's damning her. "How can you look at yourself in the fucking mirror? You met her when she was seven years old. And you wormed your way into her heart like a fucking pedophile. God, have you been preparing her for this her whole life?"

"Don't be disgusting, Henry," I snarl.

"*I'm* disgusting? That's what they're going to say about you, Cal. It'll be a witch hunt and they'll burn you at the stake."

The television which had been blaring suddenly shuts off and a quiet sob cuts through the tension. My eyes flicker to movement in my peripheral to see Maddie standing there with tears in her eyes, streaming down her pale cheeks. She's completely dressed, in yoga pants and one of my Academy t-shirts, that really doesn't do much for our case. Her wet hair, pulled into a bun on the top of her head, matched my wet hair. "Henry…"

"Maddie…" He takes a step towards her, and I grip his arm hard because, in this moment, I just see him as a man, *a threat*, that wants to touch my girl.

"Don't," I growl. He looks at me, and to my surprise, stands down. I suppose even in this moment, he knows better than to fuck with me when it comes to Maddie. "Madeline, go upstairs," I tell her. Our eyes meet, and for a second I believe she'll obey, but instead she takes a step closer to us.

She wipes her eyes and shakes her head before pointing at my brother. "Henry, this really isn't your business."

"Cal has you brainwashed, sweetheart. You can't stay here." My nostrils flare as anger courses through my veins making me feel like I could rip my brother apart. *I'll kill him before I let him take her anywhere.*

"There's nowhere else for me," she whispers.

"Maddie, you need to come with me. It's not right…you, here with him. This isn't healthy and he's ruining you."

"No!" she cries and I grip his arm harder, worried for a moment that I'll pull his arm from its socket if he tries to take another step towards her.

"What would Aria say? What would *Mom* say? To know that you've been sleeping with the girl you raised?" He stares at me. The disgust is there. The judgment. The anger. But I sense something else hidden beneath the rage.

Worry.

Fear.

Maybe deep down, he knew this was more. *But he knew.* He knew the world wouldn't let me have her.

Not without a fight.

A fight I was more than willing to give.

I'd burn the world to the ground for Maddie and the look in his eyes tells me he knows that.

"I would hope they'd understand that I love him..." Maddie interjects, her voice full of conviction. "You're acting like he's my dad, Henry...and he's not."

"That's what everyone sees him as, Madeline. Tell me you're not so naive that you think they won't nail Cal to the wall for this." He turns to me. "You can kiss your job, your praise, your accolades, all of it. Done. You're finished here, Cal."

"So, you're planning to lead this witch hunt? You're planning to villainize him?" Maddie asks. "What kind of big brother does that?"

His eyes flare with anger that I've never seen before. "The kind that is protecting a child."

"I'm not a child, Henry. And *no one* has protected me better than Cal."

"Maddie..." I nod at her, "can you please go upstairs?" I don't want her around for the rest of this conversation, as I can't be certain about what else will come out of Henry's mouth. She nods obediently before turning to Henry.

"I understand that you're shocked and confused and maybe a little..." I can tell she's struggling to find the right word, "*concerned*...but Cal has never done wrong by me. In that regard, nothing's changed."

As soon as Maddie is out of sight, I let go of his arm and he turns to me, his stance is still combative and the disgust in his eyes sends a pang of guilt to my soul. My brother and I have always been close, and I could sense the rift forming and growing in our relationship by the second. "How could you do that to her?"

"Henry it's not like that."

"Oh?" He scoffs. "Then what's it like?"

I rub the back of my neck. Despite my brother's anger, I want to try to make him understand. If he didn't, it would be the end of our relationship. I know that. I'm never going to give Maddie up, and if he doesn't understand, I doubt he would want to be a part of the narrative that included her and me together. "Things have changed."

"Yeah, no shit."

"I love her…"

"You've always loved her…that's the fucking problem," he snaps.

"You're making this into something dirty when it's not. Tonight, was the first night we took that step. Tonight, was the first night I touched her…" I rub my index finger and thumb together. It was something I always did when I felt the need for a cigarette. I had quit smoking years ago when Maddie came home with tears in her eyes that she didn't want me to die after a particularly harrowing lesson in her health education class. It took every patch, and gum, and ounce of willpower to quit, but I did. *Because she asked me to.* Although the craving still hits me in the face during times of stress. *Like now.*

Maddie will have a fit if you have one.

"I fell in love with her," I continue.

"That's bullshit. You fell in love with the idea of young pussy. Your dick got a hard-on for the teenager living with you."

My blood boils and I push him against the wall, prepared to shove my fist down his throat. "*Never* refer to Maddie like that."

"You're going to ruin her. Hell, you probably already have. In five years, she's going to be in a therapist's office, explaining about how the one man who was supposed to take care of her, the only man she ever trusted, took her virginity because she was so confused and she thought she loved him. You should have been the adult that told her that *this* wasn't it. *This* wasn't right."

"And what the fuck do *you* know about love, huh?" I snap. "You don't know shit about it. It's why you're such a fucking dick to Grant. You think Dad loved us? You still think he's coming back? Grow up, Henry. Dad didn't love us. He didn't love Mom!" I scream at him. "Grant has always cared, always put us first, and you hate him over some deep down resentment and twisted loyalty to our father who never gave a shit about you!"

His eyes widen and his mouth drops open, but I still don't stop. "You think I don't love Maddie? Then you haven't been paying fucking attention. Because I've always fucking loved that girl. Do you understand me? Always. And yes, now it's different, and some won't understand it or support it, but I'll be damned if they don't respect it. I'll be damned if *you* don't respect it. I'm almost thirty-four years old. I know what the fuck love is and I *love* her. And if you can't understand that, if you can't *see* that, then it's because you don't know what love looks like. What it means to love someone…*unconditionally*."

He takes a step forward and I go for the jugular. I speak the words that everyone says when he's not around. The worry that coats Mom's face whenever she spends time with them. The dreaded *D* word that Grant has asked if I believed they were headed towards. "You don't love Aria. You married her because she was pregnant, and then she wasn't and it sucks and I'm sorry but you should have gotten a divorce because you didn't love her.

You were scared and you were trying to please Mom, and be a good role model for me, or whatever the fuck, but you *don't fucking love her*. So, don't jump down my throat because I *do* fucking love someone and you're jealous that I feel something other than complacency and some bullshit obligation from almost a decade ago."

It was low, I know it. He knows it. Maddie, who very well may be sitting on the step, knows it. Hurt is written all over his face and I can tell he's gritting his teeth. "JEALOUS? I'm not jealous of your delusional relationship with Maddie, Cal. Get a fucking grip."

"It's not delusional and I'm not working through some fantasy of tasting forbidden fruit. I'd die before I did anything to hurt Maddie. I would never use her to fulfill some sexual deviance. I love her." I grit out. "You know that's not what this is about."

He shakes his head. "How can you not see that this is wrong? She's so dependent and afraid of losing you that she's trying to transition you out of guardian and into another role in her life. That's not how this works. You can't be both!"

I stand up straighter, puffing my chest out slightly because my aggression has kicked in after he calls my ability to protect her into question. "I am both. Maddie is *mine*. Ten years ago, she endured the most tragic experience of her life, and I was *there*. I held her tiny body against my heart as I walked her through hell and in those twenty or so steps from that closet to her front door, she latched onto me and hasn't let go. I've never let her down before, I'm damn sure not going to start now."

"What kind of life can you give her here?"

"I haven't given it that much thought what with just figuring out that I wanted her…*long term*—about twenty minutes ago."

"Aria is going to lose her shit. So is Mom. And Grant…since

you care so Goddamn much about his feelings."

"And I know I need to tell them. I'm just hoping you give me a chance to do that."

He looks towards the steps and then sweeps his eyes along the room. "I was always so proud of you. My selfless little brother who put his life on hold to help a little girl who'd lost everything. Who was alone in the world. It was obvious from the start that she loved you so much and you made her feel safe. Can't you see how difficult this will be for her if things end between you two?"

"They're not going to end," I tell him. My voice is firm and final and I don't even feel a sliver of doubt in my words.

Maybe Henry is right. Maybe all along I'd been falling in love with her. Not in a sexual way, but in a way that made me love her mind and her soul and her heart. The way that made me believe in soulmates. That the second I lifted her tiny body into my arms all those years ago, all of the weight had lifted off of me. All of the hurt of watching my father walk out of my life without another thought to me or Henry, lessened slightly. But if that was the case, if I truly had been preparing myself for the day she turned eighteen so that I could love her body the same way I loved every other part of her, then I know now this is it.

That *she* is it.

"You don't know that for sure, Cal."

"Yes, I do."

The sniffles coming from her bedroom gut me as I make my way up the stairs. I open her door, and I watch as she cries into her pillow, her shoulders shaking under the force of her sobs. "Baby," I murmur and then I'm behind her, curling my body around her petite one in an attempt to shield her from all the outside pain. "I'm here. He's gone."

She turns in my arms, allowing me a look at her face that's red and splotchy. Her eyes are glistening from her tears, turning them the brightest shade of blue, and her puffy lips look so soft and sweet. I lean forward and run my tongue across her bottom lip, tasting the salt from her tears. "The things he said…"

"Don't mean shit to me."

"He's your brother."

"And you're *everything*." I don't want to say the words. That although we are fighting the previous conventional terms of our relationship, that I do feel something parental over her. And that trumps *everything*. "There's no one in this world I'd take over you."

She bites her bottom lip and squeezes her eyes shut. "It's so unfair. Your relationship will never be the same. I know you love him. You look up to him. He's your big brother."

"He'll come around. Or maybe he won't. I don't care."

"It's been years, and he *still* hasn't come around to Grant."

"And that should tell you something. It's *him*…not us." I cup her cheeks and rub my thumbs over the space beneath her eyes, wiping the tears.

She blinks her eyes a few times and I see the tears clear from her blue orbs. "It's about your dad?"

I shrug because, to be honest, I'm not sure. I was six when my dad left, during a period when I knew something was wrong but couldn't understand the ramifications it would have on me later in life. Henry was ten and he asked our mother when he'd be back for months and when my mother finally looked at him with tears in her eyes and a glass of Chardonnay filled to the brim and told him he wouldn't, I watched my big brother break down and sob.

He didn't stop for six long months.

He remembered things I didn't. He remembered our father better than I did. I remembered the nice neighbor that taught me to fish and made my mother feel special. The one that took us to dinner and came to my baseball games. The one that fixed things in the house and taught Henry to drive because mom can't drive for shit. I remembered Grant. I saw the way he looked at my mother. The way that he loved her. It showed me how a man was supposed to love a woman. Henry was drowning in feelings of anger and resentment, too caught up in the pain to realize that Mom was happy. That Grant made Mom happy. He didn't see the signs and thus is now in a loveless marriage because he'd been angrier for longer than he'd been happy.

That wouldn't be me.

"To hell with him." She clears her throat. "Your Dad, I mean."

I smile at her because she knows my heart and my thoughts before I can breathe them into existence. "To hell with yours too."

She shivers in my arms and buries herself further into my chest, her lips rubbing against my neck as she talks. I want to finish what we started, to discover her body all over again, but the last thirty minutes had been draining and I know she's exhausted. "You're not sick, Cal. Promise me, you'll never think that what we are is anything else but love. Love in it's purest form. Nothing dirty or bad or wrong…just a man and woman that were put in each other's lives to help the other heal and grow and be happy."

I nod, but then remember she can't see me as my chin rests on top of her head. "I promise. You and me against the world."

Thirteen

Madeline

Once when I was younger, I witnessed a dog attack another dog. He latched onto the other's neck and wouldn't let go until the two owners pulled them apart.

Right now, I feel like that smaller dog with the way Cal is latched onto the space between my legs. I don't know how many times I've come from his tongue in the last hour, but I think it would take divine intervention to get him to let up his tortuous assault. He licks and bites and sucks my clit, baring his teeth every few seconds and nibbling on the sensitive flesh. A slick sheen of sweat coats my body and my heart races in my chest as I feel myself building for another orgasm. "Cal, I can't take much more."

He pulls away slightly, his mouth hovering an inch above my sex and I almost climax at the sight of him. The lower half of his face is glistening, and his eyes are dark with desire and hunger. "Your pussy thinks otherwise." He looks down at me and I follow his gaze. My sex is red and swollen from his beard and my clit is exposed from him spreading my lips for the better part of the past hour. "Just give me one more."

I bite my lip and nod because *who am I to deny this sex God another chance to make me come?* "And then it's my turn?"

His eyebrows almost shoot off his face and he licks his lips. "Your turn for…"

"Making you come?" I clear my throat and stare at him through hooded slits. "With my mouth."

"Such filthy words for such an innocent girl." He growls before lowering his face to rub his tongue through my wet sex. "You want to put your mouth on my cock, little one?"

Say it.

I let out a sigh and let my eyes float upwards. "Yes…*Daddy.*"

He groans and then he's back on my pussy, licking me to another soul-shattering orgasm as his fingers bite into my thighs so hard I'm sure he'll leave marks. Bright lights flash behind my eyelids as I come hard under the force of his mouth. It's a good thing that Cal has my legs pinned down or else I would have probably suffocated him by now. My eyes open slowly, matching the lethargic movements of the rest of my body. My vision has blurred slightly, but when Cal comes into view, he's running a hand down his face and swiping his tongue over his lips. I let out a breath and sit up slightly taking note of his sexy body and the look he's giving me. He doesn't say anything, he just stares at me, our eyes having a conversation that I don't think I fully comprehend. "Cal…" I start, wondering if he's shutting down on me.

"I can't believe…" He sits back on his heels and runs a hand through his hair. "You're *you*. How am I going to explain this to…everyone?"

I clear my throat, preparing to give him an answer although I'm sure his question was half rhetorical. "I thought you didn't care what anyone thought?" He gives me a look that I read instantly. *I lied. I care.* I take a deep breath and prepare to speak my greatest fear. "So, what this is already over? Was this all you wanted? One time?"

His eyes are hard and I'm praying I get the reaction I'm hoping for. *Anger.* He runs his fingertips up my legs, tapping my thigh in equal beats. The beats are in perfect rhythm with the hum between my legs. "You know that I know you better than you know yourself, right?"

"What does that mean?"

"It means you can't fucking manipulate me." He runs his tongue over his teeth. His tongue that has gotten very acquainted with my pussy for the past hour.

I narrow my eyes and go to move off the bed when Cal pins me to it, keeping me in place. "Get off, Cal."

"You know, I've never spanked you, but I'm tempted to change that. Don't ever insult me like that again." He growls. "I don't care if you were only saying it to get a rise out of me."

I swallow at the heat of his words. "Spank me?"

"Yes, over my knee, bare-assed."

"How very *Fifty Shades*," I smirk. I'll never forget the look on Cal's face when he found out that I had an affinity for *romance* books. He practically fled from the room and avoided my eyes for a week.

A smile plays at his lips, but it's wicked and sinister, not playful. My clit pulses in response. "This isn't fucking over." He grits out before he rubs his nose against mine gently as if he's chasing his harsh statement with gentleness.

"Okay." The fatigue of what felt like at least ten orgasms is catching up with me. Coupled with the very exhausting interaction with Henry has me fighting sleep.

"Tired?"

I shake my head, knowing that he had plans to keep me up all night, and that I had made a big promise about giving him a blow job. "No, I'm awake." My eyes flutter open but he's already moving off of me.

"Get some rest, baby." He kisses my lips and the taste of my orgasm is still on his. He pulls the covers up over my naked body and I reach for him, wanting him within reach but he's already off the bed.

"Wait…" I whine, and he chuckles.

"Just let me cut all of the lights and check the alarm, I'll be back in two minutes."

I nod, knowing that I'll be long asleep by then. *Holy shit, sex is exhausting.*

∞

"You're being suuuuper weird," Aria says as she reaches across the table and swipes a fry from my plate. Aria is always on some diet, despite the fact that she had the most perfect body. I think this week it's Keto or something. Whatever it is, it's turning her into a raging bitch because she usually treats French fries like they're their own food group. I shoo her hand away and point at her pitiful salad.

It's been three days since Henry had caught me and Cal, and we still hadn't told anyone. We are hoping to wait until after my birthday to give us one final holiday of normalcy before the Grayson family changes forever. I was shocked to learn that Henry hadn't immediately told Aria because that was something she wouldn't have been able to hide from me. Christmas is tomorrow and just like every year, Aria and I have lunch on Christmas Eve that sprouted out of Cal having to work the first Christmas I lived with him.

"You won't be here for Christmas?" My lip trembles as I notice the suitcase packed in the corner. I've been living with Cal for about two months now and this is the first time he's leaving overnight. Needless to say, I'm terrified.

"No, sweetheart. But I made sure Santa knew to take all your toys

to Aria and Henry's."

I wipe my eyes to prevent the tears from falling. "I don't want the toys. Just you." I hate seeming ungrateful, but I'm used to not getting toys. I'm also pretty sure Santa isn't real, but Cal seems to be pretty sure he is so I don't want to tell him that.

"Really? I heard you got some really nice things…"

I purse my lips as I think about the list Cal made me make of all the things I want. It wasn't very long because I wasn't even sure what to ask for, but he said he knew I'd been good this year so I would probably get everything.

"How long will you be gone?"

"I should be back on your birthday."

"You promise?"

He rubs my cheek slightly and sighs. "I can't promise you that. But I promise that I'll try my hardest."

I wrap my arms around his neck and squeeze. "Merry Christmas, Cal. Thank you for the best present."

He wraps his arms around my tiny body and rubs my back gently. "Merry Christmas to you too, Mads."

"Earth to Maddie?" Aria waves a hand in front of my face and I snap out of my memories. "What is with you lately?"

"Nothing." I shake my head. "Sorry…what?"

She sighs. "I can't get anyone to pay attention to me." She hides her hurt with her sarcasm as she pokes at her salad.

"I'm listening, I swear. Just a lot on my mind."

"Like what, Mads? Since when don't you tell me things?"

"What did you mean about no one paying attention to you?" I ask, trying to change the subject.

"Well, I guess you're practically an adult…and weirdly my best friend." She waves an arm around. "Henry's being strange."

"More so than usual?" I raise an eyebrow at her. Every once

in a while, Henry kind of shuts down on Aria. It's like he needs intermittent breaks from being married. It's sad and not fair at all to Aria. I know they got married because she was pregnant, but I always assumed he still loved her and not that...he felt *trapped?*

"Yeah."

"What makes you say that?"

"He hasn't been around much. The usual stuff, staying late at the office, leaving early in the morning. But I also feel like we haven't had a conversation in days." *Probably since he found out about me and Cal.* "And he mentioned something about not making it to your birthday dinner..." she winces. "It's so weird."

"Maybe things have changed." My guess is he's probably not enthused about being around me and Cal.

"Why? What the hell changed?"

"I don't know." I shrug. The words are on the tip of my tongue, knowing that it would probably be better coming from me versus Cal anyway, but we have a plan. A plan that doesn't involve me telling Aria in a public place on Christmas Eve. Aria would have questions. Aria would yell. And cry. And maybe throw something. Now really isn't the time "Maybe it's for the best, that he's not at dinner...since Grant will be there?"

"I guess...I feel like he doesn't even want to go to Margie's tomorrow. It's so strange." She takes a sip of her water and tucks a dirty blonde tress behind her ear. I'm about to ask her if *she'll* still be at Margie's for Christmas when a voice floats around us.

"Aria!" A vibrant redhead with dark brown eyes and breasts that make it so a guy probably never knew what color her eyes actually were comes towards the table.

"Ashley, hey!" Aria stands up and hugs her before pointing at me. "Ash, this is—"

"Maddie! Oh my gosh, you're even prettier in person." She presses a hand to her large chest and stares at me for a second, as if she's shocked that I'm really in front of her. "When Cal showed me your picture, you did not look this grown up!" She shakes her head and looks at Aria. "Guys and their daughters, I guess."

"He's not my father," I snap, harsher than I planned. But I don't know who this girl is and I'm already on edge from the conversation about Henry and now this.

"Well, I know…not technically, but he always kept me up to date on how you were doing. He's so proud of you." She beams and it makes me want to smack the look off her face.

I cock my head to the side innocently. "You're friends with Cal?"

"Well, we're a little more than friends, if you know what I mean." She giggles and Aria shakes her head. Bile rises in my throat, and I take a breath in an attempt to keep my chicken wrap from coming back up. I clear my throat and take a sip of water that I pray cools the heated anger rising within. "I haven't talked to him in a while though, I should give him a call. See if he has plans for New Year's."

"I doubt it…" Aria starts when I interrupt.

"I think he does actually. He mentioned something in passing." I shrug. I want so badly to say that he has plans with me but I don't know how to phrase it without sounding like a jealous girlfriend.

"Do you know if he's seeing anyone?" Ashley asks and I've officially had enough of this conversation.

"Aria, I'm going to run to the ladies' room." I point towards the edge of the room and she nods, probably sensing my tension over this conversation. I'm barely two seconds away from the table when I'm sending a text.

Me: Can you talk?

His response is instant and while I want to say it's the attentive boyfriend in him, Cal has always been quick to respond to me whenever I needed him.

Superhero: You okay?

As much as I want to say no, I know that will send him running, thinking I'm hurt or unsafe in some way.

Me: Yes. Just need to talk to you for a second.
Superhero: Give me two minutes.

I pace the length of the bathroom, grateful that it's empty when my phone begins to vibrate.

"I'm not exactly alone," he tells me instantly.

"Can you go somewhere to change that?"

"I had to walk out of an interrogation. What's going on?"

I sigh, knowing that now isn't the time to bring up my jealousies. I don't say anything because if we can't really have this conversation then there is no point in talking.

I hear a door opening and closing. "Spit it out, baby."

"*Baby?*" I question, wondering if anyone thinks that he's talking to me.

"I walked away."

I let out a breath and the tears spring to my eyes over something so simple. "I love you."

He chuckles. "Is that all?"

"It seemed pretty important at the time." I lean against the sink and stare at my reflection in the mirror. Not only do I feel different after taking this step with Cal, I looked different. My lips are swollen from his constant kissing and biting, my cheeks are slightly redder from his beard and my eyes are shining with excitement. I look like a woman in love. I look happy.

He doesn't say anything at first but then he clears his throat. "For the first full hour I was here, I couldn't get this morning out of my head. I've been actively trying not to think about you ever since."

This morning I woke Cal up with my mouth on his cock, the sounds of my gagging pulling him out of the last few moments of sleep.

"We can have a repeat of that later," I whisper. My voice is low and it's my best attempt at being seductive.

"Fuck. You're going to unman me, woman." I can hear the smile in his voice. "I have to go though."

"Okay. I'll see you later."

"I love you too." He tells me just before the phone goes dead. I press my phone to my heart, those four words making me forget all about the thirsty redhead probably probing Aria for information on Cal. When I make it back to the table she's gone and Aria is shaking her head at me.

"You've got to cut that shit out, Mads," she snaps.

"What?"

"It's like you can't handle any woman having an interest in Cal. It's selfish as hell, and frankly, you're getting too old for it." My eyes widen, not prepared for her to basically attack me as soon as I sit down. "Penelope is too scared to even mention Cal's name because she thinks you'll like manifest and murder her. You're not his girlfriend, Maddie. Stop." She pins me with a glare and I clear my throat nervously.

I'm not prepared to tell her the truth, which means I have to go to the opposite end of the spectrum. I swallow my pride and prepare myself. "You're being really ridiculous, Aria. Your slutty friends are embarrassing and frankly, they make me uncomfortable." I twirl a finger around a lock of my hair as I prepare to imitate Ashley. "We're more than friends if you know what I mean…" I make a face and shake my head. "Ick."

She puts a hand up. "I agree that was a little tasteless, but Penelope did nothing wrong. She was polite and sweet and you jumped all over her and therefore, Cal *couldn't* be interested."

"Cal *wasn't* interested and you were trying to force it by bringing her to a *family* dinner."

"You don't know *everything*, Maddie."

"Neither do you!"

She rubs her temples and closes her eyes. "Jesus Christ, I thought you'd grow out of this, but it's getting worse, I swear."

My eyebrows furrow and I narrow my eyes. "Grow out of what?"

"This crush you have on Cal."

End this conversation, now. "Excuse me?"

"You think I don't notice? That none of us notice?"

My blood runs cold. *Fuck, did Henry say something?* "None of us?"

"Me, Margie, Henry, Grant? We were all seventeen once too, you know. And we have seen a few things…" She points at me with her fork and I feel my hands starting to sweat under the table. I rub them on my jeans as a tremor shoots through me.

"So, what you all just sit around talking about me?"

"No, Madeline. We all think it's harmless and that you'll grow out of it. I mean obviously…"

"That's really ridiculous, Aria. I don't have a crush on Cal." *Because I'm full blown in love with him.*

She blinks her eyes several times at me. "Well, whatever this weird claim you think you have on him needs to stop so that Cal can feel free to meet someone and be *happy*. You're going off to college and—"

"Who said I'm going anywhere?"

"What? Maddie, you're going away to school. You need the college experience, and schools are basically beating down the door to get to you. You've gotten early acceptance into how many schools? Not many of which are in Oregon."

"I've gotten into some local schools."

"I don't think you should go to any of those. Maximize your potential, girl."

"None of this is even the point. You think I'm the problem? You try to set Cal up with every girl in Oregon, and he's *not* interested!"

"He never even gives anyone a chance because he takes your opinion *so* seriously!" she exclaims.

"Heaven forbid he cares about my opinion. I'm important to him, Aria. I know I don't need to tell you that."

She huffs. "I swear if I didn't know any better, I'd…" She shakes her head, her dirty blonde hair dragging along her shoulders as she pinches the bridge of her nose. "It's going to be a nightmare getting you two apart."

"What?"

"You need space, Maddie. All you've ever known is him and I think it's messing with your psyche."

"What does that even mean?"

"I was going to bring this up to Cal first, but maybe it's best if I talk to you."

My eyes dart around the restaurant. I need an escape route, and I find myself looking for the nearest exit. "About what?"

"I was thinking maybe for this second half of the year you should live with me and Henry."

"What? Fuck that," I snap.

"Okay, you might be able to get away with that with Cal, but don't forget who you're talking to." She gives me a motherly look and I grit my teeth.

"Excuse me. *F* that."

"Mads, you're going to be eighteen and…" She trails off and although she doesn't say it, I can hear the implication. *You're seconds from seducing Cal, I can see it.*

"And?"

"And…I just think you'd do better with a constant female presence."

"I don't see how the two correlate."

"Mads, I just…"

"How about you say what's really on your mind? Instead of dancing around it?"

"Okay, I think you living with Cal now will…blur some of the lines between you two."

"Meaning…?" She cocks an eyebrow at me and before I can blink, the words are out of my mouth. "So, you think I'm going to try to have sex with him? Is that what you're saying?"

She squeezes her eyes shut. "Yes."

I cross my arms over my chest and let out a breath. "I don't…I have nothing to say to that." My mind is spinning and I don't know how I'm going to navigate the rest of this conversation with someone who could practically see inside my mind.

"Well, your reaction is certainly puzzling. I figured you'd have a more dramatic response."

"To what? I'm not moving in with you and Henry, so there's no real point in discussing this further."

"Maddie." She looks at me, her face concerned, her voice even and I know, in this moment, I won't be getting up from this table without spilling the truth.

"What, Aria?" I avoid her gaze, peering around the restaurant. Memorizing my surroundings of the moment my life changes forever. Large floor to ceiling windows line one side of the restaurant. Every empty table is covered with a white linen tablecloth, complete with silverware and plates and glasses and flowers in the center. There's a couple seated adjacent to us, but far enough away that they won't be able to hear Aria's hysteria. They're holding hands over the table and I long for the day that Cal and I can do that in public.

"Look at me, Madeline." I pull my eyes away from the couple and look at Aria—the woman that had become my mom all those years ago and I see the tears in her eyes. "No."

I scoff, my final attempts to brush her off. "No, what?"

"Maddie...tell me..." she swallows. "Has Cal...been inappropriate with you?"

"No, of course not," I tell her immediately. My heart hurts at her verbiage. *How could she think he'd ever hurt me?*

"Fine, let me rephrase that..." She takes a sip of her drink and bites her bottom lip. "Have you crossed a line...with him?" I don't say anything as I wonder how to respond to that when she slaps her hand on the table. "Dammit, Maddie. Answer me." My eyes well up with tears at the harshness of her tone and her eyes immediately soften. "Sorry...I shouldn't have..." She gets up and moves around the table to sit next to me on my side of the booth grabbing my hands and holding them in hers. "I love you so much, Maddie. I always have. I always thought you...you were the daughter I was supposed to have." A tear falls down her cheek and my heart thumps against my ribcage thinking about the baby she lost. "Let me protect you. Let me help."

"There's nothing to protect me from, Aria. I swear, I'm fine."

"You haven't answered my question. Sweetheart, if Cal has touched you or...anything..." she swallows. "It's rape."

"It is not!" The knee jerk reaction to hearing that word is all the confirmation Aria needs because she bursts into tears.

"Oh my God, Maddie!"

"Oh my God." I put my face in my hands. *How the hell did we get here? Oh my God, Cal is going to lose it.*

"You can't...you can't fucking live with him! I'm going to kill him." She's pulling out her credit card and waving our waiter over when I shake my head.

"Aria, no! Listen to me, it's not what you're thinking!"

"Oh, so he hasn't touched you sexually?"

Lie. And make it convincing Maddie. At least till you get home and you and Cal can figure something out. "No! I just...I want to." I bite my bottom lip, the tears in my eyes have now moved down my face. "You're right, it's a crush. But it's harmless and I'm working through it, I swear. He would never touch me, Aria."

I think my explanation works, but she shakes her head as she gives the waiter her card. "You're moving out."

"What? Aria..."

"I remember being eighteen and feeling like I was in love. You need space to get over this, Maddie." She puts a hand over her chest. "God, you scared the hell out of me. I thought..." She pinches the bridge of her nose and runs a hand through her hair. "I love Cal, but you're my number one priority. I'd nail him to the wall for fucking touching you." My blood runs cold hearing her words. I wasn't sure how I expected her to take it. I thought maybe she'd be accepting, or support me, support *us*. I hadn't anticipated this reaction. "I know you're not crazy about the idea, but it's for the best Mads, you'll thank me one day, I promise."

Fourteen

Madeline

"Oh my God Cal, answer the fucking phone!" I bang my hand against the steering wheel as I end the call through my Bluetooth. The tears well in my eyes and they dart to the rearview mirror as I look for Aria's car. My grip on the steering wheel is so tight, I feel like they're burning as I wring my hands around it. I let out a deep breath as I lessen the grip and lean my head back against the headrest. I'm convinced Aria is going to follow me home to wait for Cal, disallowing me from explaining the situation in anything but a calm and rational tone.

I am neither calm nor rational at the moment.

I am borderline hysterical.

I've spent practically every day of the past ten years with Cal, and every day of the past week with Cal in bed, and I'm not keen on the idea of changing either trend. I bite my bottom lip as I press his contact again and a sound of exasperation leaves my lips when I get his voicemail *again*.

What if this was important?

He knows you'd call the station.

I huff a sigh of irritation as I continue to fly down the back road. It has one lane with trees on both sides for miles. I'm not far from home when I see my dashboard light up signaling a call.

"Oh my God, where have you been?" I know that's not the

way to start a phone call with Cal as it'll put him on edge immediately. I always know to be calm in the first few minutes, so that Cal won't set the world on fire in attempts to find me.

"What's wrong? Why do I have five missed calls from you? Where are you?" His voice is just between nervousness and anger and filled with anxiety. Somewhere between *"is something wrong?"* and *"there better be something wrong with the way you've got me worried."*

I let out a breath, trying to calm the adrenaline rushing through my veins. *Don't freak out because then he'll freak out.* "I'm fine. When will you be home? I have to talk to you."

"I have a lot going on today, Maddie. I don't have time—"

"Make time." I grit through my teeth. "This is important."

"I can't get home right now. I have to meet with Aria in a few minutes and—"

"Do not meet with Aria," I tell him and he's silent on the other end.

"Did you guys have a fight or something? I don't have the energy to mediate you two today and it's Christmas Eve, shut it down." I sigh as I think about the fact that he has gotten between a few of our arguments in our day, usually when I thought she was taking the *bad* cop thing too seriously, and I wanted the good cop to bail me out.

"No! Cal, it's bigger than that." I stop, wondering how to phrase my next words. Do I just blurt it out? Or do I ease into it?

"Does…does she know something?"

"She has a hunch. I just spent the last hour and a half with her and she flat out asked me if we're having sex, so, NO Cal, do not meet with her right now."

I hear the sounds of a door closing. "What!? What would make her ask that?"

"Because some whore you went out with showed up and I

got territorial, okay?"

He groans and I can already hear him pacing the length of his office. He's probably pulling at his hair, his sexy mouth pulled into a scowl.

And now I'm thinking about his mouth and everything it can do.

I continue. "Cal, she wants me to move in with her and Henry. She says living with you is too…tempting."

"WHAT?" he yells and I wince at the volume resounding through my car.

"That was my reaction. I flew off the handle and her cop senses started tingling. She started crying and…it was a mess, Cal. I finally had to tell her that she was right in that I had a crush on you but that you'd never touch me. I panicked."

"There's no way I'm letting you move in with Aria and Henry." His voice is angry, but I know it's not directed at me. I can also hear the wheels turning in his head. *How were we going to get out of this? And now that Aria has a hunch, would Henry tell her what he knows? More importantly, has he already told her and this is all a test?*

I bite my lip and nod my head. "Please don't," I whisper.

"I won't. Okay? I'll take care of it."

"Don't…don't be too obvious." Aria's intuition is usually spot on, *I mean obviously*. But Cal is quick on his feet and smart as hell. He'll take care of it. He'll fix it.

He has to.

The sound of the front door almost makes me drop the spoon I'm using to stir the chili I'm making. It's Cal's favorite and something tells me he'll want something like this after dealing with Aria. I'm just about to turn around and make my way towards the door when I feel hands around my waist and his lips at my neck. "I could get used to this," he murmurs in my ear and presses a kiss just behind it. I'm instantly flooded with feelings so intense that he may as well have kissed my pussy. His hand moves around me and slides into my sweatpants and into my panties so easily it catches me off guard. I shiver as his cold hand rubs the warm slick skin between my legs, his calloused fingers rubbing my clit so gently it makes my knees weak.

"Get used to what?" I spin around to face him effectively removing his hand from my pussy.

He sucks the two fingers that were previously inside of me into his mouth and lets them go with a salacious pop. "You in my kitchen when I get home."

"Because I haven't been for the better part of the last year?" I raise my eyebrow at him and he rolls his eyes in response.

"You had to kill it." He takes a step back and grabs a beer from the fridge.

I *almost* don't care that the moment has passed because we have important things to discuss. I don't want to get lost in Cal and I getting intimate. "So, what happened with Aria?"

"She never even stopped by, and I certainly didn't want to call her and initiate anything." He pulls me away from the stove and sits down, pulling me into his lap. "Not when I wanted to get home to you." He grabs my head and brings me closer to his mouth when I stop.

"Cal, wait."

"*You're* telling *me* to wait?" He chuckles. "You usually toss your panties at me the second I'm through the door." He tugs at the waistband of my sweatpants and peers down them before letting them go to snap against my skin.

I scoff at his comment. "Rude and untrue. *Sometimes* I make you work for it." *Rarely*. I put a finger up when he goes to respond. "Eventually you're going to have to talk to Aria. Tomorrow is Christmas, and we'll all be at Margie's...it might come up."

"She's not going to bring anything like that up in front of my mother."

"Then she'll pull you aside, Cal. You didn't see Aria today. She was like a dog with a bone and you know how she is when she fixates on something! She's not going to let this go. Come new year she wants me out of here."

"And that's not her fucking call to make. Besides, you'll be eighteen."

"I'm still under your care until I graduate high school."

"Technically, but it's a fine line. She can't really *make* you do anything…"

I let out a deep sigh. "I'm not going to be able to enjoy tomorrow or my birthday. I feel like she'll be perceiving everything differently. I won't be able to touch you or be near you without her thinking it's something more." A chill comes over me, and I push myself into his arms, resting my head on his shoulder as he wraps his arms around me. "This sucks."

"Hey, you can always be near me. No one will ever tell you differently. I know our connection is different now, but nothing could ever break the bond that we have."

I pull away from his chest and raise an eyebrow at him. "And what bond is that? Daddy and his little girl?"

He pinches my side and shakes his head, but I don't mistake the way his cock jumps underneath me. *He loves it as much as I do.* I bite my bottom lip and his eyes darken as he takes in a breath. "You're going to kill me with that. But no…" He trails off. "I don't know what it is, Mads. I just know that you've always been special to me. When we met ten years ago, obviously I wasn't thinking we'd ever get here. That thought never even crossed my mind. But after the first year, I knew I'd be in your life for the rest of it, and eventually, you'd be an adult and I thought we'd be friends...I *knew* we'd be friends. Even in passing, Aria and Henry have mentioned being there for your first. ." he clears his throat aggressively, *"legal* drink." I turn and grab his beer from the table and put the bottle to my lips with a wink and run my tongue along the opening. I feel him hardening beneath me, and I realize I don't want to talk about it anymore. I drag my tongue up the neck of the bottle before taking a long sip of his beer and then set it back down. When I turn to face him, his nostrils are flared and his grip on my hips is tightening to the point of bruising. "Maddie." His voice is hoarse and I rub against him in response.

"Cal." His name falls from my lips in a whisper, my lips ghosting along his as he grabs my ass and cups it hard. He pushes me harder against him and a gush floods my panties. "Mmmm." I moan just as his lips meet mine. "Fuck me." The words leave my mouth like a sigh and I squeeze my eyes shut as I try to control the electricity buzzing through me and creating the euphoria I've become addicted to.

Now I understand the meaning of the word dickmatize.

"I've been thinking about your sexy little mouth since I left this morning...I want you to suck my cock again..."

My eyes widen and a smile finds my lips. "Yes, please."

"While you sit on my face." I know my eyes are wide and nervous right now. We'd never done that before, although I'd seen it in pornography so I understand the logistics. I can tell that Cal wants us to try, but it makes me anxious.

"Hey, you don't have to blow me, baby." He nuzzles my ear. "You can just straddle my face and ride it."

Holy fuck. I had no idea he had such a dirty mouth.

I push back on his chest and flutter my eyelashes as

seductively as I can. "No, no I want to suck your dick, but... ummm...do I have to do the other thing?"

"Yes. That's non-negotiable."

"Cal..."

"What are you so nervous about? You were less nervous to lose your virginity. Baby, this *won't* hurt."

"No, I know I just...what if I can't keep myself up and I... you know, suffocate you?" I whisper and he rolls his eyes.

"Then what a way to go." He smirks. "This isn't up for debate, Madeline. We're doing this. Because I know you'll like it." He rubs his nose against mine.

"Okay...do you want to eat first?" He raises an eyebrow at me and I shake my head. "Food fiend." I point at the stove.

"I mean...not particularly, but I suppose I won't plan to stop once we start, so food first is smart." I climb off his lap and he slaps my ass causing me to giggle.

"I mean if you're not hungry..." My mind is already upstairs in bed with Cal, my mouth all but trying to swallow his dick as he feasts on my cunt. I'd begun craving orgasms just as much as I hungered for food and thirsted for water. It's as if in one week, Cal has changed my basic needs, skyrocketing him and his cock into the number one slot. The idea of being in that space with him gives me a heady feeling, better than being tipsy or the high of a great ballet performance. It is a full body high that I can't put into words. I just know that I want to live in that space.

Cal's already up the stairs before I can blink. I turn the oven off and I'm on my way up the stairs behind him when I hear keys in the door.

Jesus Christ, Cal needs to take everyone's keys back. What if we were already going at it?

I cross my arms over my chest and cock my head to the

side, preparing for God knows who when Aria walks through the door and I resist the urge to roll my eyes. "Mads, hey." She smiles, like she doesn't have plans to turn my whole world upside down. Like she hasn't spent the better part of lunch accusing Cal of something she considers abhorrent. She's severely dressed down in comparison to lunch, sporting only a pair of leggings and a sweatshirt under her coat and a Mariner's baseball cap with her long ponytail hanging out the back.

"Aria." I nod and she shakes her head.

"Still upset, I see."

"You think I'm upset, wait till you talk to Cal." I purse my lips.

"You told him?"

"What do you think?"

"I knew I should have talked to him first. I knew you'd get him worked up."

"Can you blame her?" Cal comes walking down the steps, in sweatpants and a t-shirt and for a second, I feel a flash of jealousy that Aria gets to see him like this. *This is for my eyes only, goddammit.* Flashes of dry humping him in those gray sweatpants because it allowed me to feel everything comes flooding back and I let out a breath.

She swallows and I can tell she's nervous. "Cal...can we talk about this in private?"

"Maddie is old enough to be a part of this conversation. She'll be eighteen in two days." He nods towards me. His jaw is hard, the angles so sharp they could cut through almost anything, alerting me that he's gritting his teeth hard. I want to reach out and rub his jaw to loosen the taut muscles before he hurts himself, but I keep my hands to myself.

"Which is exactly the point."

His brown eyes that in the past week I've only seen filled

with scorching heat, are now filled with a fiery rage. "I'm still lost."

"You're going to make me spell it out for you?" She blinks her eyes several times.

"Yep."

She lets her head drop and moves into the kitchen. "It's not going to matter if she's eighteen, Cal. You're her guardian. Everyone knows that. You raised her."

"You're talking to me like this is even an issue." From Aria's point of view, this might sound like a denial, but I can hear the true meaning. *It's not an issue because fuck everyone, Madeline is mine in every sense of the word.*

"They'll think..." She blows out a breath.

"What do you think?" he asks and I can hear the accusation. *You think I'd ever hurt Maddie?*

"I think Maddie is impressionable and young, but old enough to make decisions that can impact her life in a dangerous way. There's an impulsivity and a sense of immortality that comes with being eighteen that's dangerous and reckless and..."

"That's never been me!" I exclaim. I wasn't the rebellious teenager, I've never tried drugs, I don't sneak out after curfew, I get impeccable grades...

"You've been experimenting with alcohol for how long now?" *There is just that one little thing. But everyone does it! What else is there to do in this boring town?*

"That's so different!"

"You're right, in some ways it's even more dangerous than experimenting with sex." She looks at me and sighs. "To my knowledge, you're still a virgin, but who knows how long that will last."

"You make it sound like at the stroke of midnight, I'm going to sneak into Cal's room and seduce him." I wave her off.

"The mere fact that you can say that with a straight face, and Cal barely reacts to it makes me believe it's a very real possibility." She crosses her arms. "To be frank, I think there's already something going on, and it scares the hell out of me." The tears are back in her eyes as she shifts her gaze between us. "Well, *someone* deny it."

"Maddie, go upstairs." He doesn't look at me, probably knowing that a look shared between us wouldn't be lost on Aria. He keeps his eyes trained on her, his stance combative and assertive. *This is going to get ugly.*

I should probably start packing.

CAL

M<small>Y EYES, ONES I KNOW TO BE BLAZING WITH FURY AND ANGER</small> find the source and narrow slightly. I know that I need to reign in my temper before I explode all over Aria, but I'm livid, Maddie's emotional, and I was seconds from tasting her cunt when Aria barged in without an invitation. *I am ready to explode.*

"Sit down, Aria." I point at the table, and when she doesn't move, it's enough to push me over the edge. "I said, sit the fuck down," I growl. I rarely use this voice and I've never used it on anyone in my family so I'm not surprised when her green eyes widen and she slowly lowers herself to the table.

"Cal, before you fly off the handle, let me explain—" Her voice wavers and I notice she begins to crack her knuckles. I've worked with Aria for over a decade so I know when she's rattled and all of her telltale signs are starting to show but I hope she's not expecting mercy.

"Explain what? How you're stirring up trouble for no fucking reason?" I cross my arms and look down at her, continuing to stand to further assert my power and rattle her further.

She points at the chair across the table. "Can you sit down?"

Typical power play. "No."

"Cal…"

"Tread lightly if you still want a job."

She makes a face of confusion and raises an eyebrow. "You can't fire me, *boss*," she snaps. "This is what's best for Maddie."

"Staying with me is what's best for her."

She slaps her hand against the table. "You say that now! But you *both* need some distance from each other."

"What the hell does that mean?"

"It means *she* is far too dependent on you, and you feed off of that. You feed off of her needing you. The more vulnerable she is the more you feel it's your job to fix her. You've always been this way."

"She doesn't need *fixing*, Aria. She's perfect." I immediately regret my choice of words. That didn't particularly sound like a guy that is proud of the girl he raised. It sounded more like a man that is proud of the woman he is currently fucking.

She sighs and shakes her head. "Maddie's feelings for you are…*changing*, Cal. And the only way to help her get over it is distance. She can't live here and be in your space. She's confused and she's just going to get hurt or…" she swallows and I can tell where she's going, *"you're* going to get hurt." I hear the implications as loud as if she'd spoken the accusation aloud. *If you touch Maddie, and people find out, you're fucked.*

"I know that you love her, Cal," she continues, "and anyone with eyes can see she's crazy about you. But that's the point I'm trying to make—you two have history and it's just not right." She crosses her arms. "You shouldn't even be thinking of Maddie like that."

"Who said I am?"

She shrugs. "Years of police training."

"Aria, look. Nothing is going on so—"

"And it needs to stay that way. Maddie is moving out." She points at my door and I have to take a breath before I explode.

"You don't have a fucking say. She's eighteen in less than two days and last I checked *I* am her legal guardian."

Aria stares at me for a beat before she stands up with a long sigh. "You're right, Cal. *You* are." She begins walking towards the door before she stops and lets her head drop. "She's already lost the people that were supposed to love her unconditionally. You do something…you go down a road you can't come back from…" She turns around just as a large tear slides down her cheek. "It would break her to lose you too."

A sniffle breaks the silence after the door shuts and anxiety creeps up my spine as I think about Maddie sitting on the stairs, having heard everything that was said. I make my way to the stairs and stand at the bottom, watching Maddie sit in her usual spot when she eavesdrops. "What did I tell you about that?" A stream of tears is flowing down Maddie's face, her blue eyes almost as clear as the ocean.

She gives me her middle finger and then she's bounding down the four remaining steps and into my arms. "I don't want to leave. Please don't make me go."

I think about Aria's arguments and I feel them weighing on my chest. I could see the judgment in her eyes. The fear. The devastation. I hadn't admitted anything but the words left unsaid hung in the air and cloaked us in tension.

My body tightens around hers as I carry her up the stairs. I move into my bedroom and set her on the bed before dropping to my knees in front of her. "I'm so sorry," I tell her and she frowns. "I should have been better prepared." I shake my head, thinking about all the ways that this could have gone. "I knew it was coming, and it's as if I didn't even think to deny it. Deny *us*." I drop my head to her lap and wrap my arms around her midsection, clutching her like she's a life raft floating towards the treacherous waters of the future. "I acted like a man crazy in love with a woman."

She gasps and grabs my face, bringing her gaze to mine. "Don't apologize. Never apologize for trying to protect...*us*. I love seeing that side of you."

"I only have one side, Madeline, and it'll rip anyone apart who thinks they can take you from me."

"It's been that way for a while, I think." She licks her lips and it makes me want a taste of her tongue. "I'm eighteen, Cal. She can't make me. I can't leave you. I can't...be away from you."

The thought of her being away from me makes my heart slam against my rib cage. I get off the floor and sit next to her on the bed and her body immediately reacts, as if it knows what it means to be in bed with me. She's in my lap before I can reach for her and I hold her in place to prevent her from squirming against my dick. "I don't want you away from me. Ever. I need you by my side every morning, every night, and when I get home from work." I cup her cheeks and rub my lips against hers. "I just got you...I can't give you up." I look down at her and the pain in her eyes is a direct reflection of mine. Blue eyes that I could spend a full day getting lost in are filled with sorrow and guilt.

"Promise I can stay," she whispers as she rubs her fingertips over my lips. Her eyes are fixated on my mouth as if she's hypnotized by it. I'm thankful not to be looking in her eyes, knowing I can't refuse her anything when she bats them at me. It gives me a second to collect my thoughts.

Is it the worst thing for some space? Maybe not permanently. But maybe for a month or two just while we gain our footing? Maybe just till the end of her school year?

As if she can hear my thoughts and the fact that Aria's words affected me more than I want to admit, her eyes jerk upwards and narrow into slits. "You're gonna make me stay with Aria and Henry? Your brother who knows the truth?"

I let out a breath knowing that this is going to be a battle getting her to agree. I'd never let her go with Aria and Henry. Henry is a wild card, and I know Maddie wouldn't feel comfortable living there knowing that he knows the truth. She's already nervous to be around him tomorrow. "Would you be open to staying with Margie?"

"I can't believe we are even discussing this!" She begins to move off my lap when I tighten my grip. I need her close to me. I want her to feel that she's not the only one that's hating this idea. That the idea of living without her under this roof like she has for the last ten years guts me.

"Stop moving," I order her but she doesn't listen and continues to try and break free of my grip.

"No, let me go, Cal." She makes it off my lap and stands in front of me with her hands on her hips in that sexy as fuck way that makes me want to drill into her cunt until she loses the fucking attitude. "This is bullshit, and I don't agree with it."

"Can we take it down with the attitude? You're being a brat."

She stamps her foot and I almost chuckle at the beginnings of this tantrum. "How am I being a brat because I want to stay here?"

"Because that's not how it works!" I snap. "It's not how any of this works."

"And that means…?"

I drop my head into my hands and sigh. "Things are different between us and you living with me while we explore whatever this is…may not be the best idea."

Her bottom lip trembles and she wraps her arms around herself, rubbing her arms, and I wish I could have her back in mine. "How can you say that?"

"Because I don't want to get you pregnant for one. And the way we've been going at it the last week, if we keep this up, you'll be knocked up by graduation. We aren't using condoms and nothing is a hundred percent effective. I just mean...this much access to each other might be...dangerous."

She crosses her arms, defiantly. "And the second thing?"

"I don't regret where we are or how we got here. But we need space to navigate this. Living together this early on in our relationship...is just too soon." I trail off, and my eyes roam around my bedroom. Maddie's room is just down the hall and yet it's as if all of her stuff has moved into my bedroom. Her charger on the other side of my bed. Her laptop on my nightstand. The hair ties and pins from her dance buns that litter every surface of my room. She's even left her toothbrush in my bathroom despite the fact that she has her own down the hall. "I've never lived with a woman. For years I just had...Well, you. But living with you now is different."

"Like...moneywise?" She winces. "You've never let me have a job but I can get one."

She can't be fucking serious. I roll my eyes and move off the bed to pull her in my arms. "When have I ever not taken care of you?"

"Well, it was different before..." I wince. "Before I was a dependent and now, I'm an equal..." She trails off as a blush paints her cheeks, like she isn't sure if that's true. "I can...pay for things," she squeaks, and if I wasn't so pissed off at her questioning my willingness to take care of her, I'd find her comment endearing.

I grip her jaw and her cheeks turn even pinker. "It's not different in that regard. I'll always take care of you. You've never needed to worry about money before and you still don't, okay? Now, I don't want to talk about that again." I tell her and she nods knowing not to push me. "It's different because it is. I shouldn't have to say this, but our relationship isn't what it was. I know Maddie, the young girl who I met years ago. And now, there's this *woman*, who I want to be with…" I pause and shoot her a hard glare. "I have to think of you as two different people, Maddie, or I won't be able to live with myself. I can't treat you the same way I've treated you in the past. We're transitioning into new roles in each other's lives and I think it'll be harder under the same roof."

She lets out a breath and her lips form a pout, but at least she's not crying. "I guess I can stay with Margie."

I don't know how long I've been asleep when a warm, wet feeling engulfs my lower half. I'm vaguely aware that I'm naked, after spending the better part of the evening fucking the life out of Maddie and that was before I pinned her down and made love to her until she couldn't breathe. The tears leaked out of her eyes and slid down her cheeks as I professed that nothing would change between us if she moved. We didn't break contact once as Christmas Eve turned into Christmas Day and now, I wonder if we are gearing up for round whatever.

It's pitch black when my eyes open, and sure enough, I feel weight on top of me and hands on my chest. "Fuck." I groan when I find her hips. I'm not inside of her, she's rubbing herself against my dick, essentially using me to get off. My dick is hard and resting against my stomach as she rubs against me, letting me slide between her lips to rub her clit. "Baby, let me get the lights." I turn on my lamp on the nightstand illuminating the room and she winces at the flood of light. I lick my lips, seeing her bare tits, her nipples pebbling and begging to be sucked. I trail my gaze down her stomach to where my cock is pressed against her cunt and my mouth drops open at the erotic sight. Her lips are stretched on either side of my dick and I can see that my cock, that's leaking precum from its head is already glistening with her juices.

I swallow, and all I want to do is impale her on my dick. I'm about to suggest doing just that when she opens her mouth. "I was thinking..." she whispers. She bites her bottom lip, and for a second, I'm so concentrated on that juicy fucking lip I want to bite that I forget she is still talking. "About what you suggested earlier?"

"I'm sorry baby, what did you say?"

"About...umm...sixty-nineing?" In the light of the room, her cheeks are almost bright red, and under any other circumstances, I might ask her what about this makes her so nervous. *And maybe later...way later...four orgasms later, I'll do that.* But right now, all I care about is getting her pussy on top of my face.

"Get up here," I demand. I'd gone down on her no more than two hours ago. Her sweet, tangy flavor is still in my mouth, and yet I was fiending for another taste. I am so starved for that feeling of her quivering around my tongue when I suck her clit into my mouth, I am practically salivating. I want her to ride my face, take the orgasm and whatever else she wants from me all while she's gagging on my cock. Taking more than she can handle as I fuck her mouth, bucking my hips against those pink, wet lips that never fail to make me lose control when she wraps them around me.

She does as she's told and just when she settles, with one leg on either side of my head, I grab her ass, bringing her lower. "Don't be nervous," I mumble against her pussy that's already wet from her earlier rubbing. I press my lips to her sex, sliding my tongue between her folds and flicking her clit once with my tongue causing her to cry out. She grabs ahold of my cock and squeezes hard as the lust ebbs and flows through her. "Lick the tip, but don't put me all the way in your mouth, Maddie. Just rub it against your tongue," I tell her, wanting her to taunt and tease me, while I wring as many orgasms out of her sweet tiny body before I erupt down her throat. She does as she's told, and I go in for the kill. Spreading her cheeks and digging my nails into the soft flesh as I lap at her sex indulging in her sweetness that tastes like home. Her arousal flows out of her, and I miss some of it as it trickles down my chin and onto my chest.

Of all the women I've been with, Maddie undoubtedly gets the wettest. She's the most responsive. The most eager to please. She's everything I've ever wanted in a lover. She craves her own orgasm, chases it, tells me what she wants, and I'm thanked for my efforts with the most explosive orgasms I've ever witnessed.

Orgasms that she's dying to have every time. Not to mention, she has this incredible need to give *me* one as well. Whether with her mouth or her pussy or her asshole, all three of which I've claimed as mine. A need so great it almost rivals my need to have one which is nothing I've experienced before her.

After the first time, where she really opened up to me, I wondered if it was her age and the fact that I was the only man she'd ever been with. Or the mere fact that I'm me, and she'd always wanted to please me whether it be with good grades or good behavior. She craved my praise in all walks of life, so it was no surprise that she craves it in the bedroom now that our relationship had changed. But the more time I spend with her in this intimate setting, the more I realize how sexual of a person Maddie is in general. Although at times she's nervous and timid, she slowly transforms into a siren who craves an orgasm like her next breath the second I touch her.

A grip on both thighs alerts me that she's close. *Already*. I insert two fingers into her pussy as my tongue floats upwards to rim her tight hole. I circle it once before probing it gently, and she loses it.

Her hold on my cock tightens and she sucks hard once before letting me fall from her lips. "Oh my God, Cal!"

"That feel good, baby?" I murmur against her cheek as I kiss and nibble at her through her orgasm, all the while I continue to pump two fingers in and out of her.

"So good, please don't stop!" she whimpers. Her legs shake and I feel her pussy clench and relax around my fingers as she drops her face to my groin. A sigh leaves her lips at the very end right before she whispers, "again."

I smile against her, pleased that her body is as desperate to continue the high as I am to give her another one. I flick her swollen clit with my finger. "You're so fucking wet." My lips, chin, neck, and the top of my chest are covered in her juices and I want more.

"I want us to come together next time." She turns slightly but I can't meet her gaze. "Tell me when you're close."

I slowly begin to tongue her sex again, making love to it, like the way I kiss her after a long day. Slow, long licks that make her whimper around my dick and suck and pull so hard that I wonder if she's trying to suck my soul out through it. Her nails are probably leaving permanent marks on my thighs and just when I'm about to tell her to dig her nails in harder, loving the pierce in my flesh, she removes her hand and begins to rub my balls, *hard*.

"Oh fuck, Maddie." For a second, I lose my way and fall back against the pillows. I squeeze my eyes shut, ready for the blast of pleasure that is moments away. I spread my legs wider, wanting more of her touch and her mouth and just *her*. She's learned my balls are my weakness and she wields that power like a sovereign. She knows all it takes is her to suck one into her mouth and I'm ready to lose it, but from this angle, she settles for fondling it. She pushes herself further down on my cock and to the back of her throat and I hear her choke slightly and because I know she wants it, and God knows I do too, I push my pelvis upward, forcing myself further down her throat causing her to moan and sputter which only makes me harder. The only sounds in the room are carnal, the sounds of our mouths sucking and licking each other's slick and swollen skin. "Close, baby." I groan, but I know I have to get her closer.

She is still riding the high of her last orgasm, with a sensitive clit, so I know it won't take her long to come again.

"Me too." She speaks, though it's muffled as her mouth is full of my cock. I press my lips to her again, my tongue taking a new speed as it rapidly fucks her while I rub her clit in clockwise motions. "Oh God, wait wait wait!" She stops and I smile knowing she's close.

"I'm there, put your mouth on my dick, Madeline." I see that she visibly shivers above me when she hears me use her full name.

"Yes, *Daddy*." *Oh, for the love of fuck.*

She puts me back in her mouth and I thrust upwards, exploding down her throat instantly, that one word pushing me over the edge. I suspect her calling me that turned her on as much as it did for me, and my suspicions are confirmed when she pushes down hard on my face as her orgasm rips through her. She's squirming against my face, like she does when she sits in my lap, trying to hit my tongue at the right angles. At some point, I finish coming, and she sits up so she's kneeling over my face. I immediately trail my arms up her short body, finding her breasts and squeezing, pinching her nipples as she continues to ride my face. She rests her hands over mine before pulling my right hand to her face and kissing it before sucking a finger into her mouth just as she did my cock.

"God, I love you so much," she whimpers just as she lets me fall from between her lips. She puts her hands on my stomach for leverage before trying to move from my face. I grip her ass again, keeping her in place and she giggles when I place one final kiss on her sex. She climbs off of my face and sits between my spread legs, her cheeks flushed, her hair disheveled and her lips red and swollen.

"You're so beautiful," I tell her.

"That was so fun." Her eyes are shining with lust and love and adoration and it makes me want to have my hands on her. She must sense that because she crawls up my body and snuggles against my chest before placing a kiss over my heart. I wrap my arms around her and move her so that she's lying next to me and I'm spooning her from behind. I rub my hand down her arm and kiss the back of her shoulder. "I'll hate not having this every night."

I drag my nose down her cheek and neck, inhaling her scent and knowing that I'll probably hate not having her here even more than she'll hate being gone.

What if Aria is right, and the space between us causes her to rethink this? What if she realizes that I'm a fucked up man for touching her the way that I have?

The thought makes my blood run cold that after all of this she may end up hating me.

CAL

I LET MY HEAD FALL ALL THE WAY BACK, THE POUNDING IN MY TEMPLES giving me a mind-numbing migraine that I know will only be exacerbated the second I step inside. I snuck out of bed just as the sun began to rise over Christmas day, hoping that I'd be back before Maddie wakes up, but now I wish I had woken her up to let her calm my nerves. I slide my key into the door and I'm immediately met with the smell of cinnamon, just like every Christmas. Every year, my mother spends the morning baking every dessert under the sun and sending them to various homeless shelters, soup kitchens, and churches that hold Christmas dinner for anyone without a place to go. So, I'm not surprised to see my mother in the kitchen with Christmas music blaring.

"Hey Mom, Merry Christmas," I tell her and she spins around from cutting up her apples for her cinnamon apple strudel. Wearing her usual Christmas sweater with a picture of Rudolph and matching apron, she's the picture of festive.

"Cal?" She looks at her watch and then up at me. "I wasn't expecting you this early! Merry Christmas, honey!" She pulls me in and reaches up on her tiptoes to hug me, allowing me to dwarf her small frame. "Is Maddie with you?" She peeks around me and frowns when she doesn't see the person that is never more than a few steps behind me when I come over.

"No no, she's still at home sleeping. We'll be back later today, I just wanted to come alone first…" I rub the back of my neck and sit at the kitchen table. She pushes her glasses to the top of her head and narrows her eyes.

"What's going on with you, huh? You look like you've got something on your mind. Talk to me, Cal Michael. I didn't know you were coming this early or I would have had breakfast ready." She opens the refrigerator and I notice it's packed with food that's already been prepared and some that hasn't. "I can whip you up some eggs and bacon really quick?"

"Mom, I'm fine." I rub my head. "But do you have any coffee made?"

"There should be enough for another cup." She grabs a mug and pours it for me before pouring a drop of milk, just how we both take it. "Here. Now talk."

I let out a breath. "You know I wouldn't ask this if it wasn't… really important."

"You can ask me anything, Son. Small things or big things. It doesn't have to be *really* important for me to help." Her eyes are soft and warm to match the kind heart she has inside, despite the fact that she spent the earlier half of her life having it broken.

"Do you think Maddie can stay here with you…just until she graduates?" She blinks a few times and sits back in her chair, crossing her arms. She doesn't say anything and I wonder if she's waiting for me to continue. "Anything she needs I'll take care of—" I start and she waves me off.

"Hush, Cal. I'm more than capable of taking care of her and I love spending time with her. I'm just curious as to what brought this on exactly." She raises an eyebrow at me and I know that look. *I already know the truth, so don't bother lying to me.* "You two have a fight?"

"No, Mom." Maddie and I rarely fought, we rarely yelled,

and the few times we did I felt like shit over it and usually ended up apologizing an hour later, and that's if she didn't come to me first.

She drums her fingertips against the wood. "Okay...do you want me to guess?"

So, she knows, but how? "Did you talk to Henry?"

Her eyebrows raise. "Your brother knows?"

"Knows what?" *Okay, so maybe she doesn't?*

"You tell me."

"Oh, for the love of God, Maddie and I are..." I clear my throat, preparing to speak the words when she beats me to it.

"Screwing."

I almost spit out my coffee in my haste to swallow it down quickly. "Mom!"

She puts a hand over her heart. "What? Oh, I'm sorry is that not accurate?"

I grit my teeth and screw my eyes together. "It's accurate. How did you know?"

"First things first, when did that start, and don't lie to me." Her voice is even, not angry or judgmental or upset. But calm and rational, unlike Henry and Aria.

"Not long if that's what you're thinking. A few days ago."

She nods. "Well, that's a relief. That girl has been in love with you for so long; I'm surprised it took this long for it to happen. She thinks you hung the moon and the stars and everything else in the sky." She rubs under eyes.

"Mom..." I trail off. "Please don't hate me." I expect to see the angry look Henry had or even the devastated look Aria had, but her eyes are filled with compassion and love and understanding.

"Do you love her?"

"More than I thought was possible...I already loved her so

much but…it's just so different now. I never expected to get here, I—"

"I did." She tells me honestly with a ghost of a smile playing on her lips. "I saw it a mile away."

"When?"

She lets out a breath. "I don't know. Small things here and there. The way your eyes search for her the second you walk in a room. The way you gravitate towards her. She's always been affectionate with everyone, but with you, she was always more so. You always went above and beyond for her but as she got older… you still always went the extra mile. I wasn't sure how or when it would change into this, but it seemed inevitable."

I let out a breath as I listen to my mother paint a vivid picture of me and Maddie. "Aria thinks it'll ruin her. That I'll break her."

"Aria needs to mind her business and focus on the problems in her relationship." She narrows her gaze. "She's always got an opinion on everything but that's another story. As far as Maddie goes, you couldn't break that girl if you tried."

"I think she means if things don't work out…we can't go back to the way things were. Maddie would hate me if I hurt her and it would devastate her not to have me in her life."

"*I* would hate you if you hurt her. You planning to hurt my girl? Because you wouldn't be here if you two were just experimenting with her new legal status."

"I'm not planning on it…but things happen. What if she decides she doesn't want this? What if she ends it? It would still make it hard for us to be close again."

"True. And that's a very real risk. But you've already crossed that line, so there's no going back at this point, am I right? But if she loves you as much as I know she always has, I don't think she'll ever want to be away from you, honey."

"I don't want to hurt Maddie. I don't want to ruin her. And Aria thinks that us being together after everything we've been through…given our history, will ruin her."

"Maddie isn't your daughter, Cal. This isn't illegal, sure some will take issue with it, but to hell with them. You deserve to be happy, and I've never seen you light up the way you do except when you're looking at Maddie."

"I love her…more than my own life. That hasn't changed. But I want…I want it all. So, if she needs space to make sure that this is what she wants, then I'll give it to her."

"Did she ask for space?"

"No. She's not happy about it, but Aria has her rattled. Aria wanted her to move in with her and Henry but with the way they're both acting, I don't want her to have to deal with that."

"So, Henry knows but Aria…doesn't?"

"As far as I know, and Henry took a swing at me, so needless to say he's pissed."

"He's always been such a hothead." She rolls her eyes. "Must be why he said he wasn't sure if he was coming today."

Henry knows Christmas means so much to my mother. For him to just not come, means he's probably not sure that he'll be able to keep his temper in check. "He's not? Are you okay with that?"

"Your brother makes a point to disrespect the man I've chosen to spend my life with at every turn. If he wants to stay home, he can. I don't want drama on Christmas." She points at me as if to say, *if he shows up, keep it together*. "Anyway, when is my partner in crime moving in?"

I groan and rub my forehead, the headache forming again at the thought of all the trouble Maddie and my mother could get into. "Listen, Thelma, keep Louise out of trouble. Do not let her drink."

"Hey, you have your way of parenting and I have mine." She shrugs before giving me a pointed look.

※

When I get home, Maddie is still sleeping, which isn't surprising. If she woke up and realized I wasn't home, she would have called me immediately. I stand in the doorway of my bedroom and watch her sleep for I don't know how long. She's on her stomach, her hair splayed out over my pillow, her naked body warm and covered by blankets. I pull my shoes, coat, and most of my clothes off before I climb into bed with her. I trace the features of her face with my fingertip and she sighs in her sleep which sends a spark to my dick that has already taken notice of her naked body. I turn her on her back and lower the blanket to reveal her perfect, taut body. I trail my lips up her skin, taking time to adequately kiss her pussy and her nipples before pressing a kiss to her mouth.

Somewhere around me sliding my tongue through her folds she began to squirm so by the time I get to her mouth she's almost awake.

"Mmmm, Cal," she mumbles. "Touch me." She sighs and I know she's fighting the last few moments of sleep, on the precipice of dreams and reality when her eyes flutter open. "Hey."

"Good morning, beautiful." I rub my nose against hers before placing a kiss on it. "Merry Christmas." I hold up the small box in front of her eyes that I'd retrieved from one of my safes. "This is for you." Her eyes light up and she sits up, wrapping the sheet around her naked chest. Her eyes dart to mine and I shake my head hearing her unspoken question. "It's not what you're thinking."

She runs her finger over the red box and traces the script

on the top. "Is it a ring?" Her mouth parts and I can see her pink tongue peeking through her teeth.

"It's a ring." I nod with a smile. Some things never change. Maddie always asked what something was before she opened it. She got one guess and if she guessed right, I had to be honest.

She opens the box slowly and stares at the ring that I've had for a few weeks. Her eyes well up with tears before she blinks them back. Her breaths are labored and ragged and I see the goosebumps popping up all over her skin. "It's so pretty."

It's a white gold band that forms an infinity symbol in the center with diamonds. The inside has our initials with the words "I'll love you forever" on the inside. Simple and to the point as those four words encompass everything I've ever felt for Madeline Shaw.

"It's engraved," I tell her as I slip the ring out of the box. She reads the words aloud and then she's lunging for me, wrapping her naked body around my half-dressed one.

"I love you so much…*forever*," she whispers into my neck. She pulls back and I grab her hand, sliding the ring onto her right finger before kissing it.

"I said it's not what you're thinking because asking you to marry me—while it's what I want," her breath hitches and for a second I think stars explode in her eyes, "it's not time. You still need to graduate and go to college and—"

"You're going to make me graduate *college* before you ask me?" She frowns.

Her words make my heart race at the thought of making her mine. "I don't know yet, but we just started this and it would be easy to get caught up in the sexiness of all of it and get married to tie you to me forever, but I want to make sure we are making the right decisions at the right time. I've always put you and your well-being first and that will never change."

"So, is this...a promise ring?"

"Yes."

"A promise to what?"

"To love you forever, Maddie. No matter what happens between us."

She frowns and I cock my head to the side. "Don't let Aria get in your head, Cal. Don't think you have to push me away and give me space because you think it's the only way for me to figure out what I want. If you think it's best for us, then I'll move out. Just...just promise I can come back?"

"About that, Maddie..." I trail off. She tenses in my arms and her grip tightens on me. "I talked to Margie."

She nods. "Okay..."

"You'll be okay with staying there?"

"For how long?"

"End of the school year?"

"And then I can come back?"

Her eyes are a combination of hurt, worry, and fear. She thinks I wouldn't come back for her. She thinks *my* feelings will change. "Yes, of course."

"You promise?"

I nod, remembering that the rest of her college acceptance letters should be trickling in soon. She's already been accepted to several out of state and I know it's a conversation we'll need to have. I don't want our relationship to be a factor in where she decides to go; I want her to spread her wings and explore the world around her without fear.

But I'd be lying if the thought of going with her didn't cross my mind. Realistically, if we continued down this road, we couldn't stay here. Everyone knows the story of how Maddie and I met and I wouldn't want to put her through people's scrutiny for the rest of her life.

I'd want to start somewhere new with a clean slate. Her and me, and hopefully, if we get there, all the babies she lets me put inside her. "I promise."

"You've never broken a promise to me before."

I grip her jaw and her lips purse. "Then you shouldn't be worried."

"Will we still get to see each other?"

I pepper kisses down her slender neck, trying to calm the nerves flowing through her. "Of course, baby. Nothing can keep me away from you. Is that what you're worried about? That we won't see each other? My mother is thrilled to have you, but now even more because she knows she'll see me more." I chuckle and she pulls away from my mouth and looks at me with wide eyes.

"You…told Margie?"

"She guessed." I shrug.

They widen further and covers her mouth with her hand. "She GUESSED?!"

"Apparently, we've been pretty obvious for a while now."

"Holy shit." She drops her head on my shoulder and takes a deep breath.

"For what it's worth, she's pretty on board."

"I always knew Margie was the coolest of the Grayson bunch."

I pinch her side. "I resent that."

"So, what's going to happen today?"

"I'm not sure. I think Henry is bailing."

"And Aria?"

"I don't know, but Margie knows that Aria's still in the dark about everything."

"When do I have to go?"

"When you go back to school maybe?"

Her eyes light up. "So, I can be with you for New Year's?"

"Yes. What would you like to do?"

She bites her lip. "You."

I throw my head back and let out a laugh. "I think we can make that happen."

"I'm serious, I need to have you as many times as possible before you ship me off."

"I'm not shipping you off. Don't be so dramatic. Do you need me to come tuck you in every night?"

"Oh." She raises her eyebrows and rubs against me. "Yes, please."

∞

We pull up to my mom's and I reach for Maddie's hand and rub my lips over them. "Give me a kiss before we go in."

She casts a shy glance at the house before turning back to me. She leans across the console and presents her lips to me. I cup her face and kiss her senseless, before peppering kisses all over her face. She sighs and stares up at me like I hold the answers to all life's questions. "That better not be the last time you plant one on me today."

"Maddie…"

"Find a time."

I roll my eyes at her bossiness and get out of the car, helping her out, and grabbing the gifts we brought for my family.

The second we walk through the door my mother is squeezing Maddie so hard I'm actually wondering if she can breathe, stroking her back and whispering something to her. I can't hear what she's saying but I see Maddie nod her head in response. She pulls away and cups her face before kissing her forehead and shooing her towards the kitchen. She points at me and narrows her eyes. "No funny business, Cal." She circles her finger at me.

"I've got my eyes on you."

"You're kidding, right?"

"I am certainly not kidding." I blink my eyes a few times at her and she puts her hands on her hips. "I don't want you two shacking up on my couch or sneaking off somewhere to fool around."

I wince and groan. "Seriously?"

"Very much. I'm going to treat Maddie how I treated you and your brother growing up." She heads back into the kitchen leaving me feeling like I'm seventeen again. I roll my eyes and make my way into the living room.

Later that afternoon, I'm sitting on the couch next to Grant—who I'm fairly certain is still clueless, watching the pre-show for the Christmas game when I hear the front door open. Aria's voice floats through the air and I'm immediately on edge when I hear my brother's a beat behind her.

Fuck fuck fuck.

CAL

'M UP BEFORE I CAN STOP MYSELF AND MAKE MY WAY INTO THE kitchen where I find my brother, sister in law, my mother, and Maddie and all of their emotions encased in the small space.

Henry's eyes meet mine first and they're still filled with rage and anger when my mother speaks first. "There will be none of that today, leave that at the door, boys, I mean it." Aria's eyes flick to Henry's and then mine and I can see how clueless she is as to why we are on the outs.

"Seriously, it took all the bribery to get him here. I don't know what's going on, but it's Christmas, can everyone just chill?" Aria pulls her coat off and sets it on the back of a chair as she slides off her boots.

Henry pushes past me, banging his shoulder against mine but I let it go, not wanting to add fuel to the fire and exacerbate his anger. Maddie's eyes find mine and she looks away quickly, remembering that Aria is in the room, but in just that split second, I felt everything she was trying to say.

I'm sorry. I wish this were easier.

I want to take her in my arms and tell her that she has nothing to apologize for, but Aria starts to drag Maddie out of the room much to my reluctance. The last time Aria was alone with Maddie it didn't end well, and I almost want to follow them to make sure that things don't get out of hand.

I stare after them long after they're gone when I feel a warm hand on my arm. "Let her go, Son. She'll be okay."

I let out a breath and rub a hand through my hair. "This is going to be a disaster. Henry is at his boiling point and Aria can sense something's off."

"Would it be the worst thing for Aria to find out at this point?"

"She wouldn't understand, Mom. I'm actually pretty shocked you took it as well as you did. I know how this looks to an outsider…"

"I'm *not* an outsider, Cal. I'm in there with you. Aria isn't an outsider either." She points at me as she goes back to seasoning her stuffing.

Everyone needs a home team. I can hear Aria's words as clear as day. I trudge into the living room to see Henry and Grant staring at the television, neither of them speaking. Maddie and Aria are nowhere to be found, thankfully, but I wonder what they're talking about.

Maddie can handle Aria, relax.

I sit next to Grant on the couch and he looks at me in question, wondering why Henry didn't acknowledge my presence.

"Well, you two are certainly festive." Grant raises an eyebrow at us and Henry's eyes snap to his.

"Now is really not the time," he barks.

I look at Grant and shake my head, trying to tell him that it *really* isn't. "Listen, you two, it's Christmas, it *is* the time. You know that your mother lives for this holiday. She doesn't want to see you two like this, so whatever it is, squash it till tomorrow. Actually, not tomorrow, because that's Maddie's birthday."

Henry snorts and takes a sip of the whiskey I just realized is sitting next to him. "Yeah, can't have *that*."

"Watch your fucking self, Henry," I growl, a warning to

leave her the fuck out of it.

He narrows his eyes at me before turning to Grant. "He must not know."

Dread floods me and my chest tightens as my palms start to sweat. I'm not sure why my mother hasn't told Grant yet, but I know she would handle it, and to be honest, the fewer people I have to tell, the better. "Henry, it's not your business."

"Not my business? This shit affects everyone in our family, *little bro.*"

"Can you not do this now? On Christmas? Here?"

He huffs and looks towards the television. "I'm only here for Mom, I don't give a shit about anyone else."

Probably includes your wife. I think, but I decide that's probably the quickest way to start a full-fledged fight.

"Well, that's not a good attitude to have." Grant starts. "Just keep your shit together, Henry. It's the one day of the year where you should appreciate your family and the past year you've had with them."

He shoots me a look as if to say, *I'm still pissed at you, but Grant is still a douche.* Aria and Maddie come back into the room, and no one is crying, so I take that as a good sign as Maddie sits on the floor and Aria sits on the arm of Henry's chair.

"What's going on? Why is everyone so quiet?" Aria asks. No one says anything and she pouts before looking at me curiously. "Is this all about what we talked about? We're fine, right, Mads?"

She nods but doesn't meet my gaze. "Yes."

"Wait, what?" Henry looks at his wife then Maddie and then me.

The thing about siblings is the unspoken conversations you can have. The ability to know where their mind is going before they get there. "Henry, can I talk to you for a second?" I ask, hearing his mind begin to race.

"You knew?" He stares up at Aria before his eyes flash to Maddie and then mine.

"Henry, knock it off," Grant growls, and in that moment, I know he knows. *I guess he's the only one who can keep shit to himself.*

"Knew what?" Aria looks at my brother. "What is going on?"

"That Cal and Maddie are…" His words get caught in his throat but it's enough for Aria to put it together as she jumps off the chair and stares at me.

"I KNEW IT!" It all happens so fast, and although I'm prepared because I'm always on guard, I don't expect Aria to lunge for me.

I definitely don't expect to see her being yanked back, *hard*. "I wouldn't." My mother's voice is so quiet as she has a death grip around her arm.

"Margie, let me go. Your son is…is…IT'S MADDIE." Her eyes, filled to the brim with tears, destroy me. The devastation behind them shows me she has nothing but Maddie's best interest…but also that she'll *never* understand.

How could you? her eyes demand.

"And if you have something you'd like to say, you can say it like an adult, but no one is attacking anyone. If you need a second to cool off, then go upstairs." My mother scolds as she points towards her staircase.

Aria spins in a circle and her eyes land on Maddie. "You lied to me…to *me*."

The tears are already in Maddie's eyes, but they haven't started to fall. She stands up and shakes her head. "Look at you. Of course, I lied to you. You don't understand! That much is obvious."

"Oh my God." She puts her hand over her mouth. "He's already got you so brainwashed." She turns towards me. "How could you fucking do this to her?"

"He's not doing anything to me!" Maddie interjects and I can already tell she's ready to snap. "It's not what you're thinking."

She ignores Maddie and keeps her eyes trained on me. "She's not even eighteen! It's fucking rape, and you're a COP," she stresses. "You know better." She holds her stomach. "I'm going to be sick. You...you took advantage of a girl that trusted you! She was SEVEN when you met her!"

"He didn't take advantage of me, Aria...I love him," Maddie whispers and her eyes flick to mine just for a second. But in that second, I can read every thought that crosses her mind. *You didn't take advantage of me. I've always loved you.* "I've loved him for a while. Long before anything happened."

"You think you love him...but God, Maddie, you're so young. You don't know what love is."

I do. My mind practically screams.

"And you do?" She narrows her eyes at Aria, and I can already see this is not going to end well.

"Mads..." I start, not wanting to see things escalate even further.

She ignores me and continues. "You know what love really looks like, Aria? You're such an expert, right?" The implication is clear and everyone falls silent waiting for Henry or Aria to defend their love as fiercely as Maddie and I plan to.

No one speaks.

Aria's chest heaves up and down, seconds from breaking down when she turns to Henry. "And you knew...? You *all* knew and you're just *okay* with this?"

"I just found out...believe me, I am *not* okay with it," Henry growls. "I still think she shouldn't be living with him." Despite the fact that I already have a plan in place for her to live with Margie, I want him to know it is *not* his decision.

"She needs to be staying with *us*," Aria interjects.

"That's not your call to make," I growl. The idea of Maddie going to stay with two people that would undoubtedly make her feel wrong for having the feelings she does is *not* going to happen.

"So, you think it's right for her to stay with you...? While you're..." Henry shakes his head and Aria interrupts.

"She can't stay with you. This is disgusting and I am so...sick over this, honestly." At this point, Aria is shaking, her fists flexing and unflexing and her entire body is stiff and rigid. "If you were anyone else, I'd be bringing you in for questioning." She puts a hand over her eyes. "I still might."

"Aria, stop!" Maddie snaps. "Just stop! I am not that broken little kid anymore. I know that's how you still see me, but I'm not. And in six more hours, I'll be an adult, capable of making my own decisions. Decisions that you can either support or—"

"Support?" she exclaims. "I can't support this, Maddie. It's wrong. And one day when you're far away from here and...*him*, you'll see my point. One day you're going to look back on this with so much regret. I know you love Cal, but you can't have him this way, Maddie. It's wrong."

"It's not wrong, stop saying that! What's wrong is staying in a relationship with someone you don't love. *That's* wrong," Maddie snaps and I know she's agitated. I can feel the waves of tension flowing off of her and it's only a matter of time before she says something she regrets.

"Okay, everyone just take a breath," Grant speaks up. "Before someone says something they can't take back." He shoots Maddie a look and the pink colors her cheeks over being scolded.

"And it's Christmas," my mother adds. "I already told you to check this foolishness at the door."

"This isn't foolishness, Margie, I can't believe you're downplaying it."

"And how are you even okay with this?" Henry asks as he turns to our mother.

"I'm always okay with love, Son."

"This isn't love this is—" Henry starts.

"Careful." Grant shoots him a glare.

"I don't think anyone asked for your opinion," he growls as he throws his hand up towards him. "This is a family matter."

I put a hand over my eyes, preparing for this to blow up even more.

"And he's my family," my mother argues. "And I'm yours. So that makes him yours too, and we are the only family you've got, Henry. Now you stop this right now. I didn't raise you to be like this."

He snorts. "You barely raised me at all. Maybe you raised Cal, but you didn't raise me. By the time you decided to be our mom again, I was already pretty self-sufficient." I narrow my eyes as I try to remember that time in between my dad leaving and my mother meeting Grant. The time is blurry since I was only six and Henry was ten, but clearly Henry had a much different experience. "But hey, we know at least one thing I got from you," he raises his glass of whiskey to her before taking a long sip.

Blood boils in my veins and I flex my hand so I don't send my fist flying at his face. "Henry, enough. What is wrong with you?" I bark at him. "You're pissed at me, but don't take it out on Mom."

"And you need to watch your mouth, or you can see yourself out." Grant isn't usually confrontational, even when Henry is being a dick, but right now my mother is wringing her hands on her dishcloth, tears pouring from her face, and I know Grant has *zero* tolerance for that."

Henry snorts. "Fine. I'm out. Aria are you coming?"

Aria looks at me and then at Maddie and shakes her head. "I raised you too, Maddie, and for you to think I don't have your best interest at heart…"

"I didn't say you didn't," Maddie whispers. "I know you do."

"Then why can't you understand that I know what I'm talking about? That this is going to hurt you in the long run. It has already changed you so much."

"Because…" Her bottom lip quivers and I feel the tightness in my chest, just as I always feel when I see Maddie cry. I want to pull her into my arms and absorb all the pain she's feeling.

Fuck. I need her. I want her to rub her tiny body against me until it hums with need and want and desire. And then when she's on the edge waiting to jump, I'll fuck her so deep, wringing every ounce of pleasure from her until she forgets about this argument. Forgets about our judgmental family who we'll probably lose in the light of our relationship.

But we'll be okay.

I want to show her with my mouth and my hands and my dick that I'm all she needs. That I can be everything for her. *Always*.

That my love for her is unconditional.

"Because," she continues, "you don't feel what I feel. If you did, you'd understand. Instead, you're looking at me with judgment and disgust. You think it's wrong because you don't understand it. You're looking at me like…you don't love me anymore, and that's never been the deal. Not with us. I'm still *me*, Aria."

"Ma…ddie." Aria chokes out and takes a step towards her just as Maddie takes a step back, shaking her head as if she doesn't want her to touch her. The pain is written all over Aria's face, watching her choose me and *us* over her.

"You said hurtful things. To me and to…" she bites her bottom lip and looks at me, "the man that's always loved me and put me first. Cal would never hurt me. You can't be so angry you can't see that. That you can't see that learning to navigate this relationship is difficult enough for both of us without you being on our side."

"Because it's unnatural!" Henry jumps in and Aria puts her hand up to silence him.

"Maddie…" Aria starts when Maddie puts both hands up in surrender.

"I'm not having this conversation with you anymore. I get that you don't support it, or maybe you will one day. Maybe all you need is time. That's also fine. But in the meantime, I want space."

"What?" Aria's eyes find mine before shifting back to Maddie.

"If you can't respect my choices as an adult, if you can't respect my relationship with the man I love, then…" She shrugs and I can see the pure sadness over potentially losing Aria, but I know it's easier than the tradeoff.

Losing us.

A part of me breaks for her. Breaks for the girl that loves Aria so much, the woman that has been her mother and friend and sister all rolled into one, and it will hurt her beyond measure to not have her in her life.

But Aria is right, not having me would destroy her. Hell, it would destroy me too.

"I think everyone just needs to take some time to cool off." I look at Maddie who looks like she's seconds from losing it, and I finally do what I should have done the second Aria flew off the handle. I cross the room and pull Maddie into my arms completely ignoring everyone else in the room. I needed a second of peace amongst the chaos.

"You okay?" And it's as if those two words coupled with my arms around her causes her to lose it because she wraps her arms around my neck and pushes her face into my chest.

"I want to go. *Please.*" Her voice is so quiet, I'm sure I'm the only one that heard her.

I rub her back and press my lips to the top of her head ignoring the prying eyes of my entire immediate family. "You don't want to stay?" I cup her face and she shakes her head, as black streaks fall down her cheeks.

"I just want to be with you," she whispers. "I can't…do this."

"Go upstairs, I need to set a few things straight here." She nods and when I squeeze her hand, she looks up at me. "All the way upstairs. No eavesdropping." I don't kiss her because I'm not ready to share that part of us with my family, and I'm grateful that she doesn't push for it.

I turn my eyes back to them, and particularly Aria and Henry when I hear Maddie moving up the stairs. "You're either with us or you're not, but I'm not doing this shit with you every time we're in the same room. So, either you check your issues at the door or…don't come around."

"Fine with me, I don't want to be witness to your perversions." Henry walks by me and I shake my head.

"This holier than thou bullshit is actually getting old, Henry. Maddie isn't my daughter and she'll be eighteen *tomorrow*. Stop turning this into something it's not. Stop making this into an ugly thing. You should know by now that I would never put Maddie in harm's way intentionally. But I *do* love her and I'm not giving her up just because you two can't be adults. You need to grow the fuck up." I don't wait for them to respond before I'm out of the room and up the stairs to find my girl.

Eighteen

Madeline

It's been a week since Christmas, and more importantly, a week since I've seen or spoken to Aria or Henry. I was half expecting Aria to have reached out by now to talk, but it's been radio silence. With each day that passes, I feel even more guilty for not trying to mend the rift between us. *She couldn't ignore me forever, right?* The only communication has been a text on my birthday telling me she loves me.

My response went unanswered.

The next day my birthday gift, two tickets to see a local band we both love, arrived in the mail. But the note attached said she understood that I would probably rather take Sasha. I cried for four straight hours after that. I felt like I lost my mother and best friend and sister all rolled into one.

I was up half the night packing most of my things in preparations to move to Margie's house, before collapsing onto Cal's bed wrapped in his arms letting myself fall into an exhausted sleep. I wake up to the feeling of him stroking my hair and I dread opening my eyes because it means it's morning and more importantly that I have to go.

"I know you're awake." He rubs his finger along my lips and I part them slightly letting his digit slip inside. "God, I'm going to miss waking up with you."

My eyes pop open at that and I move on top of him to

straddle him. "You *know*...I could maybe sleep over at Sasha's sometimes?" I raise an eyebrow and he smiles, raising his pelvis underneath me.

"We'll see each other, baby." His hand touches my face and traces his fingers from my forehead to my chin. "I won't be able to stay away from you but for so long."

I lean down and rub my nose against his. "I'm holding you to that." I plant a kiss on his lips. "Do you have time to fuck me before you go to work?"

A growl rumbles in his chest and then I'm on my back with my legs wrapped around his waist. I'm wearing one of his t-shirts and a pair of panties that he rips from me instantly. "You call me." He grits out. "Day or night." He grips my face and stares down at me, his eyes boring into mine. "You need me, you call me. I'll come." He narrows his eyes to emphasize his point. His gaze is hard and demanding, almost daring me to disobey him.

I mean it, Madeline.

"I know." I try my best to keep the tears out of my voice, but it's no use and I know he can sense the sadness lurking beneath the surface. His face drops to my neck, tucking it in the space there and inhaling. Teeth nip at my skin as I wrap my arms around him and slide my hands under the waistband of his sweats and slide them down.

He pulls away to remove his sweats, leaving him naked and hovering over me. He rubs his dick against my sex, lubricating his cock and tickling my clit in the process. I watch as a bead of cum trickles out of the tip and mixes with my arousal. "This still belongs to you. You know that, right? You know that you don't have to worry about anyone else..." He trails off.

I'll admit the idea did float across my mind that me not being around as much might open up the opportunity for women to get the wrong idea. Not that I thought he would entertain anyone, but women flocked to Cal and it made me crazy. I look up into his warm eyes that shine with love and devotion for only me, and I nod. "Do I need to remind you of the same?"

"Doesn't hurt to hear it." He slides inside of me and a sigh leaves my lips when he settles against me, the base of his cock kissing my mound as he glides in and out with ease.

"I belong to you, Cal."

"Fucking assholes, think they can mess with you." He grits out as he begins to pump in and out of me harder. "If I'm not around…" He trails off.

"I don't want anyone else…and just because I'm at Margie's, I have a feeling you'll still be around and daring anyone to come within a few feet of me." I smile, despite the sinking feeling in my stomach. I've never been away from Cal for longer than a few nights at a time. Now we are preparing for six months of being apart for *every* night. I squeeze my eyes shut to prevent the tears from falling when I feel one leaking out of the corner of my eye and slide into my hair. I turn my head when he grabs it. My eyes are still closed, but I feel his tongue at my temple, tracing the trail of my salty tear.

"Please don't cry." His voice is hoarse, like he's seconds from losing it as well. I open my eyes when I feel him slip out of me, his head is lowered, staring at his hands. "I've never not been there…" He trails off. "And now you're freaking out. This is a mistake." He looks up at me and I immediately fear the worst, feeling like the wind has been knocked out of me.

My eyebrows shoot to my hairline and my eyes fill with more tears. "Cal…"

"No, no…not that." He shakes his head. I sit up and he grabs my hand, interlacing our fingers and bringing them to his lips. "Not that," he whispers, as if he can hear my thoughts.

We aren't a mistake.

"I'll be okay," I manage to whisper. This whole time I thought that this would be the hardest on me. That being away from the man I've come to love in every way would leave a void in my heart and my mind and my soul. That I had come to be so dependent on Cal, that I didn't know how to function without him right beside me, telling me that *I can*. That I was so used to waking up in this house every day, and seeing *him* every day, that the idea of going a day without seeing his smile, or hearing his laugh, or *touching* him made me short of breath. But watching this strong man fall apart in my arms at the thought of being away from me, makes me believe that I'm not the only one that will feel the emptiness over our distance.

Maybe this distance is for the best because this can't be healthy… right?

He chuckles and shakes his head. "I know you will."

I sit up on my knees and wrap my arms around him. "But I'll miss you."

He pulls out of my grasp and tucks a lock of my hair behind my ear before cupping my face, his thumbs stroking the space just below my eyes, drying the leftover wetness. "The place won't be the same without you."

"I'll come visit." I giggle.

"Fuck visiting. That makes it sound like you don't live here. This is your home, Madeline. You know that, right?"

I bite my bottom lip, my body suddenly hyper-aware that my sex is swollen, his cock is hard, and neither of us finished. "Cal…" I trail my fingers up his torso, running over every defined ridge of his chiseled chest, *"you're* my home."

Cal sets my suitcase in his old bedroom that Margie has long since turned into a more effeminate guest room once I started staying with her more frequently. The posters and sports MVP awards were removed and the once blue painted walls are now white. The full-sized bed was replaced by a queen with a fluffy white down comforter with pink accents and a mountain of pillows at the head. "I think that's everything." He looks around the room at all of my suitcases. "Anyone tell you, you have a lot of shit?"

"You. Once or twice." I giggle. But I didn't want to have to be running back and forth between Margie and Cal's no matter how badly I wanted to see him when I couldn't find what I needed.

He looks at the door and then at me before he starts to close the door when Margie's voice rings out. "DOOR OPEN!"

Cal groans and rolls his eyes. "You've got to be kidding."

"You didn't have enough this morning?" I raise an eyebrow at him.

He rubs his forehead and I take a minute to roam my eyes over him. Black jeans and a black button-down adorn his perfect form, settled underneath a black leather jacket with his badge peeking out. I bite my bottom lip and his eyes darken when they find mine.

"Did *you?*" he asks in response to my ogling. "That's precisely why I tried to close the door. I just wanted to kiss you properly."

"I think the problem is you want to kiss me *improperly.*"

He shakes his head and pulls me into his arms. "I'll call you later."

I nod, the words getting caught in my throat. I wanted him to tell me he would *see* me later. I wanted a plan in place for when I'd see him again. "When will I see you?"

He rubs a finger over my lips. "You go back to school tomorrow and then you have practice…" He trails off. "And I have to work late tomorrow."

"Will you come see me after?"

"It'll be late."

"I don't care."

"My mother might," he laughs.

I let out a huff. "I guess I'm going to have to learn how to sneak out of the house."

"No." He growls and squeezes my ass. "Behave yourself."

"Or…what?" I know my eyes are filled with excitement and mischief.

"Madeline, don't tempt me with my mother downstairs." I bite my bottom lip and rub against him, before trailing my hands up his body. Not so accidentally bumping his cock with my hands *twice* causing him to groan. He grabs my hands and brings them to his lips. "Okay, you little minx, I have to go."

I nod, trying my best to put a brave face on, but he can see right through it. "I love you," I tell him as I wrap my arms around his middle and rest my head-on his chest.

He tightens his hold around me and I let his scent surround me. He lifts my chin up to meet his gaze. "Six months," he whispers.

"And then…?"

"And then I'm *never* letting you go again."

I spend most of the day in my *new* room, putting everything away and taking intermittent naps because moving is exhausting as hell. I'm trying my best to keep up a brave face over this recent change, but the tears have been flowing nonstop. In the midst of unpacking, I come across a photo album. It feels heavy in my hands, reminding me of what's inside, and my heart sinks in my chest at the painful memories. I run my fingertips along the edges of the familiar red cover and hug it close to my chest as if the hard ridges are the soft, warm arms of my mother.

"What do you want for dinner?" Cal asks as he walks into my bedroom to see me sitting in the corner with my arms wrapped around my knees, hugging them to my chest. "Maddie?" He kneels down in front of me. "What's wrong, honey?" I've been staying with the nice police officer that found me hiding in the closet last month and he seems nice, but I want to go home.

"I want to go home." I speak, barely above a whisper. A tear trickles down my cheek. "I just want my mommy."

"What?" he asks and leans closer to my face and I reach my hand out and push him hard although he doesn't move an inch.

"I WANT TO GO HOME! I DON'T WANT TO BE HERE!" I scream so loud my throat is sore.

His eyes widen and for a second, I feel like I might have hurt his feelings. "Maddie…"

"I want my mommy! And I'll never see her again!" The tears are flying down my face at this point, the sobs bubbling in my chest and spilling out all over this sweet man that has been taking care of me.

He rushes to my bed and grabs my pink bunny and sits next to me holding it out for me and I snatch it from his hands. "MINE."

"I know." He's so calm, and it makes me wonder why he's not yelling at me. Daddy's yell, don't they?

"I want to go home." I turn to him and he looks just as sad as me.

"Maddie, I know you want your mommy and you want to go home, but… you can't." He turns to face me head-on and puts his hands on my shoulders. "I know this situation sucks and you were dealt the shittiest hand, and I'm sorry. I'm so sorry I can't make this better *for you. I would take all of your pain away if I could."*

I sniffle and wipe my eyes. "I miss her."

"I know."

"The kids at school said my daddy killed her."

His eyes are cold and hard and he looks away from me. I'm not sure what happened that night. I remember yelling and screaming and a loud bang. I think I fell asleep for some of it. But then Cal was there and my parents were dead.

"What else did they say?"

"Is it true?" I ask. I know my mommy and daddy died but no one told me why or how.

"Maddie…"

My chest feels like it's about to explode, my heart is beating so fast, and I feel like I can't see anything through the tears in my eyes. "I hid. I hid because I was scared. He was yelling and…" My lips tremble and then I'm in his arms and he's rubbing my back as I cry into his shoulder. "I let her die. I should have done something…"

"Shhh, sweetheart, there's nothing you could have done. You were smart to hide. Your mommy would have wanted you to hide."

He continues to talk but I don't hear it. All I can hear is my mother's voice floating around me. Singing to me. Reading me the story of "Madeline." Teaching me how to play Hopscotch and jump rope and giving me the warmest hugs. She smelled like honey and always came when I called.

Except now.

Cal stands with me still in his arms and takes me into his bedroom and sets me on my feet. I squeeze my pink bunny harder as he moves into his closet and pulls something out of a large bag.

"This is technically evidence, but I knew one day you would want it. I didn't want this to be filed away where you would never see them."

I take the book from his hands reluctantly and sit on the ground. I open the book and wipe my nose as the tears begin to form again when I *realize it's a photo album.*

"Mommy." I press my fingers to a picture of her and pull it from the sleeve and hold it in my hands as he sits down across from me. "Thank you."

He nods and rubs his jaw. I've noticed he has more of a beard lately. "I want you to be happy, Maddie, so if you want to go, I'll call your social worker. We can still be friends." He smiles at me and I shake my head back and forth.

"No!" I scoot closer to where he's sitting and sit up on my knees putting my hands on his shoulders. "I'm sorry I said that. I didn't mean it." I shake my head. "I want to stay. Please let me stay."

"If you're not happy here…"

"I am! If I can't be with my Mommy…" I trail off. "I want to be with you."

I press the album to my chest and let out a sigh. I bite my bottom lip, to stop the tears from falling but it's no use. My eyes drift upwards, and I let them flutter closed as I try to picture my mother smiling down on me.

∽

It isn't until dinnertime when I finally emerge to find Margie cooking in the kitchen.

"Hey Mads, I was just about to come get you! You all settled?"

I wince at her words. *It's been four hours and I already miss him.* "Yep, I'm in. Do you need any help?"

"No, I'm almost finished." She washes her hands before turning to me with her head cocked to the side.

"What?"

"We should have a little *talk.*"

"Margie..." I trail off and she points at the chair indicating that I need to sit.

I do as she says and rest my head on my fist. "Yes...?"

"So, there's going to be some rules, missy."

"Like a curfew? I assumed."

"Not just a curfew. You can't just go gallivanting off with my son whenever you feel like it."

My mouth drops open. "You mean...Cal?"

She looks at me as if to say 'don't start.' "Your *boyfriend*, Maddie." No one's referred to him that way before and I feel my sex clench on instinct. "You're eighteen, so I'm not going to put very strict rules in place, but no sleeping at his house, Maddie."

"I can't stay there?"

"No?"

"Why?" I furrow my brows in question.

"Are you insane?"

"No! That's a serious question."

"You think I'm going to allow you to go have a sleepover with your boyfriend?"

I sigh. "Fine. Well, can he stay here, at least?" She looks at me from over her glasses.

"Nice try," she says sardonically.

I gasp. "What? He's your son, you're going to tell your precious baby boy he can't stay over?" My fingers cross under the table hoping that works.

She narrows her eyes at me. "You think you're so slick, don't you?" She chuckles. "Fine, Maddie if my son is so hell-bent on staying here, then fine, in the basement and away from your bedroom." She gets up and goes back to the stove.

"Can't he stay in Henry's old room?"

"No," she says without another word or glance in my direction.

"Send me a picture," I hear growled in my ear and I roll my eyes as I run my hand along my wet leg with the one hand I've submerged in water. I grip my phone harder, careful not to drop it in the bathtub that I've filled to the brim with jasmine scented bubbles.

"Later." I murmur. "How was your day?"

"Long. Aria is still avoiding me like the plague and people are taking notice."

I groan. "Cal..."

"I mean they just think her and Henry are having issues and it's making things awkward and tense, or that we had a fight."

"Do you think Aria will say anything?"

"No...I don't, and I told you not to worry I'll handle it if it comes to that."

"Baby..." I trail off. "If it comes to that..." I clear my throat, prepared to speak my biggest fears. *That people wouldn't be forgiving or accepting or willing to ignore. They'd be outraged and it would be the end of Cal Grayson, glorified Officer of the Law.*

"I said I would take care of it." I go to respond when he cuts me off. "Oh, shit!" And I can hear the smile in his voice. "I'm going through the mail. Seems like someone has a little something from a certain Harvard University."

"Oh my God!" I sit up so fast the water sloshes over the sides of the tub. I hadn't wanted to go away to school, but Cal and Aria had forced me into at least trying. I had the grades and SAT scores and extra-curriculars for it, not to mention an essay of what happened that tragic night that's probably worthy of a bid for presidency. And now that Cal and I probably couldn't be together here in Oregon, the thought of starting somewhere else new excited me. *Pending we could afford it and Cal would come with me.* "Big or little?"

"Big or little?" He repeats in question.

"Envelope, Cal! Is it a big or little envelope! Rejections are little, acceptances are big!"

"Not necessarily, sometimes..."

"CAL MICHAEL!" I growl into the phone and he chuckles.

"It's big."

"Open it!"

I hear him ripping the paper open and then silence where I assume he's reading. "You're in."

"Holy shit!" *I got into Harvard...* My eyes widen and tears spring to my eyes.

"You did it, baby."

"I couldn't have done it without you." I smile. "Thank you for pushing me and...*everything.*"

"Mads..." He trails off, probably feeling uncomfortable under my gushing and I continue before he can ruin the moment.

"Don't make a joke. Don't ruin this. Cal, I think...I think I might want to go away...for school."

"I think that's smart. You're brilliant, Maddie, and going somewhere like Harvard will open you up to so many more opportunities." It's hard to gauge his reaction over the phone, but I hope he doesn't think that I want to go *anywhere* without him.

"I don't even necessarily mean Harvard though...I just...I think I need out of Oregon. But..." I stop. "I want you to come with me."

"To Harvard?"

"Anywhere. I don't want to leave here without you." He's silent so I take the chance to continue. "Think about it, how are we going to be together here?"

"I mean we can't exactly, but I don't know if me coming

with you—"

"Why? No one outside of here will know our past unless we disclose it. But we can go out on dates and touch in public. We can...take those steps that we won't be able to do here." *Mainly your ring on my finger and your baby inside me.* I press my legs together as that fantasy fills my mind.

"We can talk about it." My eyes widen and a smile finds my face, thrilled that he doesn't push back. "What are you doing Friday? Do you want to come over after school? I can meet you."

I lean forward, his implications clear and my sex responding to it. "Oh?"

"Yeah." His voice is low and husky and I can picture him sitting in his chair, legs spread, his hand rubbing his dick as he thinks about all of the things he wants to do to me.

"And just what should I tell your mother, who seems to think I can't be within fifty feet of your house without risking pregnancy."

"Do what I did when I lived there."

"And what's that?"

"Make something up."

Nineteen

Madeline

A SOUND OF A LOCKER SLAMMING BREAKS ME OUT OF MY AGGRESSIVE sexting with Cal. My heart is racing so fast, pounding in my chest *and between my legs* as I read the borderline obscene things Cal is saying…*and* what I'm replying. I almost drop my phone before turning to my best friend who's staring at me like she knows *exactly* what I'm doing. Cal and I downloaded one of those messaging apps, so that we could be more *colorful* in our messaging, and so far, we've been taking full advantage.

"What are you doing?" She raises an eyebrow at me before taking a sip of her coffee that I know she skipped second period to get.

"Nothing." I slip my phone into my bag and tighten the ponytail at the back of my head nervously.

She crosses her arms in front of her chest and leans against the row of lockers. "Really? Because you look guilty as hell."

"You just scared me that's all."

"Mmmhmm. So, you're coming to Melanie's party tomorrow, right?" I press a hand to my forehead and groan. *Fuck, I forgot about that and I want to see Cal.* "Madeline Elizabeth, it's her birthday! You're telling me you forgot?"

"No." I shake my head. "I didn't forget I just…it slipped my mind that's all." There's only so much I can stay focused on between school and ballet and a very sexy boyfriend who claims most of my free time and all of my thoughts.

I've been at Margie's three days and I've only seen him once since I moved in. He came over under the illusion of "staying for dinner" before the two of us made out like teenagers on the couch after Margie went to bed. Of course, not before strict instructions to *behave*, and that Grant would be awake watching television in the basement. The fact that he could pop up any moment had us keeping things *slightly* PG And by PG, I mean, his hand was up my shirt at one point as I straddled him. It reminded me of how things started between us and the memory made me weak in the knees.

I was hoping this weekend, I could convince Margie to let me stay at *a friend's* house one of the nights. I hadn't planned on lying to Margie, but I also wanted to spend time alone with Cal and she had made it pretty clear that *"high schoolers don't get to spend the night at their boyfriend's house."* Apparently, Cal isn't really my guardian anymore, but someone I need to be guarded from. Him, his hormones, and mine too. *"Mads, Cal used to panic about what would happen if you got pregnant in high school when the boys started coming around and taking notice."* Confusion finds her face. *"Not quite sure how this works now."*

I understood. Cal isn't the same Cal anymore. He didn't even call me Mads anymore. And ironically, I called him *Daddy* now.

I shut my locker and pull my bag up on my shoulder as Sasha and I begin walking towards our next class. She links her arm through mine. "So, you going to tell me who you're texting that's got you glowing?"

"No one."

"Oh my God, Mads, seriously? What's with all the secrets?" Ever since I moved to Margie's, Sasha has been on my case trying to figure out why. According to her, the hypothesis of Cal and I being together immediately went out the window. *Little does she know.* She's convinced that we had some a huge fight and I wanted out. "Oh my God, is it a secret boyfriend? And Cal found out? And that's why you moved because he freaked?"

"No, Sash. I already told you, there was no fight. I just needed a change of scenery. Cal has to be out of the house a lot more right now with this new case, and he didn't like me being all by myself."

"And I already *told you* I think that's bullshit."

"What's bullshit?" Sasha's boyfriend, Mike, interrupts as he slides a hand over her shoulder. His hand tugs on her curly hair and pulls her in for a kiss. "What's going on, Troublemaker?" He kisses her nose and she giggles.

"Nothing." She rolls her eyes and turns back to me. "I'll pick you up around eight tomorrow."

I haven't talked to Cal since our delicious sexting earlier, so I'm eager to get back to it as I make my way out of my dance studio that night. My ballet instructor even scolded me for not focusing halfway through barre method. *But I couldn't focus.* All I could think about was Cal's mouth.

Everywhere.

That sinful, sexy mouth that he has an obsession with keeping between my legs.

Even now, I'm breaking one of Cal's cardinal rules, which is to always be aware of my surroundings, particularly at night by myself. Instead, my head is buried in my phone, rereading our messages for what felt like the tenth time. Besides, I've never felt unsafe in my dance studio parking lot.

Until now.

The hairs on the back of my neck stand up as a chill runs through me and a shiver skates down my spine. I look up from my phone and around the somewhat deserted parking lot searching for anything that feels out of place. My eyes dart across all the places someone might be able to hide but my search comes up empty. I immediately reach for the pepper spray Cal makes me carry and grip my necklace as the walk feels like an eternity to my car. I take each step quicker than the last and before I realize it, I'm full-on running towards my Volkswagen. By the time I get inside and lock my doors I let out the breath I didn't realize I had been holding the entire way to my car. I immediately look in the backseat, recalling every scary movie I've ever watched and put a hand over my chest.

"Get a grip, Maddie." I let my head lean back, and shoot Cal a text letting him know I'm leaving before I start my twenty-minute drive to Margie's house which includes about fifteen minutes of a dark somewhat windy road.

I'm about five minutes into my drive when I notice headlights in my rearview mirror. It's nearing ten-thirty, so I'm not totally shocked to see another car on the road, but I've also been on this road hundreds of times without seeing one at this hour.

I turn my gaze back to the road when I realize the car is getting closer and the lights brighter, making me realize they have their high beams on. I wince at the harshness of the light and try to avoid looking in the rearview mirror. I understand driving with your high beams on while on this road, but I always switch them off when I come into contact with another car.

What the fuck?

For the next minute or so, I avoid looking up, when I realize they're *right* on my tail. *Oh my God.* I press on the gas, trying to accelerate to put some space between us, but they keep up with me, not letting more than a few feet between us.

"Oh my God, just go the fuck around me, dick!" I put two hands on the steering wheel, trying to move faster, forcing me to about sixty miles an hour on this road that I really shouldn't be going faster than forty when I decide I need backup. Or at least someone to know what's going on in case this lunatic runs me off the road.

He's going to panic.

I press the button and the sound of the ringing floods my car.

"Hey, I just saw your text. You got to Margie's fast"

"CAL." I don't even try to hide the panic. "Some…someone's tailing me. Really bad."

I can hear him shuffling instantly. "Where?" he asks, even though I know he's pulling up my tracker.

"On route fifty-eight." I look up, and sure enough, the car is still riding my bumper. "Cal, he won't stop. He's so close and he has his high beams on."

"Baby, I need you to stay calm. We've talked about this, you can handle this."

"We haven't talked about this on this windy road!" I shriek. "I'm scared, Cal." Tears spring to my eyes and I find myself shifting in my seat and I'm starting to regret chugging that whole bottle of water after my last class.

"I'm coming to you. Drive towards my house, not Margie's."

"Margie's is closer."

"Yes, and I don't want any asshole knowing where you're headed or where you live. Come to *me*."

I swallow and nod. "Okay…"

"I'm bringing the cruiser and my lights will be on. Stay calm, okay? I'm going to stay on the phone with you until I get there. Focus on the road, I see you're coming up on the first turn. Don't take your foot off the gas."

"I have to slow down, Cal, I could crash into the side of the mountain or run into the creek!"

"Sweetheart, you can do this. You're a great driver, just breathe." His voice is even, and I know it's because he's good in a crisis and I'm grateful for this because it's keeping me calm.

I look up and my eyes widen when I realize I don't see his lights anymore. I sit up taller in my seat and tears start to rush down my cheeks. *Fuck.*

I don't see his lights because he's right on top of me. His lights are almost pressed into my tail and only then do I realize they're driving some sort of SUV. But I still can't make out the face of who's driving. "Cal...I think this guy is trying to run me off the road. I...I'm scared!"

"I'm close, baby. Two miles, okay?"

My teeth begin to chatter nervously and just as we are coming up on the turn, I see the flicker of the red and blue lights coming at me. High beams come back into my rearview as he backs up and before I realize what's happening, I see him turning around and zooming back down the road. I slow down to a complete stop, pressing my hand to my chest, trying to calm my racing heartbeat as I know Cal is close and I'm safe, when I see his cruiser zoom by me. "NO! Please, don't leave me!" I scream. Tears are flowing down my cheeks and I know I'm moments from full-on sobs. I know Cal can see the taillights of the offender and could probably catch that asshole, but I can't be alone right now. I hop out of my car just as he turns around and parks behind me and I'm in his arms before he's barely out of the car.

"Are you okay?" He puts a hand on either side of my face before tucking me into his chest. "I'm here, it's okay." He rubs my back as my sobs start to slow. "What happened?" He kisses my forehead and I reach up and let his lips brush against mine.

"Don't leave me." I murmur against lips.

He lets out a breath and sits on the hood of his car, pulling me between his legs. "I'm not leaving."

"I don't know who it was. I really tried to see. Cal, I'm sorry!" I squeeze my eyes shut and shake my head.

"Don't be sorry. I'm glad you were focusing on driving and staying safe. That's the most important thing, okay? That you're safe." He lets out a breath and I feel it on my face as I move closer to him. "Fuck, I should have sent someone out to patrol this road, maybe they'd come across them. Do you think they were drunk or anything?"

"No, they weren't weaving, but then again, I don't know. They were just so close." I move to look at my bumper, holding my hand a mere inch from my car. "This close. Any closer and they would have tapped me."

"They didn't touch you?"

"No…" I shake my head.

He lets out a breath. "I'm going to follow you to Mom's."

"Wait, Margie's? I can't come home with you?"

"I'm going to go into the station for a while, see if there have been any other reports on this. I want you home and safe. I'm putting a cruiser outside her house too."

"Cal…" I whine. I didn't want all of that, nor did I need all of that to feel safe. *I needed him to feel safe.* I could have all the protection in the world, but if it didn't include him it didn't matter. I'd still have a nightmare tonight. I'd still have flashes of my father behind the wheel of the car behind me, trying to push me into a ditch.

"No, Maddie, I'll come see you tomorrow, alright? But I'm not taking you home and then leaving you alone after what just happened."

"Will you come back to Margie's tonight?"

He lets out a breath and runs a hand through his hair. "I'll be there through the night, I'm sure."

"But Cal…"

He boxes me in against my car and presses his forehead to mine. "No buts. If anything ever happened to you…" He trails off as his hand moves up and traces my face. "You're all that matters to me."

I bite my lip at his words and pull him closer, his lips hovering just over mine. "Please," I whimper and then our lips crash in a dizzying kiss. His tongue rubs against mine and his hands spread my legs so he can stand between them before he lifts me up and I wrap my legs around his waist. "Cal," I whimper.

"Fuck…" He opens my coat and steps between them, finding the seam of my leggings between my legs making me grateful that I changed out of my leotard before I left. He digs one finger into the seam, pressing against my sex and I moan, only to let out a yelp when he rips them at the center, making a hole in my crotch.

"Cal!"

"Hold on, baby." He growls as he lowers his sweatpants. He opens the hole wider and moves my panties to the side and before I can protest, he's inside of me.

Outside.

On the dark road of route fifty-eight.

My heart pounds in my chest as I can't see anything past Cal's eyes that are boring into mine. "I need your cum on my dick, Maddie. I need you to come, so that later tonight when I'm frustrated and angered by the fact that someone decided to fuck with you, I can remember you're safe and sated at home waiting for me."

A sob leaves my mouth, but it's more out of pleasure than sadness as his coarse pubic hair rubs against my clit. My mouth drops open as he pins me to the car and begins to fuck me like a wild animal.

It makes me wonder how many wild animals have given into their primal urges just off this road in the woods behind us.

"I'll literally rip the fucking limbs off of anyone who thinks they can touch a hair on your head, you know that right?" He grits in my ear and I nod. "Say you understand."

"I…I understand."

He pushes in and slides out slowly, letting me feel every ridge of his cock rubbing my walls. I touch his dick that's half inside of me and pull him back in. His cock is wet with my arousal and I hold my hand up, licking *us* off my hands.

"Give me a taste." He growls.

I rub a finger over my clit, to collect some wetness before pushing it through his lips. His tongue rubs against my finger and I feel the gentle graze of his teeth. He groans and begins to fuck me harder, faster, and more feral than before. His pumps are erratic and uncontrolled, his fingers digging into my thighs as he slams in and out of me. "You came," I whisper. "I called and you came." My eyes well up with tears as the gravity of what just happened washes over me. "In minutes."

He holds himself inside of me, even though I know he's on the precipice of his release and cups my face in his hands. "I told you. You call, I come."

CAL

MADDIE IS STILL SHAKING ONCE WE ARE INSIDE MY MOTHER'S house, so I pull her trembling body into my arms and rub her back. "You're safe," I whisper in her ear. I guide her into the kitchen and pour a glass of water for her and watch as she takes a tentative sip. "Whole thing, baby." She does as she's told, finishing the entire drink before putting the cup in the sink.

"Please stay with me," she whispers, and for the first time, I can see the fear in her eyes. The fear I'd seen when I pulled her from that closet and a handful of other times in her life. "Don't leave."

"Maddie..." I rub a hand over the back of my neck and she takes a step closer and into my arms.

"Stay in Henry's old room. I just...I need you close."

I let out a breath, knowing that she could break me down easily. *She knows it too.* "If this maniac is out there..." She bites down on her bottom lip and backs up slowly. "You're safe here, okay? Mom has a top of the line alarm system." *I know because I made her get it.* "And Peters just buzzed that he'll be here in five. You're safe."

"Nothing makes me feel as safe as being near you." She twists her mouth as if she's about to cry and I run my knuckles down her sweet face.

"I'll come back, alright? The second I leave the station." Her eyes light up and she's in my arms instantly. "But try and get some sleep while I'm gone. Maybe take a warm bath?"

"I'd rather wait for you to take one with me." She rubs against me and flutters her eyes at me.

"You're going to get us in trouble," I tell her. As enticing as a bath with Maddie is, and regardless that the idea sends a spark to my dick, I know I have to go into the station. I'm livid that someone messed with her, and even more so that this person is still out there. Antagonizing a young girl on a dark highway is shit I do not stand for.

Not. In. My. Town.

I press my lips to hers, sliding my tongue through her mouth followed by a kiss on her nose before ushering her up the stairs.

"You'll be back?" she whispers.

I nod, before heading towards the door. She blows me a kiss and as soon as I'm out the door my phone vibrates with a text

Maddie: Be safe. Come back to me. I love you.

I'm on the warpath the second I set foot in the station, barking orders at anyone I come into contact with that they need to get their ass out there and find who fucked with my girl. It isn't until I've been there an hour and called to check on Maddie at least three times when I decide I need something to calm my nerves.

"You're smoking again?" A billow of smoke leaves from between my lips as I pull it away and flick the ash into the street outside the station. Aria's concerned eyes come into view through the smoke, and she tries to pull it away from me but I take a step out of her reach.

"It's been a rough night." I grit out and she frowns and looks down at the ground before meeting my eyes. This is the most we've spoken in two weeks and I can actually say I've missed her.

"What happened?"

I prop my foot up against the building behind me. "Some asshole fucked with Maddie, tried to run her off the fucking road."

She gasps and immediately reaches for her phone. "What? Where?"

"On fifty-eight. They were tailgating her, hard. I met her just after the first bend and it spooked them. They sped off. She was shaking by the time I got to her."

"Kids? Drunk? High?"

"I don't know, but you can bet your ass I have everyone in there on it."

"Cal…it was probably just some assholes on a dare or just being stupid."

"So? They could have hurt someone."

"You mean Maddie."

"Okay fine, yes I mean Maddie. They could have hurt Maddie. That should mean something to you too, Aria." I flick my cigarette into the street and shoot her an angry glare before heading back inside.

She stops me as I reach for the door. "Fuck you, Cal. How dare you insinuate that I don't care? I'm just saying you acting like a raving lunatic over something that is literally a needle in a haystack is not using our resources properly. Do you even know what the car looked like? Could she ID the guy? Can *you*? What do you have them looking for? You said you spooked them, right? Then they are probably done with their harassment for the night. Where's Maddie now?" I don't respond as I throw the door open and storm through the entrance. "So, Margie's. Then she's safe. She's fine. And my guess is you probably have the place guarded like Fort Knox."

I turn around, and just as I prepare myself to reprimand her for her insubordination, for the first time in a week, I notice her. Under the lighting of the police station, I see the redness in her eyes, the bags that lie beneath them, and the absence of eye makeup that she usually wears. She looks like she's lost about ten pounds and her hair is pulled up into a top knot, her telltale sign that she hasn't washed it. I cross my arms in front of my chest. "What's going on with you?"

I can see the war behind her eyes of whether she wants to unleash whatever is going on before she inevitably lets her shoulders sag. "Your brother moved out."

People are moving all around us, but all I notice is the heartbroken look all over my sister in law's face. "Let's go to my office."

I shut the door behind her and lean against my desk. "What happened?"

She shrugs and looks around as if the answers are written on the walls of my office. "Life?" She bites her bottom lip as the tears slip down her cheeks but she wipes them instantly. "He wants to move."

"And that's why you're fighting?" I ask. "I assume you mean move out of state? He wants to move and you want to stay?"

"No. He wants to move *without* me. He wants a divorce."

I know Henry and I aren't speaking, but I can't imagine that he'd leave the state without telling me. I briefly wonder if he's mentioned this to our mother, but decide that he couldn't have because Margie would be beside herself at the idea of not having both of her boys in the same state.

"Why?"

"He doesn't want to be married...anymore. He said we've been trying to keep things together for years but neither of us are happy. We've been fighting a lot...and then...this stuff with Maddie..."

"Don't put that on us, you both seemed to be on the same side about that."

She looks down and then up at me. "I'm giving her space but I want to be in Maddie's life...regardless of your place in it." She sits down on the small couch in the corner as if she's crumpling under the weight of the world just as a tear slips down her cheek. She twists her mouth to try and stop the flow but they continue.

"Okay?"

"Henry doesn't."

How could he just turn his back on her? On me? "He cares about Maddie, I know he does."

"I'm sure one day he'll come around, but..." She pauses and her gaze drops to the ground. "He's said some pretty ugly things about it. I know I didn't take the news well, but in my defense, I was hurt—I am hurt. Hurt that she lied to me. Hurt that she felt like she couldn't confide in me." She shakes her head, finally meeting my gaze. "But Henry...he's angry, almost vengeful." I frown at her choice of words. I knew he's angry, but I had hoped that he would come around sooner rather than later.

"After Christmas," Aria continues, "I gave a lot of thought to all of this, and ultimately it's Maddie's life and," she shrugs, "I can't control her any more than I can control Henry. The two most important people in my life want nothing to do with me."

"That's not fair, Aria. You turned on Maddie first. You think she doesn't want you on her side? In her corner? She loves you so much and she's hurting over this too."

"How is she?" she asks, the tears making her green eyes more piercing than usual.

"Good...she got into Harvard." I smile with pride and the

one on Aria's is just as big.

"Holy hell!" She giggles through her tears.

"That's our girl." I stop. "We did a good job I think."

"She's a great girl." Aria smiles and I nod. "You'll…take care of her." She blinks rapidly and the insinuation is loud and clear.

"Of course. Always."

She nods and stands up slowly. "Tell Maddie…I miss her and I'm always on her side."

I was never an affectionate person with the exception of Maddie, so I know Aria is surprised when I pull her into a hug, wrapping my arms around her. "You're family Aria, alright? No matter what happens between you and Henry, you're family. I'm still on your home team."

She pulls away and wipes at her eyes. "Thanks, Cal."

The night turns into morning quickly, and before I realize it, the sun is rising and I still haven't seen Maddie. *And I see she has also noticed.*

"You never came," she says into the phone. Her voice is sullen and I can just see the pout forming on her lips.

"I never left the station. I had a lot of things to take care of once I got here."

"Evidently, I was not one of them."

"Maddie…"

"I told you I needed you. *Here*. With me."

"I know, baby, I…"

"Just forget it, I have to get ready for school."

"Are you okay to drive?"

"I'm fine, Cal. I'll see you whenever, I guess." I can't help my eyes from rolling at her guilt trip. I know she's upset, but *she* also knows that I'll see her before day's end.

"Today, Madeline."

"Sure, Cal." I know she wants to hang up on me, but she doesn't, yet. I wait for the inevitable words to leave her lips. "I love you."

I smile into the phone. "I love you."

"Who do you love?" The door closes from behind me and I spin in my chair to see my best friend, Ryan, biting into an apple with a cup of coffee in his other hand.

"I'll talk to you later." I hang up the phone and stare at my best friend who is currently dressed like he just came from the gym. "Can't you knock?"

"And miss out on who you're clearly having phone sex with?" *Jesus Christ, this is not what I need right now. I've been calling this asshole all night, and now he shows up.*

"I told someone I loved them, and I'm having phone sex now?"

"That wasn't an *I love you*. That was an *I love plowing you from behind, send me a picture later*." He points at my phone. "Now, who was it?"

"A woman. Why are you here?"

"Well, you rang the alarm last night over Maddie, and this is me responding to said alarm. What woman?" He takes another obnoxious bite of his apple.

"Five hours later, thanks."

"I was coming off of a ninety hour week, and you said Maddie was fine and at your mother's. It could wait. You had half the force on the street last night. You didn't need me."

"My best friend and the detective? No, I didn't need you." The sarcasm drips from every word.

"You're evading the question? And…it's making me more intrigued. Tell me about this girl."

"Ryan, it's no one."

"And now you're hiding something."

I grab my phone and keys from my desk. I was already planning to leave for the day to go home and get some sleep before Maddie got out of school and now that Ryan is suddenly very curious about my new love life it's time to go before my face gives it all away.

He follows me out of the office and the station and I'm not in the mood for this interrogation when he calls my name. "Grayson."

I turn to face him when I'm just a few steps away from my jeep. "What?"

"I didn't become a Detective at twenty-six because I let things get by me, you know."

The implication is there, I'm sure of it. But what I'm not sure of is how he feels about it.

"And I didn't become the Chief of Police by not taking chances. What's your point?"

He shakes his head and looks away from me, staring into the distance before turning his gaze back to me. "You know what you're doing?"

"No."

He nods his head. "That's honest. Do you love her?"

I let out a breath, preparing to lay my feelings for Maddie out for yet another person. "Yeah." I nod.

"Damn." He crosses his arms. "What about Henry?"

"You know about Henry?" I ask, suddenly confused that he became the focus of this conversation.

He shrugs. "Well, I can only assume he'll be pissed when he finds out."

"He already knows, and he's definitely angry, and apparently taking it out on Aria." I rub my forehead as I think about how heartbroken she looked when she left last night. I sent her home after about an hour and told her to try and get some rest because it looked like she hadn't slept in a week.

"Well, with reason, I mean she's half to blame."

I rub my chin, my eyes narrowing slowly. "What? How do you figure?"

"Well, you two are having an affair," he says matter of factly.

My eyes widen and the word escapes me in a shout. "WHAT?" I take a step back, suddenly confused. "I'm not sleeping with Aria. Why would you think that?"

He tilts his head to the side. "I mean...with Maddie moving out, and you and Aria clearly avoiding each other like the plague at work, and everyone knows she's been having issues, I just... Wait a minute, why else would Henry be pissed?" I stare at my best friend for a moment, wondering how I'm going to blurt out the truth and more importantly how he'll take it, when his realization beats me to the punch. "Holy shit."

"Ryan..."

"Grayson." He points a finger at me. "Tell me that you are not sleeping with Maddie."

"I'm not *sleeping* with her, Ryan. I'm in love with her."

He puts his hands over his face and bends over dramatically before standing up straight and putting a fist to his mouth his eyes wide with terror. "Are you out of your fucking mind?"

"I don't know. Probably." I shake my head. "But I'm tired and tense and I need to talk to her, so now is really not the time to read me the riot act."

"How long?!" I start walking towards my car and he follows closely behind.

"Not as long as you think."

"Was she at least legal?"

"Yes, Ryan. Okay? This hasn't been going on for long okay?

She's been in love with me for…a while, and I'm just catching up. Now let it fucking go."

"Let it go? Cal…"

"I know, okay? I know, no one is going to think it's okay."

"How can *you* think it's okay? You raised her. You got into her mind and her heart…of course, she thinks she's in love with you."

"Look," I bark out at him, "I've already lost a brother over this shit. I get that people aren't exactly on board, but I'm not going to sit here and argue with you over it. I love her, I want to be with her, and I would do anything for her. I would never do anything to hurt Maddie. If that's not enough for you, then that's too damn bad." I slam my car door shut and I'm out of the parking lot in seconds.

∞

Madeline

My mouth drops open when I make it to the office and see why I've been summoned out of third period. The smile creeps onto my face the second I see him through the window of the main office. I had fallen into a troubled, restless sleep last night after tossing and turning for hours. I wanted him there, and then when I woke up this morning having fallen asleep with my hand wrapped firmly around my phone, my heart sank.

He didn't come.

But now he's here.

And holy fuck does he look delicious.

But why is he here?

I sling my bag over my shoulder and push my way into the office to see Cal leaning against the wall with a warm smile splayed on his face. He's wearing jeans and a leather jacket, his badge hanging around his neck, looking like some kind of sexy cop prepared to go undercover. "Hi.. Cal." I try to stop my voice from sounding like a woman so clearly lusting after a man, but it's no use. I can only hope that the office manager doesn't take notice. I look over at her as she looks at me from above her glasses and she shoos us off. "You've been excused for the day Madeline, we'll see you tomorrow."

Cal all but drags me out of the office and towards the front door.

"You're here."

He stops in his tracks and stares at me as a smile finds his lips. "Of course, I'm here, you needed me, and I need you. I need to make sure you're…okay after last night."

"So, you broke me out of school?" I'm shocked. Cal always stressed the importance of school and the value of getting a good education. Growing up, I was rarely allowed to miss school unless I was really sick, and even then, I'm talking fever and unable to keep down solid foods.

Who is this man?

His eyes rake me over from my feet to my eyes and I watch his eyes darken with need.

Oh.

"I'm sorry I didn't come last night…" He trails off. "Can I make it up to you?"

I look back towards the school and then at him. *Fuck, I want him. Bad.* Though we had sex last night it was rushed and frantic and quick and my adrenaline was at an all-time high. It was also the only time we've had sex since I moved into Margie's. *I needed more.* "My car is here."

He looks around the parking lot and shoves his hands in his pockets giving me a wolfish grin before sliding his sunglasses over his eyes. "Wanna meet me at home?"

"So, let me get this straight, you pulled me out of school at noon...to go have sex? Are you *sure* you're not an eighteen year old boy?"

"Trust me, sweetheart, the things I'm about to do to you are not things an eighteen year old boy can do."

We're barely through the front door before his pants are around his ankles and I'm pressed against the wall, his dick pressing against my sex through my panties under my skirt. "I need to taste your pretty cunt." He growls in my ear. "It's wet, isn't it? You got wet driving home thinking about the mess we're about to make between your legs, didn't you?"

"Cal...." I shut my eyes because his words have made me dizzy and I can't keep them open. My pussy feels like it's on fire, and I know the second he breathes near it, I'm going to come all over his face. I rub my sex against his dick, trying my hardest to get closer to him. "Off—off!" I cry out as he pokes me between my legs again. He sets me on shaky legs, and I manage to pull my boots and skirt off in record time.

"Everything comes off," he tells me as he pulls his shirt over his head. He's standing before me completely naked and my mouth falls open like I haven't seen him naked before. I pull my shirt over my head and unclasp my bra and send my panties down my legs, leaving us both naked and the attraction sizzling between us.

His arms are so defined, veins protrude with every flex of his arm, making me wetter at the apex of my thighs. The slickness is becoming more intense and I feel it starting to trickle down my thigh. His chest, his abs, the perfectly cut V of his pelvis leading down to his dick turns me into a puddle of want and need. His dick is standing straight up, hard and strong and prepared to rip me in two. This man is so virile and masculine it makes me weak in the knees. On top of the fact that he is so protective of me makes me feel safe and guarded, knowing that he'd rip anyone apart that ever touched me.

"You done?" he asks, taking a step forward and I look at him questioningly "Ogling my dick?"

I shake my head. "No."

"Well, show's over for now because I need my mouth on your pussy." He lifts me into his arms and then up even higher, pushing me against the wall and letting my legs rest over his shoulder.

"Oh my God, Cal!" I squeal, just as his tongue licks up the wetness that has trickled down my thighs. The tip of his tongue traces the trail, stopping just shy of my sex before moving to the other leg. I'm just about to ask him to put his mouth where I need it, when his lips find my folds. His hands are under my butt and his tongue is *everywhere*. It's crazed, frenzied, and borderline insane the way he's tasting me. Like a starving man that's been placed in front of food for the first time in years.

But Jesus, he knows what he's doing.

I can almost touch the ceiling with how high up I am, and when I look down, I realize just how far I am off the ground. "You're so…strong…you're a god, Cal Grayson. Holy fuck."

"You make me feel like a god," he murmurs against my sex, slowing his wild movements to slow controlled ones. His tongue snakes from the bottom of my pussy all the way up to my clit, before he sucks it into his mouth and I let my head fall back against the wall. "And I've been dying for a taste of you since last night."

"Oh fuck." The sounds that Cal and my pussy are making

are so erotic and sinful that it makes me blush, and when I look down and make eye contact with him, I detonate. His eyes never leave mine as I come, and somehow, I manage to keep my eyes open the entire time. Watching him, watch me. Our eyes locked together for what seems like an eternity during this intimate moment.

He pulls away from my sex and allows me to slide down his body, to the point where we are face to face. I wrap my legs and arms around him and he presses me back against the wall. His lips are wet and smell of my arousal, and I watch as he licks me off of them. "I love you," he tells me and my heart flutters just as it always does in these moments.

His ability to swing from this possessive caveman to this sweet lover is one of the things I love about him. "I love *you,* and I hate being away from you. Thank you for coming to get me," I whisper.

He walks us into the living room, leaving our clothes by the door and sits on the couch with me in his lap. His cock is still hard as granite so I line myself up with the tip and slide down on his shaft until he's completely sheathed inside. "Fuck." He grips my hips and begins to bounce me on his cock, sliding me up and down, my breasts bouncing with every thrust. He lets go of my hips to grab both breasts, bringing me closer to his mouth and flicks his tongue against the hard nubs as he continues to fuck me.

"Cal!" I throw my head back as he fucks me deeper, harder and faster.

"You're so perfect, Jesus Christ, Madeline."

My full name sets my body on fire. My eyes snap open and I quirk an eyebrow at him. He must sense where I'm going because he lets his head fall back and a growl leaves his lips. "Say it, baby." He grabs the back of my head and presses our foreheads together. "Say it."

"Daddy," I breathe out.

"Fuck."

"Daddy, *please.*"

"Please what, baby. Tell me what you need and Daddy will take care of it. Whatever it is."

"I need you to come, Daddy…" I press my lips to his neck before flicking my tongue out and running it along his pulse point. I nibble on his ear. "Come inside me."

His thrusts get erratic as he chases his orgasm. He pulls my face away from his neck and captures my lips in a bruising kiss. His tongue thrusts into my mouth at a speed that matches our movements. I know he's close, which is why I'm shocked when he switches our position to me on my back and my leg over his shoulder. But in this position, he can fuck me so much deeper.

My eyes roll back just as his dick hits that spot that only this position allows and I begin to spasm in his arms.

"That's my good girl." He groans. "Come for me, baby."

"Oh my God, yes, yes…" I shut my eyes, but they fly open when I feel a hand rubbing my nipple again.

"Sweet girl," he mumbles. "So fucking sweet." He reaches down and grabs my face and pulls me in for a kiss, all the while my leg is still over his shoulder.

Thank God, I was a dancer or I'd be fucked later.

Our tongues battle for dominance, but he wins. He always wins. His tongue strokes mine slowly and I feel my body beginning to build again. I pull away from his lips. "Cal, *please,*" I moan.

I stretch my toes, flexing and pointing my feet as hard as they can go as my body craves the imminent release that is seconds away. "I'm there with you, baby." He presses his forehead to mine as I dig my nails into his back, my body shaking under the force of his thrusts.

"Oh my God, I'm going to come," I cry out. He groans out my name from the bite of my fingertips and I feel his cock swell and release, flooding my insides. I'm a few seconds behind him, the moment his finger finds my clit. After two rubs over the swollen bundle, I'm shattering around him and screaming his name. My body is wound so tight in expectation of the release that the relief is so delicious it makes me feel as if I'm flying. My eyes flutter closed as my body, now loose and languid, floats back down to Earth. "Holy shit, Cal."

He's still leaning over me, his cock still inside of me as he slowly pulls out. He taps his dick against my clit and I twitch and squeal in response to his touch on my sensitive flesh.

He moves up my body and nestles in behind me. Pulling the blanket over us and spooning me. "Do you want to continue this upstairs?"

Several hours later, I'm sliding out of bed trying not to wake the sleeping man who'd just fucked the life out of me not even an hour ago, when familiar warm hands encase around my middle and pull me back to bed. "Where are you going? I'm nowhere near finished with you." His lips find my neck and suck at the space that never fails to send a sizzle through me. I close my eyes reveling in the feeling of that sinful mouth. His erection presses into my backside and the space between my legs throbs with need.

It's nearing six thirty, and I know without a doubt that Sasha would make good on her promise and show up at Margie's at promptly eight o'clock to go to Melanie's. The last thing I need is for her to show up before I'm there as if she has no idea where I am.

Oh, the tangled web.
And now I have to figure out what to tell Cal.

He fucked me almost frantically when we got upstairs, almost as if I was going to disappear any second. I know last night shook him up, possibly even more than me, and he's trying to convince himself that I'm okay. That even though he couldn't prevent it from happening, he could protect me.

"It's getting late," I tell him as I reluctantly pull out of his grasp. I slide out of his bed, naked as the day I was born, and from his gaze, I can tell he appreciates what he sees. It's almost dark, but the last bit of the day's sun is streaming through the blinds and creating an orange glow on my body, illuminating the several hickeys all over my torso and inner thighs. I slide my panties up my legs, my body aching with every step as I'm reminded of where he's been.

He looks at the clock behind him. "Late? Baby, it's six thirty." He sits up, giving me a glorious view of his torso and I briefly wonder if he's been working out more since I left. "I was kind of hoping I could convince you to stay." He winks and stands up allowing his cock to stand proudly between us. My tongue darts out to lick my lips and I feel his hand wrapped around my jaw.

"Was that an invitation?" he asks, and his words send a chill through me. I look up and he shoots me a wink. *God, I want his dick in my mouth.* Despite the fact that just earlier today, I'd been on my knees in front of him in the shower, I want it again. I would never get tired of doing that to him. The sense of power I felt, despite the fact that I was beneath him, is like nothing I've ever experienced. Even though I was on my knees, I know I owned him in those moments.

Maybe I could come back later. I roll my eyes inwardly. *Fuck, I've become one of those women.*

That's the last thought I have before Cal's lips are on mine and I'm lifted into his arms. "Wait wait, Cal." I pull back away from his lips that taste like I'm not leaving this room for another hour.

"Wait?" He frowns. "I was preparing to put my mouth on your pussy, and you want me to wait?"

I let out a breath and curse Sasha and Melanie and Melanie's mom who couldn't wait another day to bring a baby into the world. "Yes, babe…I have to go."

He sets me to my feet and crosses his arms. "Go?"

"I'm uhh…" I let out a breath, "hanging out with some friends." I grab my bra from the floor and slide it on. "It's Melanie's birthday and she's throwing a party. Sasha is meeting me at Margie's so I should probably be there when she gets there or else I'm fucked." I look at my watch, watching as the time inches closer to seven.

"Oh?" He sits down and immediately I regret two things for putting that look on his face. First, for agreeing to go at all, and second, for waiting this long to tell him. "Were you not going to tell me?"

"Of course, I was. I just did."

"You just tried sneaking out of here, Maddie."

"I was going to wake you up. I wasn't hiding anything." I shrug.

"Are you staying the night at this party? I don't want you driving late at night after what just happened. Are guys going to be there?"

I put my hands on my hips and cock my head to the side. "Who wants to know?"

He furrows his brow and stands up pulling his sweatpants on. "What do you mean 'who wants to know?' *I* want to know."

"No, is the man that raised me asking? Or the one I'm currently dating?"

He takes a step towards me, invading my personal space. "Don't test me Madeline Elizabeth." His nostrils flare and his eyes darken to almost onyx. I can tell he's gritting his teeth because his jaw is sharp and taut and I resist the urge to touch him.

"Still not exactly clear which *Daddy* I'm talking to."

Before I can move out of his reach, I'm up against the wall with his hand inside my panties rubbing the wet bundle of nerves that this small back and forth caused. "You know I worry. You're not twenty-one, Maddie, and if you're drinking, I would prefer you stay there, and especially after what just happened. But as the man who's laid claim over your heart and your pussy—yes, I would like to know if boys will be there as well..." I see the jealousy and more importantly the hurt in his eyes and a flare of pain spikes in my heart.

Every once in a while, Sasha goes to parties without Mike and it drives him insane. Sasha thinks it's hilarious and taunts him endlessly. She'd never do anything because she loves that guy more than anything, but she enjoys making him jealous.

Doing that to Cal doesn't sound like fun.

"Fine you can take me and pick me up," I tell him, trying to appease him, but I know it's not just about that. "And funny you say that, because it's a good thing I don't like boys." I raise an eyebrow at him. "I like men. One man." I cup his face. "The love of my life." I press my lips to his. "You know, I've never dated anyone seriously. Yes, here and there, but no one that has ever been worthy of my attention or my heart. I've kissed what, like three guys before you, and no one has ever touched me where *you've* touched me. This isn't the first party I've been to where there have been guys and alcohol...so what are you worried about? That I'll forget about you?"

"No, I just...worry." He grits out. "About you in those environments in general."

"Ah, so the parental and boyfriend Cal are ganging up on me, I see." I pull away from him and grab my shirt, pulling it over my head.

"Baby…" he starts.

"No, that's not fair. You can't be my boyfriend and *that* Cal at the same time. You have to pick one." I demand.

"Fine. You're grounded."

I can't even stop the giggle that escapes my lips before I'm full-on laughing. "Good one."

"I mean it, Maddie. You can't go." He points at me.

I blink my eyes a few times as I wait for him to tell him that he's kidding. *Excuse me?* "I *can't?* You're insane."

"You heard me."

"So, let me get this straight: I'm grounded and that means what exactly? I have to stay home? At Margie's? Or here? Does my *grounding* include fucking you?"

"Don't be so crass, Maddie." He stalks past me and picks up his phone.

"What are you doing?"

"Calling my mother."

What!? "You've lost it." I reach for his phone and yank it out of his hand and he tackles me to the bed in response, pinning me down and pushing my hands above my head and pushing his phone to the ground.

"Watch your tone, Maddie."

"Or what?" I lift my chin defiantly and raise an eyebrow, daring him. We stare at each other for a moment, both of our hearts racing, and I can almost feel his beating in perfect rhythm with mine.

He pushes my panties to the side and slips his digits inside of me. "I don't want you to go," he whispers.

"Why?"

"Do you have to ask?"

"Maybe I want to hear it."

"Because the idea of you being around a bunch of horny guys pisses me off, okay?" He pulls his fingers out of me and takes a step back off the bed. "I know I can't stop you from going…"

Now that he's acting more rational, I see more than just the possessiveness in his eyes. "Don't you trust me?"

"Of course, I do, it's just…those guys can give you something I can't."

"There's nothing they can give me that I *want*."

"You can be out in the open with them…"

"I don't care about that." I shake my head. "I mean I would love to be able to go out on dates and stuff with *you*." I get off the bed and wrap my arms around him. "I won't stay, but I have to go. It's her birthday and I've been neglecting my friends ever since you and I got together."

His shoulders sink and I see the red tinge in his ears. "I know, and I'm sorry I've been keeping you from them."

"You haven't been *keeping* me from anything. I've wanted to be with you. I still want to be with you." I raise onto the balls of my feet and wrap my hand around his neck bringing him closer. "Every second of every day. But…that's unhealthy, or whatever." I press a kiss to his mouth. "I'm still figuring out who I am, and I have to be able to exist outside of a relationship with a man. *With you.*"

He sighs and wraps his arms around me. "Fair. I guess," he grumbles. "When did you get to be so smart?"

"I don't know. I had a pretty great father figure who taught me some pretty important shit."

"Oh really."

"Like how to fuck, for one."

"Madeline," he growls as his hand grabs my ass and squeezes.

I giggle and press my lips to his. "Am I still grounded?" I ask when I pull away.

He sighs. "Were you going to listen to me if I said yes?"

"No."

"Then go." He rolls his eyes. "Keep your phone and your necklace on."

"I never take it off, and my phone is never off."

"Good girl." The fire between my legs, that had cooled into a barely lit ember flickers to life at his words, and a whimper escapes my lips.

I bite my bottom lip and look up at him. "Okay, maybe I have like ten minutes," I say as I send my panties back down my legs.

Twenty-One

Madeline

MY EYES FLIT TO MELANIE'S BACK DOOR AS IT OPENS, AND A SLEW of guys walk in with a billow of smoke. I'm standing near the built-in bar of her basement sipping the one beer I've had all night, just to keep Sasha off my case while my friends continue to take shots like they're immune to hangovers. Melanie's house is enormous, but we usually stay confined to the basement after one wild party caused more than a few broken things, even more stolen things, and Melanie grounded for a full six months. Her father was a CEO of some huge company based in Portland which sent him and her mother away for galas, what felt like every other weekend, leaving a reckless Melanie to her own devices.

Melanie had set up a beer pong table in the center of the room, where two guys from the football team are currently going undefeated for the second hour while the rest of the team surrounds them. A group of six or seven are in the corner playing drinking games that require bouncing a quarter into a shot glass, and the rest of us are in the bar area. A few people are outside smoking—cigarettes or weed—causing me to sniff my hair every few seconds. Cal will murder me if I come home smelling like an ashtray. *And I do not mean that it in any way sexual.*

"Why aren't you drinking?" Sasha asks me as Mike walks in and makes his way over to us.

"I have a headache," I say without even meeting her gaze. A telltale sign that I'm lying, and more importantly that I don't care that I'm lying.

She rolls her eyes at me, hearing the lie, but deciding to go with it. "You know what helps with headaches? Tequila." She raises a shot to me before downing it. I roll my eyes at her when Mike approaches us with a familiar face in tow.

"There's the prettiest girl in all of Oregon." He wraps his arms around her, sticking his face in her neck and she squeals as he spins her around.

"What took you so long? I'm already drunk." She pouts as he slips his hand into her back pocket and kisses her square on the mouth. "You smell good."

I roll my eyes at my best friend and her boyfriend who rarely keep the PDA to a minimum when they're sober. They are borderline offensive when they've been drinking. *Maybe this is where I should make my exit.*

"Hey, Maddie." Brad steps next to me as Sasha and Mike continue to pretend that they're the only ones in the room. He's wearing the same letterman jacket and a pair of jeans that outline the muscles in his legs and thus seem a bit too tight. He's still clean shaven and it makes me take note that even if I wasn't with Cal, I wouldn't be attracted to him. "You're a hard girl to see. I've been hoping I'd run into you since we sort of went out last month."

"She's been MIA." Sasha rolls her eyes. "*I've* even barely seen her except for at school!"

I ignore Sasha's dramatics. "Brad...hey, how are you?" *I'm not sure how to handle this situation. Is he still interested? Or had he gotten the hint when I didn't reach out after Cal crashed our date? Is he planning to ask me out again?* I decide to wait for him to do any of those things before I just assume he wants a real chance with me.

One he does not have.

"Good, I'm glad you're here." He starts and my eyes widen in preparation of letting him down easily. "Not like that." He shakes his head. "Just...I felt bad that I acted like a dick on that date."

Phew. "Oh! Oh my God, not at all. You weren't a dick. I just...left. I'm sorry about that, I wasn't really feeling great, and Sasha dragged me out without telling me what I was walking into." I shoot her a look, but she seems unbothered with Mike's tongue down her throat. "Okay, I'm walking away from this." I point at the two who'd be defiling one of Melanie's guestrooms within the hour. Brad follows me outside onto the patio and I make sure to leave enough space between me and the smokers which dangerously enough means I'm alone with Brad. *Fuck, I didn't think this through.*

Maddie, relax you're talking to a guy. You should be able to do that without Cal turning into a caveman. The words in my brain are rational, but they don't stop me from taking a glance around the patio just in case Cal has manifested.

"Mike told me about what happened...why that guy acted like that...the one you live with?"

"Oh..." I clear my throat. "Yeah, he's just protective."

I close my eyes, my heart thumping in my chest as my brain fights to stay in the present and not return to the night that my life changed forever. I take a deep breath and for a quick second I smell my mother's perfume and the pain lessens slightly. *I miss you, Mama.*

"That must have been really hard." He shakes his head before putting a hand on my shoulder gently then letting it graze my back. He rubs it in circles and the fog of my past immediately lifts as I return to the present. "I can't even imagine."

I move so that I'm out of his grasp and try to put some space between us. *Why is this man so handsy?* "Maybe I should get back inside," I start when he grabs my arm.

"Maddie, I'm really a nice guy. I don't see why you can't give me a chance." I don't know if he drank something or did something moments before getting to Melanie's and only now is it catching up with him because I notice his pupils are dilated and slightly glazed.

Say no. Say. NO. "Brad, you seem great but…"

"Come on, Mike said you don't have a boyfriend. One date and I'll be the perfect gentleman."

"There's a lot of reasons a girl can say no that has nothing to do with whether she has a boyfriend. As Mike should have probably prefaced, I don't date much." I cross my arms defensively. "I'm super busy and I just don't have the time for a boyfriend."

"A girl has to eat though, right? I'm talking dinner. I'm not talking about the rest of your life. Or even the rest of the month." He raises an eyebrow at me and I shake my head.

I should have just said I have a boyfriend. One that didn't go to my school.

And have Sasha refute that and become even more relentless with her questioning? Pass, my subconscious argues.

"I eat plenty," I answer, before leaving him out on the patio. I grab a bottle of water from Melanie's refrigerator and down it, preparing my exit when Sasha is immediately next to me.

"You are *not* leaving."

"Watch me."

"You've been drinking."

"I've had one light beer in four hours. I'm okay." I tell her before I finish the bottle in one swig. After a series of more hugs and goodbyes followed by a million drunken, *I love you's* from Melanie and a few of our friends, I make it to my car.

"You're leaving so soon?" My hand is hovering over my

handle just as Brad appears what seems to be out of no-fucking-where looking like the suspect in an episode of *To Catch a Predator*.

"I should go home."

"Oh, come on, have a drink. It's your friend's birthday." He moves around to my side of the car and leans against my door, stopping me from opening it.

"Brad, I really want to leave, can you please move?" I smile, trying not to provoke him or push him to do anything crazy. My hand immediately goes to my necklace on instinct, just as it always does when something doesn't feel right. It makes me feel closer to Cal and usually gives me the courage to get through whatever is in front of me. His eyes move down my body lasciviously and I immediately step back. I take a deep breath, swallowing down the nerves as I reach for the pepper spray in my clutch.

"I'm not going to hurt you, Maddie." He smiles and leans closer to me. "I want to do the opposite." His eyes close, and he sways towards me. "I want to make you feel good." His hand comes to trace my face and I take another step back.

"Please...no." I'm prepared to run, when I feel something right at my back.

Oh, for the love of God. I resign myself to being thoroughly fucked, outside by myself with two men that are much bigger than me when a familiar voice fills the space around us. "Beat it, before I kick your ass." Henry comes into view from my side and stands between us. He looks like he's lost some weight just in the two weeks it's been since I've seen him and his beard is fully grown in. "If I ever hear that you've touched her again, I'll rip your limbs from your body and beat you with them. Then you won't be able to do whatever bullshit sport you think you're so good at." Brad takes a step back and holds his hands up.

"Listen we were just talking..." he begins to stammer and I

can see him getting red around his neck.

"Before or after she asked you to move? Because she asked a few times and even said *no*. Do you know what 'no' means?"

He looks at Henry and then me before he turns and practically races back towards the house. I let out a breath, my heart pounding in my chest. "Thank you. Oh my gosh, Henry! It's so good to see you." I wrap my arms around him in a hug, but he stiffens in my grasp. I pull back and now that I'm looking at him face on, I see that his eyes are bloodshot, making me wonder if he's on something.

"You too, Mads. Listen, can you give me a ride?"

I frown, wondering where his car is and then a flood of questions enter my mind. "Sure, but…what are you even doing here?"

"Friend of mine lives around the corner." He runs a hand through his hair and makes his way to my passenger side. "So, that ride? I left my car near a hotel in town."

"Oh, yeah. Sure, of course! A hotel?"

"Yeah," he says as we settle into the car. "Aria and I are taking some time…apart."

"Oh no!" I can't stop the tears from welling in my eyes as I remember walking down that aisle at their wedding, tossing flowers from a wicker basket. "I'm sorry, Henry."

"It's okay. Things happen, you know? People change. Grow apart." He looks out the window as we pull away from Melanie's house. "But I think maybe this is for the best. I've been thinking I need a change of scenery anyway."

"You're moving?" I wonder if Cal knows about any of this.

"Thinking about it. Maybe somewhere east."

"There's no chance you and Aria could work it out?"

"I don't know, Maddie. Take Tuckerman Street." He points and I follow his direction, this is the opposite way of town so I'm wondering where exactly this hotel is.

"Shit, I forgot to text Cal. I'm just going to call him really quick."

"Not necessary," he interjects. "He knows you're with me."

"He does?"

"Yeah," he says and his voice is final. It makes me want to probe, but I figure he'll be out of the car soon enough and then I can talk to Cal.

It seems as if we're driving for ages when we pull into a parking lot of a rundown tavern on the other side of town. I turn to look at him, waiting for him to get out, because, to be honest, he's kind of giving me the creeps. He's just staring out the window when he starts talking.

"You know, what you and my brother are doing is wrong, Maddie."

Great, here we go. "Listen, Henry…"

"I'm talking," he growls and I bite my bottom lip nervously. *He's never talked to me like that before.*

"I can't believe you let him take advantage of you. Were you that desperate for attention and affection from him?"

"Okay, Henry, I don't want to talk…"

I barely have a chance to react before my face is literally on fire from his fist. "I. said. I. was. talking." His voice is low and sinister as I hold my hand to my throbbing cheek, my body in complete shock that Henry just hit me. "Now, we're going to go for a little drive in my truck." He unbuckles my seatbelt and points to the black truck at the edge of the abandoned parking lot. "Get the fuck out of the car," he whispers in my ear as he leans across my lap and opens my door. "I wouldn't do anything stupid if I were you. Unless of course…you want me to shoot you with your boyfriend's gun." He rolls his neck in a circle and I cringe hearing him crack it so aggressively. The sound is the only noise in the quiet car besides my breathing that I'm trying to keep under control. He waves the gun in front of my face and my blood runs cold seeing it so close. Cal always kept guns locked and away from me, so I don't have much experience with them up close and personal. "Leave you for dead with his bullet in you. Wouldn't that be some irony." He chuckles and a grin finds his face. My heart pounds in my chest and I can hear the blood rushing into my ears. My ears are ringing from how hard he hit me, but I think I'm definitely in shock because I haven't shed one tear yet.

"Why…why?" I manage to whisper.

His finger traces gingerly down my face and I flinch at his touch and try to move further away from him. "Your skin is so smooth. God, no wonder he's so enthralled with you." He cups my chin and jerks me towards him. "Right, so you asked, why?"

I nod. The tears have started to slide down my face now, the shock wearing off and my mind and body realizing that I'm in huge fucking trouble. I pray to God, Henry forgets about my necklace and lets me leave it on, allowing Cal to find me sooner, but my guess is he'll remember and take it from me.

"Because you and my brother need space. Trust me I thought about just exposing everything and ruining Cal's reputation. But then I realized, I would much rather ruin his life."

My lip trembles as I think about how I might never see him again and then my eyes widen in realization at his words. "Where…where's Aria? Did you hurt her?" My voice is quiet and meek.

"Out," he growls and he pulls his gun out of his pocket and points it at me. "No fucking games, Shaw."

I gulp and slide out of the car, gripping my clutch for dear life. I start walking with him right behind me when he rips the clutch from me. "Not so fast." He opens my bag and grabs my phone before turning it off and slamming it hard into the ground. My heart sinks, knowing that the GPS is now turned off and I put my hands over my eyes and almost fall to my knees. He's killed my phone and he's taking me away from my car that is programmed with a tracker. If he remembers about my necklace I'm done. I spin away from him and reach up as stealthily as I can to rip the necklace from my neck. The chain digs into my skin but I welcome the bite as the clasp breaks. At least, if he doesn't see it, he might forget that I have it.

I slip the necklace into the pocket of my coat when I feel him right at my heels. As soon as we approach the car, he binds my hands in front of me, tightly. The rope digs into my wrists and I wince at the burn. "Don't pull, they bite, little one." He winks at me before shoving me into the back seat. "Lay the fuck down."

"But…"

"NOW," he growls and I do as he says, fresh tears springing to my eyes and sliding down my face. I realize once I'm inside, I don't recognize this car and I've been in Henry's car at least a thousand times, which makes this scarier than anything.

Has he been plotting this all along?

"Wait, Henry…this isn't your…car…?" The conclusions are forming in my brain before the words are even out. *He's the guy that almost ran me off the road the other day.*

"You were always a smart girl." I hear as he starts the truck.

A shiver runs through me and I turn on my back, staring up into the roof of the car. *Keep him talking Maddie.*

"You…you could have killed me last night…" My teeth are chattering together in the frosty car, and I see my breath.

"I barely even touched you, don't be so dramatic." He waves a hand towards me.

"But…but it was *you*." It's so dark, I can't make out

anything as we continue to drive. We could be going North to Washington, or hell even Canada. I manage to get my bound hands in my pocket, so I can hold my necklace and onto the hope that Cal will save me.

"Madeline, you have become so reliant on my brother. He's sheltered you so much. You're not even the least bit prepared for the real world, and that should scare you. Me tailgating you isn't the scariest thing out there, you know." My fists flex instantly, wishing I could just hit him once for speaking about this whole situation like it's nothing. I watch as he unscrews a fifth of what smells like vodka and brings it to his lips. "Want some? I know you're a bit of a lush."

I ignore him and go back to his earlier comment, not wanting him to think that *he's* the scariest thing I've encountered. *Never let them see your fear.* "I'm fully aware you're not the scariest given that I was in the house when my father murdered my mother."

"Your mom was probably a slut too," he grumbles. "I'm sure that's where you get it."

I see red. I've always heard that expression, but I didn't think people actually *saw* red clouding their peripheral vision. I had no idea rage could manifest into a color and take over your senses until you're so blind that all you can see is the color most associated with anger. "Fuck you, Henry." I spit out. "You're going to burn in hell for this."

"Oh, sweetheart. I'll see you there."

CAL

"**W**HY THE FUCK IS HER PHONE OFF?" I SLAM MY FIST AGAINST Aria's dashboard *hard* as we make our way towards the location of Maddie's car. I've sent cops to Melanie's house and told them to strip that house of every inch to ensure Maddie is not there. *And all those fuckers are coming in for questioning.*

"Cal, calm down." I watch as Aria swerves into a different lane, missing a car by a mere millimeter. But I don't care, nothing matters in this moment but getting to my girl. *Hang on, baby.*

"I'm not going to calm down. Something's wrong with Maddie, and I'm not there. Maddie needs me, Aria." I feel my chest tightening as the thoughts of letting her down overwhelm me. Why else would her phone be off and her car reporting that she's on the other side of town when she was supposed to be at her friend's party.

She would never get in the car this late at night without letting me know where she's going. Something's wrong.

I rub my face, and my leg begins to bounce nervously. "Can't you go any faster?"

"I'm going eighty, Cal. We won't be any good to her if we crash." My phone rings and I answer it on the first ring.

"What do you know?" I bite out.

"Cal," Ryan's voice comes over the phone and immediately

I fear the worst, "the kids are all wrecked, but they're saying she left."

"Where the hell is Sasha Parker?" I ask about Maddie's best friend.

"She was…occupied with her boyfriend when we got there. When they were fully clothed, she said she left about an hour ago. But she's borderline hysterical now. She's freaking out that you don't know where she is."

I press a hand to my forehead. "Let her go. Issue citations to everyone else." I bite out. Even though Sasha is a troublemaker, I know she cares about Maddie and has been a good friend to her. Maddie was quiet and reserved her freshman year and didn't talk to anyone. Sasha came bulldozing into her life and decided they were best friends and ultimately helped bring her out of her shell. She's a sweet girl, she just gets into too much trouble.

"She wants to speak to you."

"Put her on," I grunt. I don't have it in me to deal with her, but maybe she knows more than she told Ryan.

"Cal!" I hear the tears in her voice. "Cal, you have to find her."

"I know, Sasha. I'm fucking trying. But her phone is off and her car is in a bad part of town. Was there anyone at this party that you didn't know?"

"No! It was just the usual crowd. Melanie said no randos after the last time. Cal, we should have made sure she got to her car safely. I'm sorry!"

"It's okay, Sasha," I say even though it's anything but fine. *All those fucking guys there, and no one could have seen her to her car?* I know Sasha's boyfriend was usually a standup guy, which makes me think that he was too busy thinking with his dick around the time that Maddie left.

"Listen, I'll call you if I hear something. Please keep your phone on in case she calls you."

"She won't call me before you Cal...You know that." She sniffles. "She loves you so much."

I swallow and clear my throat, hearing her unspoken words. *Did Maddie tell her? Or is she reading between the lines?* "Right, well, just keep me posted."

"Okay."

We make it to the bar that looks like a crime scene. Maddie's car is parked in a spot, and I immediately spot her phone next to her car. *No.*

I'm out of the car instantly, and reach for it when Aria screams for me to stop.

"You're not thinking clearly. Prints Cal," she says before she pulls on a glove and picks it up before putting it in a bag. "We need to get this back to the station."

"I'm not leaving Maddie's car here." I notice the keys are still on the seat, making me wonder if it hasn't been long since she's been here. I'm honestly surprised no one has fucked with it. "I need to keep following the tracker. Her necklace is still sending me a signal." When I realized that her necklace was moving, but her car and phone were staying in one place, I wasn't sure which one was actually with Maddie. It seems that they're moving west but they're not far from us. "I'm going to take Maddie's car."

"You sure you want to go alone?" Aria looks at me with her signature look and shakes her head.

"I'll send for backup."

Aria reaches for her radio and sends out an SOS for a missing person on Madeline Shaw. As soon as I hear her name, I lose it. I almost collapse where I stand, and if it wasn't for Aria within arm's reach, I probably would have hit the ground.

"You're not going anywhere alone."

"I'll—"

"No, this is too personal for you, and you'll lose it whenever you find her, regardless of the situation."

"If someone has my girl, they are going the fuck down."

Flashing lights surround us, and before I can blink, yellow police tape is moving in front of the bar, they're dusting Maddie's cherry red Volkswagen for prints and already have Maddie's phone in custody.

I guess when the police chief's girl goes missing, everyone reports for duty.

"Let's go, Grayson," Aria says as she gets in the car. I get in the passenger seat, the adrenaline starting to slow and my heart feeling heavy in my chest.

Aria must note my somber mood because her words slice through the tension in the car. "Cut that shit out, Cal. Now is not the time to give up. Maddie needs you to keep it together."

"I looked in her car, Aria." I shake my head as I prepare to speak my thoughts. "There weren't a whole lot of signs of struggle. No tire marks. Maddie's car looked the same." I let my head rest against the back of the seat. "She might be wherever she is… willingly." Maybe she ran. Maybe this was all too much for her, and she ran *from me.*

"Bullshit, and you don't believe that."

"I would rather that than someone taking her. You think I want to think about her ending this? But it's better than the alternative. It would hurt me to lose her *now*, but it would kill me to lose her forever."

"Cal, she's going to be okay. We're going to find her. But I need you to come back from the dark side. I need you to stay positive. Where does her necklace say she is?" I look down and see that it's stopped, in a town not too far from us.

"Fuck, it stopped." My heart races wondering if she ditched her necklace or if maybe we're close.

We're driving for another twenty minutes when the one lane road becomes narrower as we come to the edge of a forest.

"We can't take the car in there, it might spook them," Aria says. "I'm calling for back up."

"Tell them to stand down," I tell her. "I'm going in."

Madeline

I'm tied to the ceiling, the burn of the tight ropes cutting into my flesh. My arms are raised above my head with a rag stuffed in my mouth and I'm missing half of my clothes in a freezing cold room. My feet are frozen solid as Henry removed my socks and forced me to stand on the freezing cold floor. My body almost feels numb with how cold I am and my vision is starting to blur. I blink my eyes several times, trying to regain focus. *Stay awake, Maddie, don't pass out.* He took off my pants, which was scary as hell, watching his eyes burn into my exposed flesh as he pulled my jeans off. A wicked chuckle slithered over me as he snapped my underwear against my skin like a promise of what was to come.

So, that's how this ends? Bile rises in my throat at the thought. I'm grateful I am still wearing a shirt, allowing me to keep a modicum of modesty. My eyes float over to my coat that was tossed in the corner with my other clothes and I just pray my necklace is still sending a signal to Cal's phone. My cheek still hurt from his punch and I can see that it's already started to swell when I glance downwards.

My mind struggles to stay in the present, and I can feel myself slowly disassociating from the trauma and the state of this situation. The promise of death and destruction is everywhere

I look in the small room and I find my head returning to the last time death breathed down my neck. I can hear my father screaming, my mother crying, the crash and bang of things breaking and then *nothing*.

The door slams open forcing my drooping lids back open and Henry puts a bottle to his lips. "So," he slurs, "you asked me why." We've been here for about an hour at this point, most of which I've been in here by myself. *Not that I've minded.* I've spent the majority of the hour wondering how I'm going to get out of here, and if it were possible to get out of these ropes. Short of breaking my wrists, no. My arms are exhausted, my muscles burning despite the icy temperatures. "I figured, I owe you a biiiiiiit of an explanation." He takes another sip and moves closer to me.

My chest moves up and down rapidly. "Cal…your precious Cal ruins everything." He puts a finger up and snaps them. "You need pictures."

Tears stream down my face as I realize what's about to happen. He wouldn't confess unless he didn't plan on killing me. The water that I chugged just before I left the party starts to catch up with me, coupled with the feelings of terror has urine sliding down my leg and into a puddle on the floor. Henry comes back into the room and shakes his head, a disgusted snarl on his lips. "Are you a dog? You can't keep it together?"

I sniffle and he holds a picture in front of my face. "History lesson. This was before your time. Before precious Maddie came in and became the center of everyone's universe." He rolls his eyes and the obvious disdain and resentment is so evident, it makes me wonder how I never picked up on it before. *Was he that good at hiding his feelings from* everyone? My thoughts are interrupted when he thrusts a picture in my face.

"Look, bitch," he snarls. "You wanted answers so bad. THIS

is *my* father." He points at a tall man standing next to Margie and him and Cal when they were much younger. "Obviously Margie." He points. "Me and Cal. The little bastard that ruined everything."

I wince at his harsh words. "Note that I didn't say *our* father. Nope, just mine. Turns out my dear old mom had a little boyfriend. She got pregnant and had Cal and then my father left. He abandoned me because she gave birth to that little shit!" My eyes widen when he produces a knife from his back pocket. He runs his finger up the blade and pokes the blade through the photo and through Cal's young face. I squeeze my eyes shut to forget the image of the knife going through the picture. My mouth is sore from having this rag stuffed inside but I feel my bottom lip wobble slightly. "Now, of course, this is all new information." He tosses the photo to the side. "I had no idea any of this until last week. My father fucking *died*, Maddie. He died and I never even got a chance to know him. I never got to say goodbye. Because of HIM! My father left me and it's all Cal's fucking fault!" He puts his knife in my face. "And then *you*."

I whimper. *What did I have to do with this? I wasn't even born yet, let alone in the Grayson's life.*

"You came into the picture and then all of a sudden Aria wasn't concerned with having children. She had *you*. Even though YOU WEREN'T OUR CHILD. I waited and waited for her to be ready, for years. Then I realized that you were enough for her. Having you filled the void of the child we lost. The one *we* created. God, I've hated you for so long." He growls and I sniffle. "I felt like an asshole for hating a child but you just ruined fucking *everything*."

He slides his knife across my arms and down my legs and he presses it in slightly. I scream into the rag when I feel a pierce of the blade

...and then I hear *his* voice like a boom. "Drop it or I'll fucking shoot you."

I don't have much range of motion based on how I'm tied up but I hear his voice and then he's in front of me, a gun pointed at Henry who's kneeling in front of me. Cal doesn't look at me, my guess because he knows it would throw him off and he needs to stay focused.

"Baby brother," Henry slurs. "Oh wow, I'm shocked you found us so quickly. I had no doubt you would, you were always like a bloodhound when it came to this one." He chuckles and stands up. "I will say though, I finally get the allure about her. She smells...fucking decadent." Cal cocks his gun, holding it to his forehead.

"Madeline, close your eyes."

I do as he says but I can still hear. "Why?" Cal's voice wavers slightly, but still mainly full of conviction.

"Again, with the *why*. Maddie and I already had this nice little talk about our slut mother."

I hear a punch and the sound of bones cracking and I open one eye to see Henry on the ground. "Don't you ever speak about my mother that way."

"God, you are such a mama's boy. Well, for the sake of everyone being on the same page." He spits out some blood. "Your mother had an affair." He chuckles. "You're not really a Grayson, I guess."

I open the other eye slowly. "What?" Cal takes a step back, his eyes wide with confusion, devastation, sadness. *Everything*. I can't imagine what Cal is going through in this moment. Henry has officially lost his mind, kidnapped me and I'm tied up in the corner. Now, on top of everything, he's about to learn that he and Henry have different fathers. I just want to wrap my arms around him and shield him from the pain that is seeping into his veins like a poison he'll never be completely free from.

"Margie fucked some guy and got pregnant with you. I don't know who, neither did *my* father."

"How...how do you know this?"

"Because he DIED you fucking dick! He died, and I never got to know him! His current wife reached out to me a week ago. I flew to Boston to meet her, and she told me everything. Mommy Dearest broke his fucking heart when she had an affair and he never got over it. God, he wanted to hate you. But he couldn't. But he also couldn't look at you every day and see what she'd done." My heart breaks in my chest hearing Henry put the sins of everyone on Cal's head. Margie's infidelity, Henry's father leaving and then never reaching out.

None of this is your fault, Cal.

I watch as Cal looks away for just a second, his guard lowering as Henry's words hit him hard. Under normal circumstances, he wouldn't have. He wouldn't have blinked twice. But it's his brother, and I'm here, and I know it's throwing his police intuition off. There's no other reason why he'd let his guard down and give Henry the opening. Henry, who's now standing, kicks him in his chest sending him and his gun flying from his hand and they both reach for it. Henry gets to it first and manages to get to his feet which sends a feeling of dread and terror through me. I thought he was drunker, but I wonder if I was confusing it with being high because now his eyes look almost manic. I'm screaming over the rag, and I'm trying so hard to push it out of my mouth so I can scream or cry or tell Cal I love him. Henry points the gun at Cal, keeping it a mere inch from his forehead. *Kill me first, please. I can't watch Cal die.* "So, here's how it's going to go. Trust me, I would love to kill you first, but I want you to watch what I do to your precious Maddie first."

"Fuck. You," Cal growls. His eyes are angry, but I can see

the pain in them and it weighs heavily on my heart. I don't think I've ever seen Cal cry, but his eyes are glazed and my legs almost give out from underneath me when I see the first tear escape and trickle down his face. "I can't believe you did this." He blinks his eyes, clearing the tears from his eyes. "I've always looked up to you."

"I didn't do anything, dear brother. *You* did this. Your rotten fucking existence. You and your slut dug your own graves." He cocks the gun and the sound is almost deafening.

I love you. I love you. I love you. I chant in my head, as I squeeze my eyes shut and prepare for the end.

In that second, something whizzes past my ear so quietly, I thought it was some sort of flying insect. My eyes open and I try to turn and look to see what it was just as the door flies open, and Henry sinks to the floor, red pooling from his chest as his mouth falls open and his eyes are wide with horror.

Oh my God!

I squeeze my eyes shut and scream so loud and so hard over the rag, I think I'm going to throw up. I vaguely hear Cal call for me, but the sounds are all running together. My vision is blurred and black spots encroach my sight. The weight of the day comes crashing around me and I suddenly feel the inability to stay standing a second longer. Cops are surrounding me in an instant and before I realize it, my arms are free and the rag is expelled from my mouth. My limbs feel like they weigh at least a hundred pounds each, and they must realize that I'm seconds from collapsing because before I hit the ground, I'm in familiar arms.

"Maddie, stay awake for me, baby. Eyes open." I can't even lift my arms to wrap around his neck. I just want to lay down on a flat surface. My body feels so weak and I pray it's just the adrenaline wearing off and nothing more serious.

"So…tired." I hear voices surrounding me. *"Victim not shot,"*

"No wounds," "Suspect confirmed dead."

"No. Stay awake," Cal grits out and my eyes flutter. I feel something brush against my lips and I think it's his lips, but I can't say for sure.

"You came," I whisper, I'm trying to force a smile but I have no idea if my lips are turned upwards at all. *I love you*, my mind thinks, and I try to speak the words, but I can't even muster the strength to open my mouth again.

"I NEED A CART." I hear him scream and then I'm floating. Floating away into nothingness.

Darkness.

Black.

Twenty-Three

Madeline

The second I open my eyes everything hurts, and the beeps from the machine next to me feel like a tiny hammer to my temples as they throb with every beat. I feel like I've been run over by a car and my muscles feel stiff as a board. My eyes float around the room as best they can without moving my head, and they immediately fall on Cal who's sitting next to my bed with his head in his hands. I notice that he's bouncing his leg nervously, and his hair is sticking up in a million directions making me wonder how long he's spent pulling on it.

Right on cue, he runs a hand through his hair. "Stop pulling," I whisper and his eyes shoot up to mine.

"Maddie," he whispers and then he's out of the chair and sitting on the edge of the bed next to me. He grabs my hand and pulls it to his mouth before pressing it over his heart. "How are you feeling? Does anything hurt?" He reaches his hand to my face and gently strokes the bruise causing me to wince despite the fact that I relish at his touch.

"Does it look bad?" I ask.

He shakes his head and presses another kiss to my palm. "No. You're still so beautiful."

A sad smile finds my face as I look around the hospital room. At least two dozen balloons fill the far corner. There are plants and bouquets of flowers lining the window sill and tons of stuffed animals in all sizes and colors, the words *Get Well Soon*, printed across their chests. "How long have I been out?"

"A few hours. Not long...well, objectively. It's been a long few hours for me." His eyes look exhausted and I note he has more facial hair than usual, making me wonder if it's morning, or if it's still the middle of the night.

"I'm so sorry," I tell him. I let out a breath. "It's all my fault."

His eyebrows pull together and he shakes his head. "Not at all, and I won't have you thinking otherwise. You trusted Henry, there was no way for you to know..."

His voice drifts off and tries to move off the bed but I grab his hand. "Don't go."

His eyes find mine and they're full of sadness and remorse and *guilt*. "I let you down. I should have found you sooner. Before he touched you...fuck, Maddie. *I'm* the one that's sorry." He moves in closer and his lips brush against my cheek, and I force my face towards him and let his lips graze mine.

"You got to me in time." I force a weak smile and he shakes his head. "You always get to me in time."

"I hate that you had to see that."

I grimace at the memory of seeing Henry go down and that gruesome look on his face. The look of death will haunt me alongside the sounds of my mother's screams the night she died.

"Did...who killed him?"

Cal sighs. "Aria should have because she has the best shot on the force, and I'm glad I wasn't on that side because I wouldn't have been okay with them taking that shot so close to you. I honestly thought they'd hit you. But Aria was in hysterics. They had her sedated for a while." He swallows.

"They didn't get me. I swear. I felt the bullet go by." I tell him honestly and although it's the truth, I'm still shaken up by how close it came to piercing my flesh along with Henry's.

Cal must read my look because his voice cuts into my thoughts. "We're going to see someone when we get out of here."

"Another shrink?" I wince.

"Yes, Madeline, another shrink." His voice is firm and it sparks something inside of me that I haven't felt since I woke up.

I give him a small smile and a deep breath. "Okay, Daddy."

His eyes darken and he's about to speak when a rush of people enter the room. Some in police uniform and some in plain clothes.

"Oh my God, Maddie!" I hear her voice before I see her and then her arms are around me, squeezing me.

"Aria…be gentle," Cal scolds and I see her lift her middle finger.

"Back off, Grayson." She pulls back to look at me and cups my face. "Maddie." She kisses my forehead and pulls me into a hug. "I'm so…sorry," she whispers in my ear. Her eyes are puffy and red, and her skin is splotchy, all evidence that makes me believe she's been sobbing for hours. She sniffles and rubs her nose with a tissue and I hold my arms out to hug her again. I can't even imagine what Aria is going through right now. When I pull back her chin trembles slightly. "We'll talk later, okay?"

I nod, as the tears well in my eyes. "You've been…" I hiccup despite the lump I feel lodged in my throat, "the best friend… and mother I could have ever asked for." I smile at her through the tears. I knew I couldn't be blamed for Henry's sins, but Aria shouldn't be either. Besides Cal, Aria loves me so much; seeing me in that position in that tiny cabin probably gutted her as deeply as Cal.

"Okay, Maddie, a few things…" one of Cal's subordinates, Officer James, speaks up. He moves to the other side of my bed, opposite of Cal and Aria, and they both shoot him a look. "Hey, effective immediately you two are off this case. You shouldn't have even proceeded without backup, Grayson."

He snorts and gives him a look. "I'm sorry, who do you report to? And he had *Maddie*. You think I wasn't going in? You're insane."

"Exactly. A big conflict of interest." He taps his pen against his notepad before pointing it at all three of us.

"Is this really necessary?" Aria asks.

"It is if a rape kit exam is in order." Instantly, I freeze despite the blankets on top of me and I want to burrow under them and sleep through the rest of winter.

Aria and Cal look at me and I watch as the blood drains from both of their faces, but my eyes stay focused on Cal. I shake my head slowly, letting him know that he didn't. That no one's touched me but him. *I'm yours.*

"Not necessary," Cal says.

"Cal…" Officer James warns.

"I don't need one." I speak up. "He didn't touch me, like… that."

"Listen, I know you have a different relationship with Cal and Aria, so if they need to step out of the room so we can talk to you privately, we can do that."

"No." I shake my head. "They stay. He didn't touch me, but we can do one if you don't believe me?"

"That's not how this works," Cal growls. "And they're invasive and often times a little traumatic. You've been through enough. If you say you don't need one, you're not taking one."

I bite my lip and look at Officer James. "I don't need one, I swear," I whisper.

"Well, we do have a few questions to ask if you don't mind."

"Do we have to do that now? The suspect is…" he pauses and clears his throat as he prepares to speak of the suspect who just so happens to be his brother. "deceased." Cal says and I watch as Aria flinches. She looks down and I reach out to grab her hand giving it a small squeeze. Her eyes meet mine and a flash of sadness floats across her face.

I'm sorry, I mouth.

She shakes her head as if to tell me that I'm the last person who has anything to be sorry for.

"And this is precisely why you two are off this case. This is personal for both of you. Your brother, your husband." He looks at them and shakes his head. "And from what few of us have noticed, *you're* romantically involved with the victim." He points at Cal and then turns his head towards me.

How did they know? I vaguely remember him calling me *baby* earlier and maybe a kiss, but I thought I imagined that.

"We should remove you both from the room while we speak with her," he continues and I freeze.

"No!" The word bursts out of me like an explosion. "What part of I don't want to be away from them do you not understand? They saved my life and they're my family." I look over at them; Cal's posture is rigid and tense and Aria looks like she's on the verge of tears. I turn back to Officer James. "They're two for two for saving my life."

He lets out a sigh and flips his notepad up before pinching the bridge of his nose. "You'll need to come down to the station when you're strong enough, alright?"

"Okay." I nod.

The room starts to clear out after a few of the officers take turns hugging me and giving me even more flowers and stuffed animals. I realize that my pink bunny is next to me and I wonder where it came from, when I remember who I *haven't* seen.

"Where's Margie?" Aria and Cal exchange a look and then turn back at me and I frown. "Where is she?"

"She's...in the waiting room. She's...not taking this well," Cal tells me.

"Can I see her? I mean...does she want to see me?" *Is she upset with me? Does she wish Henry was alive over me? He was her child...and I'm...not.* I feel the familiar prickle in my scalp at the idea of being resented by Cal's mother for the rest of my life.

Cal frowns and shakes his head, assumedly at my question. "Of course, she wants to see you. She's worried that you hate her. Hell, she thinks we all do."

"I'll go get her and give you guys a second," Aria says as she slips out of the room.

"How are you feeling about...everything?" I ask, and Cal sighs before sitting next to me on my bed.

"I haven't really given it a ton of thought yet. I haven't been able to focus on anything except you," he whispers. "Seeing you tied up like that gutted me. When I walked in the room and saw you like that...I had to force my gaze away from you because I was seconds from losing it." He raises the sleeves of my gown and kisses my wrists that are wrapped in gauze. "Does it hurt?"

"I'm okay, Cal. I promise."

He shuts his eyes, but I notice him wince. "I'm never letting you out of my sight, I swear to God."

"Does that mean you'll be coming with me to college?"

His eyes fly open and he rubs his jaw. "If you want me to."

"I want to be wherever you are," I tell him. "This...was scary." I let out a breath. "But it doesn't change my feelings for you. If anything, it just makes them stronger. You really are my superhero."

"I'll always protect you, Maddie. Don't feel like you have to be with me for me to keep you safe."

"What!" I screech and my throat screams in response. *Fuck, that hurt.* "No. Cal, I want to be with you because I don't want a day to go by without waking up in your arms. Because I want to spend every day of the rest of my life with you. Because I'm so in love with you. The fact that you keep saving my life…" I give him a small smile. "That's just a bonus."

Margie enters the room just as I'm getting reacquainted with Cal's mouth and she clears her throat. I peek my head around him and smile at Cal's mother. *My future mother in law,* I predict.

"Oh, my sweet Maddie." She rushes to my other side and is wary to sit on the bed with me, but I make space for her. "I am so sorry for…everything."

"Margie, it's not your fault."

"It is my fault…the sins of my past." She lets her head fall. "I've let you both down."

"People make mistakes…it doesn't justify Henry's behavior," Cal starts.

"It wasn't a mistake," I whisper. "Cal wouldn't be here otherwise. I don't see how anyone could see that as a mistake." I look at him and his ears turn slightly pink and I smile at the ability to embarrass him, but my heart hurts that he thinks of himself as a mistake in light of recent information.

"I thought it was best to keep it from you and I shouldn't have."

"I definitely have…questions," Cal starts. "Mainly…do you, I mean, who is my father?"

"Oh my God, is it Grant?" I blurt out and I mentally slap my head as Cal's eyes dart to me and then to his mother, his eyes wide and unblinking. "Sorry, I've been watching too many soap operas."

She shakes her head. "No, not Grant. He didn't even know

that I've had an affair. He was under the impression that Patrick Grayson was your father as well." She clears her throat and the tears well in her eyes. "Cal, I... that might be a story for another time, okay?"

"Is he...alive?"

"No."

My eyes dart from Cal to his mother and I wonder if this is a conversation I'm old enough to hear. But then I remember my place is much different in their lives, and Cal would confide in me anyway.

"I want to know," Cal says. "Please."

She lets out a breath and blinks away the tears before turning towards the window. "Your father was...the love of my life." She clears her throat. "He was my high school sweetheart."

Both Cal and my eyes widen and I reach for his hand, giving it a gentle squeeze alerting him that I'm here. "I loved him so much."

"What...what happened?"

"I was so wild about Nathan Solomon. I wanted to get married as soon as we graduated. But he wanted to enlist, and my parents wanted me to go to college. Hell, I wanted to go to college. I got into Sarah Lawrence in New York. We both had things we wanted to accomplish before we settled down. He was only supposed to be gone for a year," she whispers, and the tears flow down her cheeks. "A year turned to two and then to four and then to six and I just didn't want to wait any longer." She bites her bottom lip, and I watch the regret wash over her face.

If I went to school, and he didn't come with me...would we find our way back to each other? Or would it be too late? I feel a sickening feeling sinking to the pit of my stomach at the thought.

I can't let that happen.

Margie takes a deep breath and continues. "When he finally

returned home, almost a decade later, I'd met Patrick...and I was pregnant with Henry." She shakes her head. "I did love him, don't mistake what I'm saying. I loved Patrick and it destroyed me when he left. But you just never forget your first love. Your first love takes power over you that never relinquishes. It takes hold of your soul and never lets go. Some people learn to ignore it, or the power lessens slightly, but it's never completely gone. Especially when things are left so open."

My mind reels thinking about what would happen if Cal and I ever separated. I would never forget him, and at this point, I was completely convinced I would never love another as completely and selflessly and irrevocably as I love Cal Michael Grayson. If she loved Nathan even a fraction as much as I love Cal, then I don't know how she's even managed to go on—twice.

"Where...where do I fit into that picture?" Cal asks.

"We stayed friends." She tells us. "It was a dangerous game. I spent time with him, more than what was appropriate." She blinks a few times, allowing us to fill in the blanks. "I was falling in love with him all over again. So, I had a plan to leave Patrick. I wasn't being fair to him or myself or Nathan." She clears her throat. "And then I fell pregnant and I knew it was time to come clean about everything." She sighs. "But..." she trails off. "I'll never forget the call I got in the middle of the night." I feel like I'm frozen as I prepare to hear her words. I hold my breath waiting for the bomb.

"There'd been an accident." She sniffles. "He was killed instantly."

"Mom..." Cal chokes out.

She brushes the tears from her cheeks. "He was so excited about you."

"He...he knew about me?"

"Yes." She nods. I feel like she might expand, but she doesn't and I wonder if years later it's still painful to talk about. "I know I kept things from you and..." she pauses before she chokes out his name, "Henry, but I told Patrick early on. The guilt was eating me alive and I didn't want him to think I was trapping him if and when the truth came to light. It was the hardest thing I ever had to do. Henry doesn't exactly remember this because he was only about four, but Patrick moved out for a while. But he was there when I gave birth to you and I think he fell in love with being a dad again. He was a good dad, Cal. His issues were with me, not with either of you. He loved you both so much."

"Until he didn't," Cal grits out. "He left us too, Mom."

"Honey...you have to let that anger go."

"I know." He grunts and looks at me.

Margie turns to me. "I had no idea Henry or Cal would ever learn the truth. Cal's father wasn't alive, so I didn't think it was necessary to tell them, especially after Patrick left. I made a mistake in judgment. Then you get older and you learn from your mistakes, and then it feels too late to tell the truth. I didn't even tell Grant." She lowers her head. "Of course, he knows now. I hope neither of you hate me, and Cal, I hope you can find it in your heart to forgive me."

"Margie, I don't think any less of you." I put my hand on hers and squeeze. "I still love you so much and I don't blame you at all. You did what you had to do for your family. You did what you felt was best at the time."

Her eyes float to her son, whose eyes are fixed on the ground. "I don't hate you, Mom. Never think that. I'm just caught off guard, of course." I can see the confusion in his eyes. He's not sure what to feel or what he's *allowed* to feel. "It's been a long fucking day."

"I know. I can't imagine what you both have been through."

She squeezes my hand. "My sweet babies. I love you both so much."

"We love you too." I look at her.

She nods and stands up, staring at us both. "I'll let you get some rest."

I wake up a few hours later to arms wrapped around me and a hand stroking my shoulder. My head is resting on Cal's chest after I basically begged him to climb into my hospital bed with me. I would be released in the morning, and as the sun peeks up over the day, I wonder how long I've been asleep.

"I think a fresh start would do us both some good." Cal speaks and I sweep my hand over his torso and raise my head slowly to look up at him.

"A fresh start, together?"

He rests his hand on the back of my head and kisses my forehead, keeping me close to his chest. "Yes, you and me."

"Where are we going?"

"Wherever you want."

"I can pick?" I look up at him.

"Well, you'll be enrolled in college young lady, so make sure you like one of the schools in the state." He smiles.

"You're coming with!" I squeal, and it's like the thought has my weary, aching body feeling brand new, as if I'm floating.

"I'd follow you anywhere."

Epilogue

Madeline

Four Years Later

"**B**UT CAL..." I WHINE INTO THE PHONE, THE EFFECTS OF THE multiple shots I took on the last day of the semester catching up with me. "I have plans that include my mouth...on your dick." I giggle, even though I'm slightly irritated that my man won't be home when I get home from the bar.

The transfer to the Boston Police Department was much easier than we thought it would be. Not that I was too shocked. Cal was a well-decorated officer and his reputation preceded him. Despite the fact that the majority of the force in Oregon knew that our relationship had changed, they didn't seem to paint him in a negative light. They believed he loved me as much as I loved him and that our bond had been unbreakable from the moment we met. He wasn't the Chief of Police *yet*, but I was certain it was coming in the next few years.

I had just taken my final exam of my senior year at Harvard and I was due to graduate college this weekend. Cal and I wasted no time getting acclimated into our new life in Boston leaving behind the scars and the skeletons of our past back west. Margie and Grant had gotten married and were still living in Oregon, though I had a strong inkling that they would be looking at a permanent residence in Massachusetts, the second a certain ring found its way onto my finger.

Aria, who I talk to every day, is somewhere in the middle. She moved to Michigan to join their police force, after needing a change of scenery and wanting to be closer to her family. She comes to visit all the time, and we've flown to visit her just as frequently. It's been four years since Henry died, and only now is she feeling like she might be ready to move on. The pain of losing her husband so tragically, despite how it happened, stayed with her for a long time. She was married to him for almost a decade, and up until the end, she believed things were good. *Great* even. It makes me wonder if he always had something evil lurking within or if he really did just snap upon learning the truth.

I'm standing in line for the bathroom when I hear a familiar voice floating around me.

"Ew, can you not talk about your mouth anywhere?" I spin around to see Aria standing behind me with one hand on her hip and a beer in the other.

"ARIA!" I squeal as I launch into her arms, almost sending her backwards. She looks amazing. After she moved to Michigan, she dyed her hair almost black making her look like a badass version of Snow White when she donned her uniform.

"Maddie!" She squeezes me hard and gives me a loud kiss on my cheek. "I can't believe you're a college graduate!"

"Well, not officially, and what are you doing here?! I thought you weren't flying in until tomorrow like Margie and Grant!"

"And miss the party tonight?" I hear Margie's voice as she and Grant come into view, and I squeal even louder.

"Oh my God! All my favorite people!" I cheer as I shoot my hands into the air. "We need to do a round of shots." I realize I'm still on the phone with Cal and I put my phone to my ear. "Hello?"

"Hey," I hear in my ear behind me and I jump.

"Oh my God! How did you pull this off without me knowing?" I raise an eyebrow and he wraps his arms around me.

"You don't know all my tricks."

I narrow my eyes at him and cock an eyebrow at him. The words are on the tip of my tongue, and I try to keep them at bay but the multiple Fireball shots have them falling out of my mouth. "Like the ring in your safe?"

I hear Aria snort from behind me. "I'm going to go get us a round. Tequila, Mads?"

"Please!" I cheer and watch as she, Margie, and Grant disappear.

"You're so nosy." He pushes me up against the wall and presses his lips to mine. "I'm changing the safe number again."

I roll my eyes and finger the necklace Cal got me after I broke the old one. The one that never came off without any exceptions. "Were you planning to ask me after graduation? That's so cliché."

His lips form a straight line. "No, I was planning to ask you while I was balls deep inside of you tonight, smart ass."

"Oh." I raise an eyebrow and my mouth waters at the visual. "Can't wait."

"You just couldn't let me surprise you, could you?"

"What's the fun in that?" He rolls his eyes and grabs my drink from me taking a long sip. "Sure you want to spend the rest of your life with me?"

"The last fourteen haven't been too bad." He winks and presses his lips to mine.

CAL

Two Years Later

The sounds of screams fill the room. Both Maddie's and a smaller version of her with stronger lungs and warm brown eyes that match mine. "It's a girl!" the doctor pronounces and I watch as Maddie bursts into tears.

"You did it, baby." I kiss her sweaty forehead and she grabs my face, bringing my lips to hers.

"I love you," she whispers and I smile, remembering the very different tune she was humming about twenty minutes ago.

"Enough to make another?" I ask.

She bites her bottom lip and shoots me a wink that sends a spark to my dick. "Okay, Mom, Dad, ready to meet your daughter?"

The tears are still flowing down her face when the doctor hands her to me in the exact moment she opens her eyes. I hold my breath and it feels like time is standing still as I watch her blink her eyes several times and open her mouth in a yawn. She has a head full of brown hair, with ten perfect fingers and ten perfect toes. "Let me see!" I hear Maddie as she's straining to see and I snap out of the trance brought on by our daughter.

"Sorry, I was just a little…speechless." I look at her and our baby, back and forth several times. "We made a baby."

She lets out a breath and takes in the small pink bundle in her arms. She gasps when she lays her eyes on our daughter for the first time. "Oh my God, Cal! She's so beautiful!"

"Just like you," I murmur as I kiss her temple. Her blue eyes are shining with love despite the fatigue I know is running through her after seventeen hours of labor. I push her hair back away from her face and kiss her again.

"I didn't know it was possible to love someone you just met this much..." she trails off. "But I guess I did feel that way about you," she whispers and my heart feels like it might actually explode with the love I feel for these two.

"Alright, Mom and Dad, any thoughts on a name for baby Grayson?" the nurse asks as she taps her notepad. Maddie and I had gone back and forth before we got married about whether we wanted to take my father's name since technically I'm not a Grayson. Margie and Grant had gotten married, so she didn't have that last name either. But in the end, I kept Grayson, not because I had any strong ties to the name, but because Cal Grayson was the best man Madeline Shaw had ever met, and *that's* who she wanted to marry.

I shoot a look at her and she smiles with glee at the name we picked out if we had a girl. "Callie Amelia Grayson," I tell the nurse.

"Callie! Oh, like your names combined! I love that." She smiles.

"And Amelia was...my mother," Maddie says, and I watch as the goosebumps appear on her skin. I rub her arms and press a kiss to her shoulder and stare down at the sleeping bundle in her arms. I didn't think I could be any more in love with Maddie, but watching her with our daughter makes me fall even deeper for her. The room clears out leaving the three of us, and I sit next to her on the bed. She rests her head on my shoulder and a sigh leaves her lips.

"I can't believe we got here. Everything I ever wanted...it came true." I look down at her to find her beaming up at me, something she's been doing ever since the day we met, if I'm being honest. "Thank you, Cal. You saved my life...and then gave me a perfect one."

The End.

If you liked the tortured forbidden romance of *Unconditional*, then check out *Bittersweet Surrender,* part one of the Bittersweet Duet! Here's a sneak peak!

BITTERSWEET SURRENDER

PROLOGUE

I was a good wife.
I was loyal to a fault, playing the perfect, doting wife to a man I married at the naive age of twenty-one, when I viewed the world through those rose-colored glasses they warn you about. I loved him, supported him, and I was undeniably faithful to him.

I was a good wife.
Until one day, temptation presented itself in the form of a broken marriage and the beautiful man whose job it was to fix it. I never imagined myself capable of infidelity until the man I married lost all interest in me, just in time for another to take notice.

Now, here I am opening my mind, my heart, and now my body to a man who isn't my husband.

How did I get here?

I feel as if I'm having an out-of-body experience, my soul floating above my physical self as I watch myself in complete fascination. I watch as a man shoves me up against the wall of the large corner office on the fourteenth floor of a building on Clinton Street, in Midtown Atlanta. I watch myself wrap my arms and legs around him as his lips find my neck. I hear the clash of our teeth as our mouths ravage each other, our tongues intertwining furiously. His hands move out of my wavy tresses, down my face to grope my breasts. My hands slide down his torso, my fingertips dancing over every hard ridge hidden beneath his cashmere sweater. I watch as I fumble with his pants, desperate to get them down his legs. My body is on fire for his touch. I'm desperate to feel him inside of me, to feel the connection of our bodies becoming one. The arousal pumping through my veins is something I've never experienced. I've never had this kind of passion with anyone.

Not even my husband.

You may think you know my story, but you have no idea.
I was a good wife…until I wasn't.

Author's Note

Full disclosure:

Unconditional was one of those stories that took hold of my soul and refused to let go. I was writing another book, and Cal and Maddie started speaking—loudly. I would jot down notes here and there but I tried to keep them at bay until they started keeping me up at night. When I finally started writing their story, I told myself I wouldn't publish until late 2019. I wasn't sure if I was ready to publish their story; I wasn't sure if you as readers even wanted something like this from me. Truthfully, I was scared as fuck. *Still am.* But Cal and Madeline are on my heart so much still long after I've completed their story, that I don't think I would have been able to focus on anything else until I put their story out in the world. So, I hope you enjoyed it as much as I loved writing it. For those of you that have been with me from the beginning, and would probably follow me over a cliff, I love you forever. *You're my home team.* For those of you that are new to me and my books, a million thank yous for reading!

Xoxo,
Q.B.

Acknowledgements

This book wouldn't... *couldn't* have happened without some pretty fabulous people. Your input, your love, your support is invaluable to me. As I, (and Carrie Bradshaw) have said probably a million times—sometimes family is the one you're born into, and sometimes it's the one you make for yourself.

Carmel Rhodes, at this point, I'm fairly certain I talk to you more than I talk to half the people I see every day. Our "sis-mance" goes so much deeper than our pennames and I'm so lucky to have you on this journey. I love you for life. Thank you for reading every version of *Unconditional*. For being the first one I told I was ready for this story. For telling me to stop freaking out when I *finally* wrote it. And for holding my hand when I released it into the wild. I'm fearless because I've got you in my corner.

Helen Hadjia, Leslie Middleton, Melissa Spence & Kristene Bernabe, my insanely thorough betas, you've been with me for quite a while at this point and I don't think you even understand what it means to me. I love you guys so much for everything you've done and do for me every day. You continue to show up for me and for that I'm so grateful!

Erica Marselas & Danielle James, you were the first eyes that read this story from start to finish, and your feedback was everything!

Thank you so much being that final push at the end that told me I could do this. You're amazing!

Jeanette, where do I begin? Thank you for helping me bring Cal and Maddie to life. The cover is gorgeous and thank you so much for all the pretty things you made for me!

Kristen Portillo & Stacey Blake, thank you for making my books sparkle and shine every time. Your magic never ceases to amaze me!

Author Friends & Romance Rookies, I love you guys to pieces. I'm so excited to squeeze some of you in May!

To everyone in the Hive, my sassy babes! Some of you have been with me, what, almost five years? Where does the time go? Thank you for your love and your support and making me feel like I *can*. I love you!

And finally, to the readers: Thank you for going on yet another journey with me. You guys rock my world every day!

About the Author

Write. Wine. Work. Repeat. A look inside the mind of a not so ex-party girl's escape from her crazy life. Hailing from the Nation's Capital, Q.B. Tyler, spends her days constructing her "happily ever afters" with a twist, featuring sassy heroines and the heroes that worship them. But most importantly the love story that develops despite *inconvenient* circumstances.

Sign up for her newsletter to stay in touch!
eepurl.com/doT8EL

Qbtyler03@gmail.com

Facebook: m.facebook.com/author.qbtyler

Reader Group: www.facebook.com/groups/784082448468154

Goodreads:
www.goodreads.com/author/show/17506935.Q_B_Tyler

Instagram: www.instagram.com/author.qbtyler

Bookbub: www.bookbub.com/profile/q-b-tyler

Wordpress: qbtyler.wordpress.com

Also by
Q.B. TYLER

My Best Friend's Sister
Bittersweet Surrender
Bittersweet Addiction

CAMPUS TALES SERIES
First Semester
Second Semester

Coming Spring 2019:
Spring Semester

Printed in Poland
by Amazon Fulfillment
Poland Sp. z o.o., Wrocław

22656138R00174